HOLDING THE LIGHT

HOLDING THE LIGHT

A Meryen Saga

Gloria Cook

This first world edition published 2008
in Great Britain and in 2009 in the USA by
SEVERN HOUSE PUBLISHERS LTD of
9–15 High Street, Sutton, Surrey, England, SM1 1DF.

British Library Cataloguing in Publication Data

Cook, Gloria
  Holding the light. - (The Meryen series)
  1. Inheritance and succession - Fiction 2. Cornwall
  (England : County) - Social life and customs - 19th century
  - Fiction 3. Domestic fiction
  I. Title
    823.9'14 [F]

ISBN-13: 978-0-7278-6706-3   (cased)

All Severn House titles are printed on acid-free paper.

Typeset by Palimpsest Book Production Ltd.,
Grangemouth, Stirlingshire, Scotland.
Printed and bound in Great Britain by
MPG Books Ltd., Bodmin, Cornwall.

To my dear, wonderful daughters,
Cheryl and Tracy

One

Why would anyone wish to live in this bleak, lumbering old house? Poltraze and its estate had been forsaken two years ago by Meryen's young squire. To Clemency Kivell, facing the desolate grey building on the weed-strewn gravelled court, it was inconceivable that her father's sudden intention was to buy the house.

The squire, Michael Nankervis, a condescending individual who had once cherished his ancestral home, had recently placed all his Cornish property on the market. The abduction of his infant son and heir – Clemency had played a major part in the child's rescue – had seen him remove his family to Truro, never to return. Clemency's father, Seth, could never raise the funds to secure the land Nankervis leased to the local copper mines owners for mineral rights, but he wanted this house and the grounds. Another old house, formerly the dower house, was part of the property.

Seth was a respected elder of the Kivells of Burnt Oak, a self-contained community of some sixty men, women and children, a mile and a half distant. He bore the intractable and autocratic traits of the Kivells in every inch of his brooding, Goliath frame. Today, after calling a meeting of the men, he'd ridden the long miles to Truro to seek an audience with Michael Nankervis. Why, Clemency wondered, did he desire to live as insignificant gentry? That was all Michael Nankervis and his uncelebrated forbears had been. Poltraze was a museum, no, a mausoleum. Its chambers, corridors and passages and its thoughtlessly added extensions echoed with the sorrowful or complaining voices of the unfortunates who had met violent deaths within them. Tragedies could be numbered on the fingers of both hands.

Clemency tilted her head in challenge to the ghosts said to stare out woefully, or with malice, from the numberless windows. She knew exactly what Poltraze was like inside. She had first slipped into the house just days after its desertion. As an unperturbed fourteen-year-old, she had wandered through the house with a sense of derision, and some wonder at its finer things. She had been here a number of times since, when she was in a maudlin mood or when she wanted to be completely alone. Poltraze satisfied that need; it offered a sense of total separation. Clemency did not fear isolation; she lived as comfortably within her thoughts as she did in the security and pleasure of being part of a large, close-knit, protective family. The ghosts of Poltraze had been welcome to keep her company or not. She didn't leap in her skin over a sudden slammed door, a mysterious creak or smell, or what seemed deliberate footsteps. By pretending to be a lamenting spirit herself, she had scared away a couple of gawky village youths, copper miners' brats, braving the scene. How she had laughed, watching those scruffy boys fleeing through the grounds as if a horde of demons were on their heels. Fittingly, the 'apparition' had been attributed to her late great-aunt, Tempest Kivell, the family matriarch, who had met her death in the updated west wing while thwarting another Kivell, the land-scaper here at the time and a sadistic murderer, embarking on a massacre. The house was merely a curiosity to Clemency, but she always respectfully acknowledged her great-aunt's presence in it. Only Clemency, and a steward who carried out a monthly inspection, now dared set foot inside the house.

She had made up her mind that if her father succeeded in his desire, she would not live in Poltraze, not under any condi-tion or threat; and her father was apt to be great and prolific with threats. She could belong nowhere except Burnt Oak. Her mother and her five older brothers and their families, and any other like-minded Kivell, could pack up and leave the community – and many had over the past decade – and go out into the greater world, but she would refuse to go and nothing would change her mind. Michael Nankervis's wise decision had turned her father into a fool.

Moving round to the side of the house, Clemency eased up a loosened window on its screeching sashes and climbed into the musty, heavily curtained library. Would Michael Nankervis also forsake his *Chronicles of the Nankervises* history, so pain-stakingly researched and scribed? She had once flicked through the pages of the first volume in its heavy, carved pewter cover; such headings, such footnotes – tedious entries arrogantly set down in copperplate handwriting. There was one reason, Clemency thought, why Seth might want ownership of this house: old scores. In the eleventh century the manor of Poltraze had been prize to the winner of a two-man horse race. The competing Kivell had met with an accident; a recurring bitter wound to the proud, tough breed. Every successive generation of Kivells had produced a resentful sceptic or two who spoke of Nankervis having cheated. Seth was one of those. Did he believe he had a right to be here?

Clemency gazed round the broad, gloomy room. It had an ugly fireplace. The overmantel was grotesquely sculpted with children's faces obviously in the sleep of death. What a dreadful way to remember little ones who should have been left to a dignified rest. Much of the house was dreary and poorly endowed. However, the approach to the building was not too ill considered. It had not been denuded like many other big houses by the removal of terraces and balustrades. Otherwise, the only way Clemency could see to improve Poltraze was to demolish and rebuild it. Her father would soon hate living here. She had told him so, but he'd said he had plans for it. In consequence of her bringing the squire's brat home safely, he was expecting to be successful with a low bid.

Clemency was confident Seth wouldn't gain the house. Tehidy, one of the foremost old county houses, would surely succeed in its bid to tag the whole estate on to its nearby sprawling lands. These stretched all the way to the North Cliffs, and included the tram road which was used for transportation of ores from the local mines, and which ended at Portreath harbour where the ores were shipped out. The gardens at Poltraze, although stripped of their priceless and rare collections, were, Clemency conceded, still rather splendid in neglect, but nevertheless this was mere dressing. It was unlikely the house would be wanted for habitation. It was grim. It held the night. Permanent abandonment or destruction was its likely future. No one except her father would care what happened to it.

She left the library without closing the door – as the steward must have done on his latest inspection – in an act of defiance that was unnecessary. Her mother, who indulged her after having so many males to cater for, often remarked quite proudly that she'd look to rebel against any old stone in the road. Seth and his sons ran Burnt Oak's one-hundred-acre farm, and Clemency had pitched in on the land and in the yards from the day she could walk. She was doted on by her father, who tolerated her rebelliousness almost every time, to her brothers' chagrin.

She was a gifted scholar and, contrary to her free nature, had recently taken over the teaching of lessons for Burnt Oak's children. She was proving to be a good and patient teacher. She was due to return shortly for the afternoon classes, but punctuality was not one of her strongest characteristics. First she would return for a while to her favourite world, which was anywhere outside. She had made her way here to the house on foot through the fields that adjoined Burnt Oak and Poltraze land. Under a neighbourly autumn sun that had burnt off the morning haze, she had ambled under red, copper and orange-leafed trees, kicking her feet through the crackling fallen leaves, moving past banks of huge docks, stringy, blackened nettles and saggy, forlorn ferns, all to her, the finest and the sleepiness of the season. There had been widespread big-leaved clover still showing the odd pink and white head. On the branch of a naked hawthorn a buzzard had perched, as still as midnight, before suddenly showing off its glorious wingspan in flight. Clemency had marvelled at tall colonies of gorse spun over by multitudes of spiders, their webs as fine as muslin, as fine as a young bride's lace. It was like a whole universe of fairy palaces. There was so much natural beauty and life outside and clean fresh air. She'd waste no more time inside this musty old house.

Her hurried footsteps sang out as she strode the Long Corridor. The house emitted a variety of strange sounds today; sounds like objects being shifted about and footsteps overhead and even the echo of a sighing voice. She laughed at this spectral accusation of trespass. According to Michael Nankervis's first *Chronicle*, one of the house's most persistent ghosts occupied this corridor: Septimus Bloomsbury, one of the architects, who had expired from heart failure. Clemency considered it served him right for his philistine approach. Filtering into her mind came the images of long-dead Nankervis faces peering out from lacklustre portraits upstairs in the picture gallery.

She supposed they would soon be removed. They were a drab lot mostly, she thought, the men and women who had lived here, although a few had been dark and handsome.

She would gain the outdoors by way of a small gothic door in the narrow passage that led to the kitchens, but she was closing in on the music room, the one place she appreciated. She had played all the instruments, the pianoforte, the spinet, the violins, and the wind collection. She couldn't resist a quick foray into the room.

She sat down at the spinet and tossed back her tumbling amber-coloured hair – she would knot it up appropriately when nearly home. Then she flexed her long, tapering fingers and plunged into a turbulent piece of music of her own composition. She followed it with a favourite Kivell reel. Before the end she was inspired to her feet. She had to dance. With light steps she spun and floated back down the Long Corridor and into the great hall, unaware that she was being watched.

Kingsley Faraday was fixed to the spot, spying down over the banister rail at the top of the stairs. For the past half hour he had been looking over the upper rooms. When he'd reached the west wing he had fancied his ears were picking up strange noises but that was not unusual in an empty old house. Then the music had started and his breath had locked inside him; he'd been struck motionless, compelled to listen. *A ghost playing . . .?* No, someone was downstairs. He couldn't guess what sort of someone. The first tune was wild and free with a touch of fierceness in it, and the next, gleeful and equally wild, and both had stirred and disturbed him somehow. When the music stopped he'd gone to investigate, and although neither expecting nor fearing the supernatural he had proceeded with caution.

The surprise had been utterly thrilling and delightfully captivating. Surely he had stepped into another dimension. *Please God, don't let this spectacularly beautiful young creature be part of the spirit world.*

He had never seen anyone so stunning. The dancer was almost unreal, a nymph-like being. Not yet quite a woman, she was as graceful as a cat, her movements purposeful and unrestrained. Rippling curls of dark amber flounced on her creamy shoulders. As fresh as the spring and full of light, she was dazzling, vibrant, beguiling. She was absolute perfection.

Kingsley felt sure she must hold mysteries unique. He suspected from her poise that she was obstinate and sharp and would be hard to hold down, but that only added to her delights. She filled him with exquisite tiny explosions of bliss. He just had to have her.

Clemency glimpsed the figure looming high above her and was almost caught off balance. Her heart suddenly constricted and her thoughts whirled. A ghost had materialized and was spying on her! Then she saw that the watcher was not a deceased former occupant but a mortal; a gentleman in a long black frock-coat and silk necktie finished with a jewelled pin. His sideburns were neat, his dark brown hair thick and wavy.

She pressed her hands to her hips. 'Who are you? What do you want?'

'It is not I who have no right to be here.' Kingsley's rich tones were imbued with pleasure. She had a biting spirit; he liked her resentful challenge. He started down the stairs. She did not disappoint him and stood her ground. 'The question is, who are you? You have no right to trespass here.'

Clemency sighed in irritation. What a boor. 'Are you an acquaintance of the squire? I am.'

'Really?' he raised his brows high, continuing down the stairs towards her. 'In what capacity?' Nothing carnal, he was sure. This girl wouldn't give herself to any man, let alone a shallow sort like Michael Nankervis, until she was ready. Until she was sure she had found an equal, so disdainful was she.

'That's none of your business. Well, who are you?'

'I'm the new owner of Poltraze,' Kingsley enunciated firmly. That should bring her down a little. It didn't. She wasn't a bit impressed. He found her more and more intriguing.

Clemency hid her surprise. Everything about this man spoke of wealth and high society. He had the confident air of the successful and a rock-solid demeanour. He was altogether too polished. It didn't make sense that he should want Poltraze. 'Then you're either a fool or very peculiar.'

'Aren't we all, up to a point?' The words rolled off Kingsley's tongue. He could enjoy bantering with this girl all day. 'Tell me your name.'

Clemency lifted her chin. 'I'm a Kivell. Have you heard of that name?'

'Indeed I have.' He descended the last stair but moved no closer to her. Others were required to pander to him, even this astonishing beauty whom he wanted to know all about. 'Mr Nankervis's agent has informed me of all the characters in the locality. You dwell in a quaint place with the quaint name of Burnt Oak; witches were once put to the stake there, apparently. Many of your breed have infiltrated the village of Meryen, all running small businesses.'

'Important businesses,' Clemency corrected him. 'And all are of the highest skill and eminence. They have servants. Be careful how you describe my family, sir. We are not a breed and certainly not quaint. We come from noble blood.'

Kingsley narrowed a sardonic eye. The mighty Kivells were very much their own people and thought themselves above the lower orders. He should have known this haughty young miss was one of them. 'Gypsies, rogues and thieves have intermingled with your blood. You have skills, I grant you, and they include poaching, wrecking, smuggling, brawling and forcing innocent young girls into marriage. Not to mention that there have been murderers in your ranks.'

Clemency merely heaved her chest in boredom. Did he think he could put her down? Her kin, male and female, had done all he had said and more, but the gentry had more tainted blood in their veins than any other class. 'Do you have a name, new owner of Poltraze?'

Kingsley felt he could easily adore her. No woman of his association was as arresting, as vital. She could easily become intoxicating. It was time to put things on a friendlier footing. 'I am Kingsley Faraday. Do you have a Christian name, Miss Kivell?'

'Clemency,' she eyed him with suspicion. Why the change in tack?

'From a word that means an inclination to show mercy,' he mused. 'It hardly suits you, I think. So you're the resourceful saviour of the young Master Nankervis, fated never to become squire here. I'm very pleased to meet you. So, you feel you have a right to wander this house.'

'Why on earth do you want it?'

He was pleased she did not consider him right for this dreary old place.

'Kingsley! Are you down there? I'm afraid I got myself lost.'

He winced at the carefree trill. Damn it, he was so unused to Hattie's company he had quite forgotten he had given in to her pleas to accompany him here. Where the hell had she slipped off to? Maddeningly noisy and nosy, always a liability, she had probably been up to the attics.

His annoyance magnified Clemency's curiosity. 'And who is that?'

She reflected that she would be very late taking her classes this afternoon, but her father would forgive her if she gleaned information about Kingsley Faraday and his companion. Seth was going to be absolutely furious to have lost out on Poltraze before even putting in a bid for it.

'The young lady is my sister. She's on her way down to us. She will be fascinated to meet you, although we must leave soon and you must go.'

Clemency caught him in a note of unease. 'Is there anyone else lurking about the place?'

'No – no one at all.'

Clemency was unconvinced. She had seen Kingsley Faraday's eyes dart towards the door that shut off the little-used east wing.

Two

Clemency stayed on late in Burnt Oak's well-equipped and spacious schoolroom, situated inside the largest house of the community, Morn O' May. She was making notes for an essay on famous explorers that she intended to set for the older children. Her mind was hungry for knowledge and she found it deeply enjoyable soaking up facts from her research. Reading about adventurers determined her, once again, to branch out and seek new experiences. She wasn't restless in the sense of wanting to travel and see the world's wonders for herself; she was content to enjoy them vicariously through books and memoirs. One day she would strike out on her own and, whatever that way might be, she was confident it would present itself to her at the right time.

Verena Kivell joined her.

'Mother, this is a surprise.' Clemency smiled, sorry there was no reciprocation, for Verena, statuesque and elegant in a half-length fur-trimmed mantlet and kid gloves, glowed serenely when she smiled. While the men worked the land, Verena was kept above drudgery with the aid of milkmaids and general help employed from the village. Her complexion, which was like pure marble under her lacy cap and ruched bonnet, showed only tiny signs of ageing; her immaculate, centrally parted hair still had the same glossy tints as Clemency's. Kivells prided themselves on taking lovely brides.

'Clemmie, you must come along at once. Your father has just got back from Truro and he's in a strange mood.'

'He's always in some sort of mood.' Clemency got up, packed her work into a leather folder and tied the thongs.

Verena appeared agitated. 'He says he has something important to say. He was furious earlier today after receiving almost total lack of support, and some disrespect, from the community for his notion about the big house. He feels betrayed. Be careful what you say to him, dear. He's gathered the boys and their families together and he's impatient for you to come home. Why are you so late?'

Clemency explained that she had stayed on after taking liberty with the time earlier. 'Actually, I've got something to tell Father.'

'All in good time, Clemmie,' Verena cautioned. Her daughter's frank opinions could easily provoke Seth to fierce anger while he was in one of his brooding moods.

Now that there was no question of her being uprooted to Poltraze, Clemency acknowledged that she would never have distressed her devoted, uncomplaining mother by refusing to move. She would have gone to live at the old house, protesting all the way. Her father and all her brothers, particularly Logan, the only one still unmarried, had a tendency to be prickly. They were dedicated carousers, bawdy and ready to pitch in with fights, but they were also protective and caring, and she loved them for it. They didn't view her as 'just a girl'; they were proud of her intelligence, and her courage in saving the

Nankervis boy. She wasn't ready to leave her family yet for any reason.

Clemency threw a wool shawl over her shoulders and pulled on a plain bonnet without troubling to tie the ribbons. She didn't bother with gloves at all. She was eager to reach home and acquaint her father with all the details of her encounter at Poltraze. 'Has Father said anything at all?'

'Only that there is to be no new squire.'

No new squire? So Kingsley Faraday, the pretentious man, had lied to her – and so had his sister. She was disappointed to learn this about Hattie Faraday, a vivacious girl of sparkling wit, with a wicked sense of fun. Apparently uncaring of society's rigid conventions, she had soon exasperated her brother with her constant interruptions. On thinking it over, Clemency decided that Kingsley Faraday had probably lied to Hattie too. Hattie had said she fully expected to be living in 'this riveting old place, full of the most wonderful hidey-holes' by the end of the month. 'There's no reason why we can't become great friends, is there, Clemency?' she had prattled excitedly. 'It's wonderful to find someone of my own age, just like me, in the area.'

Kingsley Faraday had rolled his eyes at that. Well, Clemency thought, whatever wonderful, superior ways he believed he possessed, as far as she was concerned, he was merely dull. Still, she wouldn't have to meet him again. It was a pity she wouldn't see Hattie again though.

Burnt Oak was set in the basin of a huge sweeping valley and formed a sizeable hamlet. Of its several dwellings, the earliest half dozen, including Morn O' May, and the forge and many craft workshops surrounded a gravelled court. There was also a graveyard, although in more recent years some Kivells had chosen to be buried in the hallowed grounds of St Meryen's church. All were protected within high rambling walls of chunky stone. Burnt Oak Farm was a short distance outside the walls, furthest from the lane leading on to Meryen; in the other direction was a back way to Poltraze.

The farm nestled behind its own dominant walls. Clemency strode home with her arm linked affectionately in her mother's, aware of solemn looks from cousins, uncles and aunts they encountered on their way; their wary expressions provoked by memories of past clashes with Seth. There would be some who knew they might never be forgiven.

Clemency was unconcerned about the shouting and cussing that doubtless lay ahead. It was an everyday occurrence with all six men of her immediate family. They said exactly what they pleased, and the women were expected to behave as if they had not heard anything untoward or offensive. Thankfully, her three eldest brothers had good-sized cottages for their young families across from the front yard. Nevertheless, with various family members wandering in and out of the farm-house, it was always noisy, sometimes contentious. Her mother let it all wash over her and managed to stay composed. She loved Seth, as he did her, and she dutifully complied with all his biddings.

Clemency and Verena went straight to the spacious dining room. Smelling the delayed supper, of roast gammon and spiced apple pudding, keeping warm in the kitchen, Clemency remem-bered she had not eaten since breakfast. Her grumbling tummy would have to wait.

Seth was at the head of the long mahogany table, drum-ming his thick fingers in tense expectation, still wearing his long riding coat and riding boots. His mass of black, silver-stippled hair, his bushy sideburns and beard were wild, his rounded cheeks near to puce. Clemency was sure he had ridden home at a reckless rate and was burning to tell his news. He seemed like a great throbbing engine with the brake only just holding him in check.

'Here at last.' He pointed gruffly at Clemency, motioning to Verena to sit on the vacant chair at his side.

Extra chairs had been brought in and all were occupied. Clemency looked for a space to squeeze in between her five brothers and four sisters-in-law, one of them pregnant with her first child. All the infant grandchildren were present, seated on adult laps, with the exception of Logan's, her unmarried brother. He was lounging nearest the door, with his long legs stretched out, a roll-up cigarette perched on an ear. He shifted on his seat and pulled Clemency down to share it with him, eager to get this meeting done with and to eat. She made a face at him. Doubtless he had an assignation ahead with some woman, to be followed by a long session of roistering at the Nankervis Arms in the village.

Seth banged his hand on the table for silence. It was un-
necessary, for everyone was attending to him.

'I saw Squire Nankervis today. He graciously accepted me
into his drawing room. We downed a convivial amount of fine
cognac while I put my proposition to him.' He inhaled mightily
and everyone leaned towards him to hear the outcome of his
visit. Seth breathed out a long, scorching breath. 'I was too
late.'

'You said before, my dear, that there's to be no new squire.
Is Mr Nankervis not selling Poltraze after all?' Verena asked.

'Oh, he's doing that all right. He's sold everything to fund
a new life away from Cornwall – where, he didn't care to say.'

Clemency gave a short gasp. It seemed then that Kingsley
Faraday had not lied to her. 'I met him today, the m—'

'Hold your tongue, Clemmie.' Logan elbowed her, hurting
her ribs. 'Let Father speak.'

Seth glared at them. They both set their mouths in a straight
line. 'It's as simple as this. Nankervis has sold off everything,
but in chunks, and has made more out of it. Tehidy's got virtually all the land. Some fellow from London has bought the
big house and parkland. He's also got the downs where the
Carn Croft and Wheal Verity mines are, so he'll be getting
the mineral rights, and rents from the miners in the village, but
he hasn't enough land to call himself the new squire. Apparently,
he doesn't want the title. He's not interested in the village.
There will be no more patronage from Nankervis or the new
owner. From now on Meryen will have to rely on poor relief.

'But,' Seth pulled his lips back in a triumphant grin, 'but,
my dears,' he crowed, playing up to his family as a self-important
actor would to an avid audience, 'I haven't come home to you
empty-handed. No, not indeed, not for one moment. You see,
I've bought Poltraze Farm. What about that? It's more than
twice the size of this one. The stock is healthy, the fields in
good order. The house is much larger too; there'll be enough
space temp'rary if some of us bed down in the downstairs
rooms until we build a home for each of you family men. The
place won't be as comfortable as here but we'll soon put that
right. The manager and labourers can either work for us or
move on. I beat Nankervis down well in price in respect of
what he owes our Clemmie.' Seth acknowledged Clemency's
past deed with a nod and, ignoring the stunned reactions to

his smug declarations, he stilled a rush of questions or protests with a jubilant raised hairy paw, crushing the air.

He got to his feet heavily, breathing like a dragon, his voice roaring. 'We're going to set up on our own! God knows, I was shown little respect by some of our kin today. Those concerned, and some of those living out in the village, have lost their proper identity. They're courting respectability, following on after the coat tails of the likes of the vicar, seeking out those society buggers. There's talk even of building a little sister church here.' Seth mouthed the last accusations as if the guilty had committed hanging offences. 'If you ask me, it won't be long before we true Kivells will be seen as the poor relations, an embarrassment to the others' high and mighty notions. Well, I'm not waiting for that sorry day to come. Today history has taken a momentous turn. The pale-blooded Nankervises have split us apart. I'll not dwell here among turncoats from the true Kivell way of ruling ourselves. If my own blood isn't for me then it's against me! We can move into the new farm, which will be called Trenbarvear from now on, as soon as we please. Tonight we shall eat then start packing up straight away.'

Seth let out a mighty growl of grim satisfaction, throwing up his wide jaw in scorn for those he imagined had injured him. He bellowed in pride and stamped his feet, waiting for the cheers of triumphant agreement. All he saw was a sea of blank faces. Then his sons were glancing at their wives and each other. Logan seemed bemused. Clemency looked, in the phrase sometimes used of her, 'as mad as hell'. Verena was shooting anxious eyes at everyone.

'Well?' Seth roared, crestfallen at having his moment of glory so quickly dampened. 'What's the matter with all of you? I thought we were in agreement over us moving out and starting up on our own.'

'Not entirely, Father,' answered the eldest son, Tobias. 'It was never really talked through. I, for one, thought you wanted to live at Poltraze House – you, Mother, Logan and Clemmie. There was no mention of us giving up the farm here. I understand your disappointment with some of the family today, but I've no wish to separate from them altogether. In fact, I shall stay on here with my family and keep this farm going.'

'Oh, you will, will you?' Seth said sourly. 'Any more of you feel the same way?'

Logan got up suddenly, nearly toppling Clemency off the chair. 'I'm with you, Father. I'll go because it's what you want, but I don't want to break from the wider family.'

'It wouldn't make sense, falling out with any of our own.' Benjamin, the son next in line to Tobias, spoke. 'I wish to stay on good terms with all, and to stay here. My family are settled and happy in our cottage.'

'Anyone else choose to stay behind?' Seth growled, twisting his side-whiskers, something he did when particularly riled.

The last two brothers, Jonas, and Adam, the expectant father, shook their heads, but they clearly weren't happy in their decision. Seth took it churlishly. 'Tobias and you,' he glared at Benjamin, 'take your families home. The rest of us are going to be busy, we don't want you under our feet.' The women were not consulted. It was taken for granted they would follow the wishes of their men.

Clemency no longer felt inclined to share her information about the Faradays. It didn't matter about them, they had Poltraze, and it was none of her father's business. Now she had to face moving to a different new home. *Trenbarvear?* Words that meant *farm of the,* and *top* and *great.* Her father might believe he was proving a point but he was about to cause an acrimonious split in the community, and even among his own sons. What her father had accomplished today was verging on the irrational. How could he be so stupid, so pathetic?

She gazed at her mother. Verena seemed resigned but her serious expression gave away her concern. She had said goodbye to the two young families who were staying at Burnt Oak, and was now leaving the room with her two remaining daughters-in-law, the younger one Adam's pregnant wife Feena, to serve the meal.

Clemency marched up to Seth. 'Do you expect me to give up teaching in Morn O' May?'

Seth lowered his grizzled face to her. 'Damn right I do. Why would you want to carry on with it? You can do whatever you choose as the daughter of an important landowner. You can live like a young lady till you get married.'

'Surely you don't mean for us to shut ourselves off from here?'

'Not entirely, but don't forget we owe nothing to those who

showed me disrespect today, or them who think they're now too grand to carouse and cock a hoop at the law. Now off you go to your mother.'

'I've got my own money, the squire's reward. I could buy my own house, live anywhere I like.'

Seth eyed her, severe as hoar frost. 'But you won't, will you?'

Clemency was humiliated in front of her family. Her father knew such threats would not be carried out. She was simply wasting his time. He knew too that she would never leave her mother. Anyway, she couldn't make any life-changing decisions for herself until she at least came of age. And she had no real reasons for complaint. She was given unwarranted freedom for a young, unattached woman.

Logan was drinking from a flagon of ale, his mouth wet from a long quaff. He was like a handsome stag, his broad body tense and his black eyes straining for action. 'What were you going to tell us before, Clemmie?'

'Nothing, really. Tell Mother I'm not hungry. I'm going up to my room to start packing.'

She was too on edge now to eat. She needed to be alone to take in the enormous and unwanted change in her future.

Three

'If that's not pretension for you then I don't know what is,' Blythe Knuckey sniped. She was the counthouse woman at the Wheal Verity copper mine, on Nansmere Downs, the miles of heath and scrubland behind Meryen village. Responsible for cleaning the mine office, dealing with the laundry and cooking for the managers, she wasn't expected to leave her post, but when she had tittle-tattle and rumour to distribute, the downfalls of others to gloat over, or trouble to make, which was virtually every day, she dismayed the bal-maidens by wandering across to the crib-house and spoiling their meal times.

'Who does Seth Kivell think he is? Signposting his new home just "Trenbarvear" indeed! "Farm" should be added. A farm's a farm, can't be ignored as such.' Blythe smirked, having barged in through the crib-house's planked door. 'Even one as big at that 'un makes a glorified scratching for a living and 'tis dirty, smelly work. Someone should go and paint "farm" on his fancy piece of wood.'

'If you're so concerned about it, why don't you go and do it, Blythe Knuckey?' Betsy Angove muttered, lowering her mug of tea and biting into her tiny pasty of potato, onion and sparse bit of meat. There was little in the way of seating in the crib-house and this was reserved for the older women, so Betsy sat on a sack on the ground. She worked in one of the ore dressing sheds with some of the older girls and young women, using spalling hammers to break down the 'hures'. These were masses of ore and waste rock that had been brought up from underground and ragged by the surface men into lumps. Along with the entire workforce, Betsy had started at the Wheal Verity at its opening, nearly two years ago. Because Blythe Knuckey's family, of whom she was the last, had lived in Meryen for over half a century she saw any newcomers to the parish as 'furrenners'. Betsy's family came from Perranporth, about six miles away. Most of the villagers had filtered into Meryen during the past decade or so as the copper mining had expanded. If the wretched woman felt that strongly, Betsy thought, she should have stayed working at the Carn Croft, which had come into operation just after her own family's introduction to Meryen.

Like all the women, girls and boys munching on mainly poor fare, Betsy loathed the strife-greedy Knuckey hag. The counthouse was perched in a prominent position on the high, exposed ground where the three managers could keep an eye on all proceedings. Blythe Knuckey thought herself above the other female workers; counthouse women were sought from among those of 'good character' who were 'experienced in housework and plain cooking'.

'I'll tell you why you won't go,' Betsy went on. 'Because you're afraid to upset any of the Kivells, same as the rest of us are who've got any sense. Who cares what that great ox Seth Kivell does anyway? It means he and some of his lot are further away from Meryen and that's for the better.'

'You sure you mean that, maid?' Blythe puckered her lips, so that they looked like two ragged strips of blood-drained meat. Her usually restless, darting eyes were fixed on Betsy in a hard, searching stare. Her face was long, with a wide, cow-like jaw.

She was a grey-haired, childless widow, ungainly even in her clean plain skirt and blouse with starched white apron worn over them. In comparison the bal-maidens wore calf-length dresses under dusty, gritty hessian towser aprons. The few who could afford them wore sturdy boots. All the bal-maidens had strips of canvas cloth wound round their legs for decency and protection, plus crossover shawls and cotton working bonnets – gooks – which had long flaps attached, again for protection from flying debris. The workers reckoned Blythe's husband, the late purser of the Carn Croft mine, three miles away, and a Methodist lay preacher, must have given thanks to the Lord for the galloping consumption that had taken him to an early grave.

'Why shouldn't she mean it? What are you getting at?' demanded Serenity Treneer, a cheerful, eye-catching girl who was sitting next to Betsy, her best friend. Why, she wondered, couldn't this shrew just leave everyone alone? She thrived on causing bad feelings. She soaked up gossip then spewed it out with spiteful sarcasm.

'Well, it means that he-goat Logan Kivell is further away now.' Blythe tilted her head towards both girls then included the whole gathering. She had everyone's attention. Anyone who made a point of ignoring her would be her next target. 'He's been sniffing round the pair of you and no wonder either, you both give him the glad eye.'

'We do not!' Betsy huffed indignantly. 'Me and Serenity aren't interested in getting ourselves a young man for a long while yet.' This wasn't strictly true. Betsy and Serenity were both taken with a young underground miner, Abe Deveril, of good looks and nature. 'We're happy to support our families. Both of us have fathers who can't work no more.'

'They could fend if they wanted to.' Blythe snorted. 'They're just idle, happy to take advantage, like so many others in the village.'

'That's not fair, Blythe Knuckey, and well you know it,' chipped in elderly widow Mary Ann Barbary, rubbing a swollen arthritic shoulder that was now aching even more due to the hard work. 'Both Mr Angove and Mr Treneer's got miner's lung. And Betsy and Serenity are good girls. They go to chapel, same as me, and I can vouch for their morals. Better if you watched your mouth. The Good Lord knows what's on your mind before you even say it. The tongue is deadlier than fire. Judge not lest ye be judged.'

'Go and get back to your own work.' A little voice, from one of the numerous child labourers, some as young as seven, mumbled against Blythe.

'Well, those maids doesn't fool me.' Blythe arched her bristly eyebrows and stalked away, but not before leaving a sting. 'Logan Kivell always gets his way. Just wait and see.'

'Of all the nerve! I'm going up to the counthouse right this minute and make a complaint about she,' Serenity seethed.

'I'll come with you.' Betsy was getting up. 'We shouldn't have to put up with her.'

Mary Ann held her back. 'Take no notice of her, my handsome. Don't you worry, just sit back and wait. Vengeance is mine, saith the Lord.'

Four

She was lost in what seemed like a wilderness. The countryside was strange and friendless, and not the lovely soothing picture described in so much poetry, including the poetry her brother wrote.

She should have listened to Kingsley an hour ago. 'You can't possibly want to take a ride in this inclement weather, Hattie. What do you mean, it's not very wet out there? Do you want to catch a chill? You know how you hate being confined to a sickbed. Very well, I concede it looks as if it will brighten up before too long, but I'd rather you stayed in the house so I know what you are up to. Hattie, please don't argue. Why must you always argue with me? Why must you be so awkward?

Oh, very well, go out if you must but don't wander from the grounds. You're not familiar with the area.'

Kingsley was a fusspot but her predicament proved that his anxiety was not without good reason. Poor Kingsley, it wasn't fair that he had to contend with a family of misfits. Hattie knew she was a constant worry to him, but she couldn't help her bubbly nature. Her parents were an embarrassment to Kingsley, her widowed sister Jane a lost cause, and then there was Matthew . . . In all, they were a bane to Kingsley, and she couldn't blame him for his eagerness to offload them from his everyday life. It wouldn't be for ever in her case. In two years' time Hattie would join him in London for her first season. At least he would then be able to place her in the hands of etiquette coaches, dressmakers and a chaperone, his function merely to be her escort. He had threatened that if she disgraced him or ruined her prospects of a good marriage he would exile her to Poltraze for good. She wouldn't risk that, but she would enjoy the occasional diverting visit to the strange old house with its dark history and curious nooks.

The light shower of rain had eased by the time she was seated side-saddle in her bottle-green riding habit, in which she had paraded to impress the young officers at St James's Park. She berated the weather now – a hefty downpour or a cruel rise in the wind would have sent her home while she was still able to find her way back. She had abandoned the parkland at the outset, trotting down bridleways and byways, peering over the hedges in the lanes at fields shorn of crops. She had headed up hills in an attempt to locate Trenbarvear, formerly Poltraze Farm, where the fascinating Kivell girl had taken up residence a fortnight ago. Her confidence that the farmstead, the only one hereabouts of any significant size, wasn't miles away and would be reasonably easy to find, had been misplaced. The only clues to the farm, goodly numbers of cattle and sheep in the fields and a meadow too large to belong to simple folk, had also proved to be false ones. She had followed trickles of streams. Surely one of these streams would lead to some sort of habitation where she could enquire the way to Trenbarvear. After all, people settled near a water supply, it was fundamental to survival. But she came across nothing and no one. She must have been going round in circles.

Now she wanted only to get back to Poltraze. She had

reached a sort of crossroads. The way ahead petered out from
being any sort of thoroughfare and on either side of her the
scrub was narrowly trodden down – although, unbeknown to
her, only by the scurrying feet of foxes. She must find some
really high ground and hope to work out where she might
be. She had meant to bring her opera glasses to scan the
horizons but had characteristically forgotten them. She should
have known better. She was hopeless at directions.

She looked up at the low sky streaked with an angry purplish-
grey. It was growing darker, threatening to let loose drizzly
rain at any moment. If Kingsley was forced to send out a search
party for her he was going to be absolutely furious. Dear
Kingsley, he was longing to return to his Italianate villa in St
John's Wood, to the serious business of banking, to his artistic
and intellectual clique, and doubtless to the arms of his
beautiful mistress.

Hattie decided it wasn't all her fault she was lost. Kingsley
wouldn't countenance employing locals for fear of gossip or
ridicule of (with the exception of herself) his family. This
meant that there had been no one of whom she could have
asked, in a roundabout way, the directions to Trenbarvear.
Poltraze was staffed entirely by loyal and trusted Faraday
servants. It would have exasperated her to learn that if she
had turned off into the woods on the first bridleway she
would soon have reached Trenbarvear on the other side of
the trees.

She rubbed at her brow. She chewed her lip. If she were on
a Poltraze mount, it would most likely find its way back, but
although Squire Nankervis had sold Kingsley the house and
furnishings, taking away only his personal possessions and the
contents of the library, he had also stripped the stables of horse-
flesh. Needles of alarm prickled inside her. Don't worry, she
told herself. There are some hours of daylight left; time to spy
something that hints of the way home. The best course, she
decided, was to retrace her route and hope to see markers that
would put her right.

'Try to find the way back.' Prodding her pony to turn round,
she did what she always did when faced with dread. She set
her face to stone, thrust aside common sense and anxiety and
used mere instinct. It usually worked.

She rode as hard as she dared, heading off in directions

without pause, uncaring whether the ground seemed familiar or not; shutting out the thought that, in the past, if this scheme failed there had always been someone there to put everything right.

After what seemed an endless time she recognized the entrance, passed through by her earlier, of the bridleway that would lead out into Poltraze parkland. 'Thank goodness!' Now Kingsley would only scold her about her unpunctuality. No longer in danger, she was disappointed at not finding Clemency Kivell.

The sudden noise of a pheasant scudding out from the trees made the pony rear up. A scream issued from Hattie's lips as she was plunged backwards to the ground. She landed with a tremendous thump, which slammed the breath from her body. She lost consciousness as a shadow was cast over her.

Clemency clamped her mouth shut to prevent a yell of anger and frustration. This spartan, draughty space was her temporary bedroom. It wasn't large enough for a bee to gather nectar in. Greying whitewash stained the misshapen, sloping walls; there was neither paint, wallpaper nor friezes in the whole house. It was as cheerless as the village morgue. The privy belonged in the stone age and a trek outside was necessary to access it.

For the time being, she kept quiet, not wanting to trouble her mother with another complaint. Verena endured the cramped, outdated conditions with quiet fortitude, repeating each day that they were only short-term. The two young wives followed her lead, but Clemency had bitten her tongue during all the unpacking. The result was good furniture and fine things in the wrong setting; it was a shambles. Clemency found herself resenting Logan's unthinking acceptance. He bedded down on the settee, caring about nothing as long as his belly was full; and he stayed out most nights, drowning his innards with strong spirits, whoring and participating in fights, the old-time male Kivell rite of passage. He showed off his fresh bruises and thickened red knuckles as if they were medals of glory. Their mother would hurry to fetch hot salt water and salves. He smirked when Clemency sighed at him in ridicule. He'd mentioned that as soon as there was more room he'd take a bride. Heaven help the poor creature.

Sites had been chosen either side of the paddock for the new homes of Clemency's two married brothers, and work had begun on Adam's, the expectant father. The men were throwing themselves into the construction, leaving the farm work to the former Nankervis manager and workforce, who had decided to stay on following a reasonable wage rise. Two cousins from Meryen, Jowan and Thad Kivell, who owned a thriving carpentry and cabinetmaking business, were involved. More family from the village and some from Burnt Oak were also pitching in, but those who had disrespected Seth had been told by him to 'stay away and go to hell'.

The incessant hammering, banging and sawing, as well as the loud voices, laughter and singing, drifted across from outside. There was constant bustle in the house. But it wasn't the same, and never would be, as the wonderful busyness and closeness of kin at Burnt Oak. The promise of a bedroom the same size as her former one, with new curtains, carpeting and drapes, was all very well, but the change of home was permanent and Clemency hated that. She was bored and lost and missed her teaching. She went outside to tackle her father about it.

She found him taking a breather, thumbing fragrant Turkish tobacco into his pipe. 'You're being churlish, Father. Why shouldn't I carry on teaching as before?'

'The matter's not up for discussion, Clemmie.' After a brief smile he turned away. When Clemency began an argument she'd keep it up for ages, determined to have the last word, just like him, and Logan, the most headstrong of his sons. She would never know how hard it was for him to say no to her. He doted on her because she was so much like his beloved Verena, brave and clever and so very beautiful. After the blessing of five fine, healthy sons (although he was finding it hard to forgive the two who had stayed at Burnt Oak) his little girl was a joy and a credit to him. He noticed with amusement that she had slipped on Logan's overcoat as protection from the cold day, and it was trailing on the ground. It was things like this that endeared her to everyone.

Clemency moved round to face him. 'Why not, Father? It doesn't make sense. Not all the family went against you, and it's not the children's fault. I miss teaching them.' She wouldn't let this go if they stayed here all day. 'It should be my decision.'

'Well, it isn't, Clemency. I'm the one who makes decisions for you.'

'That's not fair!'

'Your mother needs you to be here.'

'Not all day long, she doesn't.'

Having lit his pipe Seth considered her, putting a hand on her shoulder. 'The teaching's been taken over by someone else, Clemmie. Forget about it. If you're restless go for a ride.'

'But I could still teach the music. The children enjoyed my music lessons.'

Seth tossed his great head to puff smoke away from her face. 'You can badger me day and night but the answer is still the same. You're as bright as the stars, my princess, seek something else to do.'

'In that case I will. I've my own money. I'll start a business in the village.' It was something she had been considering for a while.

'Don't be silly.'

'Hello, Clemency.' Jowan Kivell, another who had the clan's strong build and dark good looks, joined them.

'Hello, Jowan. I'm off for a ride.' Tight-faced, she stalked away. Her father wouldn't listen to her now.

'She's in a huff.' Jowan grinned, watching the retreating figure, conspicuous in the oversized coat. 'That's women for you.'

'Clemency's just a girl.'

'Not any more, haven't you noticed? She's very much admired, inside the family and out. It's a wonder no one's approached you yet.'

'Approached me for what?' Seth roared, but he understood Jowan's meaning. It hadn't occurred to him before that Clemency was a young woman. With her looks and intelligence, of course she would be greatly sought after. It was probably his territorial leanings that had kept suitors at bay so far but that was bound to change, and soon. It wouldn't be as easy to protect her now that they lived outside the community. Clemency was always hell-bent on getting her own way. If she were to fall in love with someone unsuitable . . .

'Clemency! Where are you going?'

Her father had never questioned her like this before. Clemency kept walking.

'Clemency! You heard me. Don't you dare ignore me. Come back here.'

Whirling round, she checked her impatience. 'Nowhere in particular, just for a ride.'

'Stay on the farmland. Be no longer than an hour,' Seth bawled.

'What?' she was astonished, angry. She had never been restricted before. 'Am I to be a prisoner now we've moved here?'

'You'll do as you're told. You've been left to go your own way too long. I shall talk to your mother about you, girl!'

Puffing indignantly, Clemency went inside and changed into her waterproof riding coat; no fancy outfit for her. A simple rimmed hat sufficed, she hated bonnets. She saddled up – not side-saddle for her – and raced off before her father forbade her to go out at all. What had got into him? Kivell women were expected to be as much homebodies as women anywhere, but her father had always allowed her as much freedom as she liked. Was moving out of Burnt Oak to this awful place going to ruin her life?

She decided to call on Hattie Faraday, curious to see how she was, to meet her family and view changes to the big house. Kingsley Faraday did not figure in her thoughts. Closing in on a bridleway, an approach to Poltraze parkland she had used before, she heard a shrill scream. Startled for a moment, she galloped off towards the sound.

'Keep still, it's better you don't move.'

Hattie heard the voice as if in a nightmare and was aware of being touched. She fended off the intrusion. 'No–o.'

'Shush, I'm trying to help you. Keep still.'

'Leave me alone!' Hattie shrieked.

Clemency saw Hattie Faraday sprawled on the ground and her attacker about to do his worst. She threw herself off her pony and launched straight at him. 'Get your hands off her!' She could fight nearly as fiercely as her brothers and landed a fist on the side of his face then got an arm lock round his neck.

She was shoved back on to her knees but immediately lunged at the man again. 'Get away from her!'

'Stop it!' Abe Deveril held up a fortress-strong restraining arm, glowering at her. 'I'm trying to help her, idiot! You'll hurt her more this way. She took a fall from her pony. Look.' He shot a look at the refined animal pacing and prancing agitatedly some yards away inside the bridleway.

Hattie stirred and moaned, opening her eyes and blinking. Clemency abandoned her assault. The stranger, a labourer rather than a ruffian, she realized now, was telling the truth. She should have taken a moment to judge the situation instead of charging in under a false assumption. She could have been responsible for adding to Hattie's injuries. Nevertheless, whoever this man was he had no right to be here on Poltraze land. By the evidence of the long-strapped leather bag he had not quite managed to hide behind a hazel bush he had poached a brace of pheasants. The villagers, her family included, had made free with Poltraze game during the estate's desertion. She would take over from the poacher now. 'I'll see to Miss Faraday. You fetch her pony.'

'Don't think to give me orders, Clemency Kivell.' He edged her away from Hattie as if she were no more than an annoying insect hovering about the scene.

Clemency elbowed her way back to tend Hattie, unsurprised at his knowing her name. After her celebrated rescue of Squire Nankervis's son, everyone in Meryen knew her; she was considered a local heroine. 'Fine,' she shot back at him. 'Let's not argue. We must put Miss Faraday's needs first. She must be taken home. I shall test for broken bones.'

'Done it. I think she's just bruised and stunned. I'll lift her up on her pony and lead her most of the way. Can you manage the rest? It won't be far.'

'I know, and of course I can manage. Why could you not fetch the pony in the first instance? I understand why you don't want to escort Miss Faraday all the way safely to the house. Samaritan act aside, you might end up being transported for poaching.' She nodded towards the bag.

He got up from his haunches and stood over her, like a proud young stag, reminding her of Logan. His dark looks were similar but there the comparison ended. This man's power came from a quiet self-assuredness and not from arrogance or steaming brute force. Clemency thought he had yet to reach his twentieth year.

He shrugged his broad shoulders. 'I'm not worried about

the new people. They choose to shun Meryen and I've no wish to meet any more of 'em.'

'Clemency, how good that you're here.' Hattie was still groggy. 'I've had a little accident. Oh, who's this man?'

'My name's not important,' Abe said simply, then walked off to fetch Hattie's pony.

'What did he say?' Hattie croaked.

Clemency got Hattie up a little unsteadily on to her feet and supported her. 'He wants to remain anonymous.' Clemency righted Hattie's hat and picked dirt and leaves off her habit.

'But he did come to help me?'

'Yes. He found you just before I did. I heard your scream.'

The girls watched Abe bringing the pony.

'Thank goodness it didn't run off,' Hattie said. 'Thank you, Mr . . . um. You needn't worry. I won't mention seeing anyone except for Miss Kivell. You are not one of Poltraze's staff so I gather you are a trespasser. I'm sure I can guess why. I suppose you have a large family you help your parents to support. I think I can mount if you would kindly hold your hands together for my foot.'

'As you please, miss.' Abe's voice, with its soft rural accent, had a pleasant tone.

Hattie saw that he had a devil-may-care look about him but with not too much of a devil in it. She considered herself fortunate that he was not a thoroughgoing rogue. She might have suffered a dreadful fate.

Her aches and pains necessitated more assistance than she had anticipated and he helped her to ease herself upright in the side-saddle. Clemency placed both her hands on Hattie's back until she was sure she was able to remain seated. While Abe fetched his swag and gun she swung herself up on to her own mount. Once they were on their way through the oak and beech trees, Clemency keeping close to Hattie's side, Hattie said to her, 'I was on my way to see you but failed to locate your farm and got lost. My brother ordered me to stay in the grounds. He is going to be very angry with me. Were you by chance out with the intention of calling on me?'

'I thought I'd ask if you had moved in comfortably. We can tell Mr Faraday that I came across you in the parkland.' Clemency was curious about their companion's identity. He was leading Hattie's pony without looking behind. 'You, sir, do tell us who you are. Neither I nor Miss Faraday should have travelled so far from our homes today. Neither of us would wish to admit meeting you so your name is safe with us. Do tell us who you are.'

'Indeed, sir,' Hattie, recovering now from her shock, urged, 'I am most grateful for your kind assistance. I would never wish you ill.'

Abe already knew of Clemency Kivell's free spirit. He summed up the other young lady as being from a similar mould. He turned to them. 'I charge you both, on your honour,' he mocked lightly in the nature of a gentleman; then, as an uncouth Kivell might say, 'to keep your mouths shut. My name is Abe Deveril.'

'You are a miner?' Clemency asked.

'I am.'

'At which mine?'

'The Wheal Verity.'

'Have you lived in Meryen long?' Hattie enquired.

'All my life.' Abe was enjoying what had slipped into friendly banter with the two girls. He felt they were intrigued by him. Taking a long look at the pretty face behind him and the gorgeous one at her other side, he was of the same mind. 'I would advise you to be careful if you wander down to the village right now. There is sickness there.'

'There always is. You have family?' This was from Clemency.

'Just my parents.' He smiled. 'Are you ladies enjoying your new homes?'

Both girls warmed to his open, honest smile. It flowed all the way to his eyes, which glimmered with humour. Hattie smiled back at him. 'I love it, ghosts, mysteries and all. It's not as if I'm going to live there for ever anyway.'

'You are fortunate. I hate everything about the farm,' Clemency said, but she too allowed a smile to form. Today she had made two firm friends and that more than offset the stinging chastisement she expected from her father when she returned to Trenbarvear, in her own time.

Five

Kingsley Faraday ran down the steps at the side of the house as the girls came into view. 'Hattie! Where on earth have you been?' He turned accusing eyes on Clemency. 'Was it you who kept her out, Miss Kivell?'

Hattie had made the effort to sit upright in the saddle but she was too tired to answer.

'If you would take a proper look at your sister, Mr Faraday, you will see that she has met with misfortune and is in fact hurt.' Clemency's words were edged with frost. 'She needs quick attention.' Glancing at the house she saw faces, females she thought, at an upstairs window. At once they drew back. From somewhere within dogs barked.

Opening and closing his mouth in horror, Kingsley hurried to Hattie, while shouting for the servants. He lifted his sister down carefully, she a compliant bundle in his arms. 'Hattie, dear, I'm so sorry. Please forgive my remark, Miss Kivell. Come in, please come in with us.'

Clemency knew she should make her way straight home, but instead she allowed a stable boy to lead her pony away. She followed Kingsley through a small gothic-style door. As she tried to keep up with his long strides, she looked for changes in the house. There were none here save for some blank spaces on the walls where paintings had been, and the servants now gathering were in light green and silver livery instead of the Poltraze colours of pale blue and buff. Vigorous attention had been given to the cleaning. There was the smell of beeswax and metal polish. The odour of dogs was also strong.

Kingsley carried Hattie into the winter parlour. He laid her down gently on a plush sofa and sat next to her, rubbing her wrists. 'Bring the medicine box, the brandy, and hot water and towels, Mrs Secombe,' he ordered the housekeeper, a chunky woman with thread-veined cheeks, and peering eyes behind wire-rimmed glasses. 'See that Miss Hattie's bed is warmed through.'

'Oh, I will, sir, right away. Oh, poor Miss Hattie. Shall I order tea for the young lady?' Mrs Secombe indicated Clemency.

'Yes, do that,' Kingsley said. 'Do take a chair by the fire, Miss Kivell. Thank goodness you were there to come to my sister's aid. Where did she take the fall?'

Clemency wove the lie while easing into an armchair. Nothing had been changed or added to the room. The same curtains, fireside rug and wall lanterns were there, along with the old lace chair backs, antimacassars and runners. A log fire glowed in the grate but the house's air of gloom could not be denied; it was ingrained in the timbers, the walls and every individual thing. Clemency found it so and she was sure Kingsley Faraday did too. It was curious that Hattie didn't, but she had led a sheltered life and was innocent of the violence and cruelty in the world, and the drudgery of the poor that Clemency was only too aware of. Clemency thought miserably that whatever her parents did to Trenbarvear the Nankervis bad history would haunt it too. Her father had done his family a terrible wrong. Kivells would never belong there.

'I was pleased to have come along at just the right time to help Hattie,' she said.

'We'll always be in your debt,' Kingsley said. He glanced at the door, anxiously so, Clemency noted. His forehead was creased with lines.

'I don't need to take to my bed, Kingsley,' Hattie said, heaving herself up straight, still a little breathless. He helped her. 'I was shocked more than anything. I'm almost recovered now.'

'If you are sure—' he was brought to a halt by a flurry of scuffling and strange taps out in the corridor, growing ever louder.

It was obvious to Clemency that he was holding his breath. Why the anxiety?

A horde of spaniels burst into the room, barking and yapping as they set the occupants under a chaotic bombardment, jumping at them, worrying their feet, tugging at skirt hems. A large droopy-eyed male sprayed a table leg. A black, white and tan puppy squatted and relieved itself. Another knocked over the brass tools at the fender. Hattie screamed in joyful hysterics as a small dog leapt up on to her lap and furiously licked her chin. Clemency was used to dogs but was overwhelmed by so many at once. There had to be at least a dozen cocker spaniels, of all ages, including four puppies.

'Father! Mother!' Kingsley cried, swinging his arms in agitation and shaking his leg to dislodge one nuisance from his ankle. His face and neck were the colour of blood; he looked about to burst.

Clemency was stunned by the oath he uttered under his breath. The next shock she received was so great that she jumped to her feet, her eyes as large as saucers. Into the room came an old gentleman, with an old lady on his arm. Their mouths were stretched in grins that showed grey teeth. With a sing-song command the old man silenced the dogs, except for the unheeding puppies. Clemency knew she was being rude but she couldn't help staring. The couple, younger than she had first thought, perhaps racing towards sixty years, had a tailor and dressmaker not to be recommended. Their mismatched clothes were garish in colour and fabric. They reminded Clemency of some of the circus performers who came to Meryen every summer. Mr Faraday senior's waistcoat was floral, as if cut from curtain material, and from it hung a preposterously sized gold and diamond watch and chain. He had just a few wisps of bristly grey hair. Mrs Faraday seemed weighed down with pearls, all ugly pieces. She wore an orange feathered turban, and the hair that escaped from beneath it on to her high, rounded forehead was silvery as moonlight. Both had red-circled eyes and were lagged in layers of dog hair. They each carried a long, thin staff, held out straight in front of them; his had a mouldy-looking rabbit's foot dangling from the top and hers was decorated with a tatty red bow.

It was almost unbelievable that they could be the mother and father of the handsome man and pretty girl in the room. This explained Kingsley Faraday's horror; no one would readily care to admit that such people were their parents. It explained also why no outsiders were employed here. Kingsley Faraday had brought his parents down to Cornwall to hide them away. And what of his other sister? Hattie had mentioned the widowed Mrs Jane Hartley, who wished only to keep herself to herself. Was she one of the faces Clemency had seen at the upstairs window?

'What is going on here, dear boy?' Mrs Faraday asked in a rasping voice. Clemency was to learn that she always spoke before her husband. Kingsley flinched at the 'dear boy'.

'Nothing Mama.' He cleared his throat – of his shame and embarrassment, Clemency suspected. 'Hattie has received a visitor, that is all.'

'And one most charming, I see.' Mr Faraday grinned, bowing to Clemency. She didn't usually bother with this style of etiquette but felt compelled to answer with a curtsy.

Mrs Faraday scanned Clemency up and down as if she were studying a dog for pedigree. 'And who exactly is this divine young lady?'

'This is Miss Clemency Kivell. Miss Kivell, this is my father, Mr Clarence Faraday, and my mother, Mrs Ophelia Faraday.' Kingsley was unable to meet Clemency's eyes, wishing he were a million miles away. He had hoped to get to know the farmer's daughter intimately, to be her first lover, but she would never take him seriously after this. 'We were about to take tea.' It was a dismissal to his parents.

'Oh, we're going,' Mrs Faraday said, turning watery eyes to her husband. 'Aren't we, my old croak?'

'Oh, we never stay anywhere long, do we, my old rosebud?' Making strange sucking noises, Mr Faraday gave Clemency a lopsided smile. 'We're Clarry and Phee. Call us that, if you like.'

The puppies were still tearing about. Phee Faraday reached out with her staff to stop one chewing a corner of the carpet. 'But first, young Clemency, let us introduce you to our family.'

'I've only Mrs Hartley left to meet,' Clemency said.

As if not hearing her comment, Phee Faraday began pointing to the canine collection with her staff. Although Hattie seemed unconcerned, Clemency could almost feel Kingsley's humiliation as his mother rattled off a long list of nursery rhyme names: 'Bo-peep, Georgy Porgy, Jack, Jill, Wee Willie . . .'

'They're lovely dogs,' she said admiringly at the end. They were all very well kept.

'Miss Muffet is in pup. You must have a puppy, Clemency. We insist, don't we, Clarry? Come to the morning room at any time. It's where Clarry and I are usually found. Now, off we go, time to walk our little family outside. God bless you, Clemency.' The elder Faradays went out amidst a raucous dash of spaniels.

Clemency could think of nothing to say. Clarry and Phee Faraday had brought a theatrical atmosphere, merriment and fun with them. Hattie had brightened considerably, but her brother was rigid with mortification.

In the throes of an awkward blush, Kingsley turned to Clemency. 'My parents are . . . um . . . they are . . .'

'Unconventional,' Clemency said, feeling sorry for him.

Hattie laughed in an unladylike manner. 'You are very kind, Clemency. Our mama and papa are absolutely eccentric. They adore each other. They are cousins and were childhood sweethearts, and never really wanted to associate with anyone else. They are rather childlike and don't really see us as their children. We were sent away to be educated.'

'I'm sure Miss Kivell doesn't want to hear the whole family history, Hattie,' Kingsley cut in sharply. Mrs Secombe and a footman brought in the medical things and a tea tray. 'Entertain your guest. I have things to do. Excuse me, Miss Kivell.' He left the parlour with taut, rapid strides.

'Poor Kingsley,' Hattie murmured.

Clemency was burning to learn everything about this mystifying family. It was understandable that Kingsley Faraday wished to keep his parents away from the public eye. However, Hattie disappointed her. After sending the servants away and pouring the tea, she chattered about other things. 'I can't wait to have more adventures with you before I enter the whirl of balls, parties and soirées, then settle down as a wife. We might see Abe Deveril again. Do you dream about the man you will marry, Clemency? In a moment you must come upstairs and see my room. You'll notice a great many changes.'

'I can't spare any more time today,' Clemency said.

'But you will call on me again? Will you take me to your new home? Kingsley is adamant that I mustn't go down to the village, but I could disguise myself and go with you. You've got lots of relatives in Meryen, haven't you, Clemency? Do say you agree.'

Hattie's simpering expression bore out how naïve and immature she was in comparison to herself but Clemency was happy to assure her on all counts. If her father forbade her to come here again she would come in secret.

Kingsley went upstairs to the west wing, rebuilt fairly recently, after its destruction in the fire that had seen the dreadful end of an old squire. His sister and her companion had taken over the principal suite of rooms, of neoclassical style and pleasingly light and airy, unlike the rest of the house. However, Jane had deliberately ruined the enhanced effect by hanging heavy, dark curtains and draping every seat and table in black. There were black tasselled cushions and runners, and black ribbons surrounding the pictures. His sister took her widowhood seriously – to the absolute extreme, considering her husband had been dead for six years.

Kingsley hated the sight of Jane's petite figure muffled up to the neck in shapeless black, wearing the same single strand of jet beads and teardrop earrings she had put on the instant she had heard of Hugh Hartley's tragic death. On her small bosom, which still frequently heaved in grief, was a silver filigree-framed brooch from which Hartley's wan likeness, with curving black moustache, peered out as if he were a prisoner. And, in a way, he was. He had certainly not been allowed to rest in peace. Jane had built a shrine to him here in just the same way as she had done in his parents' old home in rural Hampshire, where she and Hartley had lived.

Kingsley had hoped that the one good thing to emerge from his parents' debts and the family's subsequent enforced removal to this out-of-the-way property would be that Jane would finally stop existing in the past. It was not to be. Indifferent to the county she was now living in, the house and its location, her only concern had been to recreate Hartley's temple. Photographs of her dead husband abounded and almost every one had been copied in oils, magnified up to four times in size. Candles of prayer and remembrance were lit, making the air thick and cloying. Marble flowers under glass domes, of the sort found on graves, took pride of place.

Kingsley felt depressed just being in the presence of Jane and her lifelong friend and companion, the dull Adela Miniver, who seemed to sleepwalk through life. It seemed to him that Miss Miniver's former life had been so meaningless that she had found a calling in joining in with Jane's way of self-harming.

He found them looking through a funereally decorated scrapbook of photographs and details of Hartley's life. How many
times he had witnessed this. He had feared it would be
difficult to drag Jane away from Hugh's grave, but she had
declared to Miss Miniver, 'We can take my precious husband
with us in heart and spirit.'

'May I interrupt you, Jane?' he said. He did not greet Miss
Miniver, who was more or less invisible to the family and
preferred it that way.

'What is it, Kingsley?' Jane asked, in the sombre, ethereal
voice she had cultivated on her bereavement. 'You look worried.'

'I am, about Hattie. I shall have to take her up to London
with me; set her up under the wing of some respectable people
for the next two years, or perhaps place her in a young ladies'
academy. I cannot possibly leave her here. Mama and Papa can't
be trusted with the right care for an impressionable young
girl. And you . . .'

'What about me, Kingsley?'

'Well, you're hardly suitable to advise and correct her.' He
threw up his hands in vexation. 'All this mourning; it isn't
healthy, Jane. Can you not move on and begin a new life at
last? Surely Hugh would not have wanted you to spend every
waking moment in such morbid reflection. Think of Hattie.'

Anticipating her friend's response, Adela Miniver passed Jane
a black-edged handkerchief.

Jane sniffed and dabbed her eyes. 'I can never forget my
darling Hugh. I only had him for a year. He was everything
to me. He was my life, and you know that. I am nothing
without him. I am empty. I wish only to be left alone. I am
sorry that I cannot be of any help to Hattie. She is too spir-
ited for me to contend with anyway. I'm sorry to say it but I
find her annoying. She is noisy and disruptive. I agree she
doesn't belong here. It was wrong of you and Matthew to
think she could reside here for a whole two years. She would
soon grow mad with boredom, and who knows what kind of
trouble she might cause. By all means take her up to London.
There, you have your solution.' Jane bowed her head then
turned away, the handkerchief up to her mouth. In the
darkened room she appeared a silhouette of drama.

Kingsley sighed long and hard, revealing his irritation. The
people under this roof were his only family; why were they

all such a liability? He tried to care about them but it was becoming increasingly hard. 'Have you seen Matthew today?'

'Of course I have not.' Jane sounded close to tears, overcome by the hurt she had complained of before, of not being understood. 'Matthew comes out of his rooms less than I do.'

'I'm sorry to have disturbed you,' Kingsley said, fearing that if he stayed here a moment longer he would be infected by the malaise of the two women. It offended him how lifeless they looked; like cadavers, their skin dead white, deprived of sun and fresh air. They were wilting, waning and shrivelling by choice, wholly selfish and utterly pathetic. It was macabre. They might as well be dead now.

Out in the corridor he hurried to a window and opened it for air. Clemency Kivell was on her pony and waving goodbye to Hattie. Kingsley not only welcomed the blast of damp coldness, he sought to steal a little of the beautiful girl's magnificent life force. If only there was someone like her waiting for him in London, or if he could take her there and make her his new paramour. He'd lavish her with her heart's desires.

No, he would marry her, parade the young rural delicacy as his wife, and every man of note would envy him and every woman would rage with jealousy, for Clemency could never be matched. Marriage had never entered his head before. He shook himself to eject the idea. Clemency Kivell had infiltrated the essence of him; he wouldn't allow that to happen again. He had nothing to inherit so he had no reason to desire a son and heir. As it was he supported the two illegitimate children he'd sired with his long-standing mistress. He wanted nothing save to be rid of the outlandish characters here. His mother, father and Jane could do without him.

But there was Matthew. He didn't want to leave his brother here, he would miss him. He cared about Matthew, he didn't want to admit it but he cared for all his family. But coming to Poltraze had been Matthew's choice. The sooner Kingsley got away from here the better. He needed to shake off the horrible sensation of grave cloths wrapping around his ankles. He was afraid. Afraid that this peculiar place would get a grip on him in a way he could never shake off; just as he could never shake off the guilt of what he had done to Matthew and Hugh.

He saw that Clemency Kivell was now trotting away through

the grounds. Good for you, enchanting girl. Don't come here again. Don't get involved with the madness here.

He heard Hattie's sparkling voice calling another goodbye to her. Hattie, his dear young sister, must leave with him in all haste. She mustn't lose her delightful sense that life was for living to the full.

Six

After slogging underground on the morning core at the Wheal Verity, Abe walked the three miles home. He ate a quick meal of bread and cabbage, then tended to his hens and pig, chopped a week's kindling wood, repaired the shed door, and did the hated filthy task of clearing the outdoor drainage to avoid disease. He scrubbed himself down in the tin bath in front of his mother's little black iron cooking slab. For modesty's sake she had surrounded the bath with laundry drying on the wooden clothes-horse.

In a clean shirt, a waistcoat and long jacket, his cap tucked inside a pocket, he made his way to the Nankervis Arms, which despite its grand name was on the rough side. He usually patronized a beer shop in a short side-street, but a serving-maid in the inn was accommodating, and the heat was on him. After twenty minutes in a back room with bosomy, red-haired Lizzy, who was old enough to be his mother, he'd down a couple of tankards of ale, return home, fetch his gun, then bag some more Poltraze game. The vicar's housekeeper was among his willing back-door customers. The florin a bird helped him see his parents through the Great Dread ahead, the winter. Something put by from his honest labour was a comfort for times of sickness or injury. He was the family's only breadwinner. His parents had had him late in life and both were now frail and just about able to cope with a few chores around their home.

Abe sauntered along Meryen's inaptly named narrow High Street with his hands stuffed in his coat pockets, his blue and white neckerchief fluttering in the chilly wind. His boots echoed on the cobbles, scraps of pavement and dirt road as he passed rows of little cob and killas cottages and many single dwellings and shops. The more recently built rows of homes, like Edge End, where he lived, roughly in the middle of the village, veered off at angles to High Street, the front-to-front houses running straight and parallel. Set back behind important-looking wrought-iron railings or stout walls were the proud villas of the wealthy – mainly Kivells now. He glimpsed showy gardens but, come the swell of spring and summer, many humbler dwellings also showed off Nature's glory.

Occasionally, Abe broke off whistling to exchange cheery greetings with children playing, housewives chatting over back walls and fences, men at work in gardens and smallholdings. He grinned on overhearing two elderly housewives, fervent Christians, agree that he was 'a good boy, but tes a pity he mixes with they wicked lot'. They meant the customers at the inn or beer shop. Abe liked a drink and joining in with the roisterous singing or card-playing, but he was equally at ease with just his own company, when out wandering the downs or poaching. Perhaps later today he'd encounter either or both of the two delightful girls he'd met recently on Poltraze land.

It was Saturday and up ahead, beside the Kivell-owned iron-monger's, was a string of people climbing down from a carrier's cart, having arrived back from Redruth market. They headed off in various directions for their homes. Soon to pass the Nankervis Arms, in their home-made Sunday best dresses, bonnets and knitted shawls, were two giggling bal-maidens, Serenity Treneer and Betsy Angove. Trailing behind them was shy Jenny Clymo. Barely fifteen, ginger-haired and freckled, Jenny had the dubious honour of being counthouse assistant to Blythe Knuckey. Each girl carried a small parcel, a cheap treat bought from her monthly wage of less than one pound. All the girls lived near Abe in Edge End.

'Hello, Abe!' Serenity and Betsy cried out together, waving and swinging their hips flirtatiously as they walked past him.

'Get yourselves something nice, did you?' he called back, rolling a smoke to light up in the inn.

'Wait and see,' called Serenity, and she and Betsy fell into more giggles. Jenny managed a small laugh. It was safe to tease Abe. He saw it for what it was, a little innocent fun.

Net curtains blew into an open bedroom window across the road. Blythe Knuckey was watching and listening smugly.

There was more laughter, loud rollicking male laughter, coming from the wide porch of the inn. Seeing who was responsible for it, Abe sighed, guessing what would happen next.

Logan Kivell and two drinking mates had lurched outside on to the flagstone court. They weren't drunk but were intent on acting out a foolish local ritual, of climbing up on to the inn roof by mounting the grimy, uneven whitewashed wall without using the porch pillars or any other support. Over the years, men and youths had slipped, fallen and been injured. A young boy had broken his back and died young as a cripple. As he pushed the others aside to be first to climb, Logan saw the girls. Angling his dark head to the side he waited until they were about to pass.

Serenity and Betsy glanced at each other, lifted their chins and carried on walking, determined to ignore the Kivell braggart. Jenny hung back, edging to the side, ready to run across the road.

Logan planted his big feet directly in front of Serenity and Betsy. 'Ladies,' he began with mock gallantry. His mates roared with bawdy mirth. Over his shoulder he told them to shut up, which they did instantly. No one dared to cross Logan. He had a mean way of hurting with every part of his huge hands. Logan's deep brown eyes swept the girls' bodies from their feet to their pelvic areas, then up to where their breasts were tantalizingly hidden, and finally to their necks and faces. They both turned several shades of pink; so delectable in the young and innocent. He liked girls like that. Even the little mouse trying to make herself unseen behind them was a sweet little thing. He'd like to cuddle her in his arms, feel her quivering, over-awed; a little bundle of mortified flesh being held for the first time by a man. 'Any of you want some company?' he drawled, flicking to each horrified face. 'I'll take you anywhere you'd like to go.'

Serenity was the most desirable of the three. He had noticed her before and taken the trouble to find out all about her. She was wholesome, she liked fun, and he could show her a lot of that. Standing so close to her, he felt her appeal growing by the second. He was sure that once he had peeled away her layers of respectability he would expose quite a lot of passion. He shifted directly in front of her then leaned forward until his face was only a breath away from hers, and whispered huskily, 'Come with me, Miss Serenity Treneer. Come for a nice quiet walk.'

Serenity felt her cheeks burning out of control. Every nerve in her body was racked by excruciating embarrassment, but she couldn't move a muscle to get away from his shameless assault on her dignity and her peace. If only Logan Kivell were not so powerfully masculine. His rugged good looks, his chocolate-brown eyes, and the thin scar running past his left eye and cutting through his straight black eyebrow made him attractive in the most awful, dangerous way. The decent village girls feared him for his potent attraction as much as for his hard, belligerent manner. In tremulous whispers they agreed that 'there was something about him'. That something, what-ever it was, Serenity was reluctant to acknowledge.

'Come with me, Serenity,' he repeated. 'I won't hurt you, I promise.'

For one terrible moment she thought she was going to nod in agreement. Then she came to her senses. 'No!' she gasped, feeling that she had only just snatched herself back from the flames of hell. She whipped back a stride. 'Leave me alone.'

Blythe pushed her head past the curtains, sure that no one would notice her spying. Her sharp features were full of malicious glee.

Scared for Serenity, Betsy pushed her friend into the road. 'Come on, we must go.' Quickened into action, Jenny pulled on Serenity's hand. Serenity managed to make her feet move.

Logan stepped to the side in front of Serenity, bringing all the girls to a terrified halt. 'Don't be like that, Serenity. It's unfriendly, and people really should be friends with me.' He pierced her to the spot with a glowering smile. His mates guffawed, calling lewd encouragements.

'Get out of her way, Kivell!' Abe's threat pierced the air.

Blocking Serenity again as she made a frantic move, Logan glanced round. 'This is none of your business, mining dross.'

'I say it is. Stop annoying the girls. Move aside from them now. *Now!*'

Holding Serenity a prisoner with his eyes, Logan reached out slowly and cupped her arm with his hand. He swung round to Abe, now coming up fast. 'What do you think you can do to me?' He didn't add an expletive or insult and it made his challenge all the more deadly.

'I'm not afraid of you, you damned bully. Call yourself a man? Forcing your attentions on decent young women who don't want you nowhere near them.' Abe's words were as sharp as daggers. 'Let go of her.'

Blythe thumped down her stairs, thrust open her front door and banged on the doors of her neighbours. This was worth an audience. A brawl was brewing.

Stung by the jibes, Logan removed his hand from Serenity's arm. His accuser was now on the court. Customers were spilling out of the inn and villagers were gathering. Logan pounded towards Abe. 'You've made a big mistake, poking your nose into my business, miner's whelp.'

'It's a mistake for anyone to breathe the same air as you, Kivell.' Abe could also sneer in a menacing way.

Logan was impressed that the youth wasn't to be faced down. Most of the local men would have taken care to be at a safe distance before ordering him to stop bothering the girls. It wasn't exhilarating fighting someone who was no match for him, which was nearly always the case. All else forgotten, he was excited to encounter an equal. Well, not quite an equal; the youth lacked his strength and experience. He drawled, 'A fair fight, just you and me?'

Abe nodded. 'It'll be my pleasure.' His father had taught him to fight bare-knuckled and to wrestle. The combination gave him force, balance, swiftness and a watchful eye. Logan Kivell was unaware that he was challenging the Cornish wrestling youth champion for mid-Cornwall.

In unspoken agreement, Logan's mates and some of the other men hurried off to the stables and returned with armfuls of straw, which they laid out in a circular bed to form a ring for the fight.

Serenity, although relieved to be out of danger, was horrified to be the inadvertent cause of this fight. Worse still, it was going to be quite an event. Word was getting round and newcomers, mainly men, about half of them Kivells, were adding to the spectators. They were fickle men, the miners; wagers were swiftly being placed on how long Abe would last. It was a foregone conclusion that Logan

Kivell would win. Serenity prayed that Abe wouldn't end up too badly hurt.

A hand landed heavily on her shoulder. It was her father. 'Home, you, and take the two other maids with you. I've heard what's going on. This is no place for you all now.'

'Father, it wasn't my fault,' she whimpered. She would never get over the shame if he thought she had deliberately encouraged Logan Kivell.

'I know that, maid.' Mr Treneer stayed to watch grimly, not placing a bet. He was sickened by the proceedings, and he hoped the fight would soon be over. He had badly arthritic legs and couldn't stand for long.

The landlord of the Nankervis Arms, lump-bellied, bull-necked Dilly Trewin, a former wrestling champion, was to act as stickler. He was rubbing his meaty hands in delight, for the drinks would flow after this. 'Right then—'

'No rules, it's a free fight,' Logan bawled. He stripped off his shirt, drawing gasps of admiration and some shyness from the women.

'You agree with that, Abe?' Dilly boomed.

'It's fine by me.' Abe was tearing off his shirt and flexing his muscles. His physique was smaller and less mature than Logan's, but his body was toned and perfectly proportioned, with sinewy muscles, and won just as much female admiration.

'Flatten the bugger, Abe,' a miner roared. 'Break his bleddy back. 'Tis time someone put a stop to un tormenting decent folk.'

'Logan will spit that ounce of scrag end out into the middle of next week,' yelled Cary Kivell the watchmaker, his respectable middle-class persona readily thrust aside for this event. Clemency was with him, having been calling on him and his family. He didn't suggest she leave; he knew it would fall on deaf ears. She would want to see the outcome of her brother's fight, and she had witnessed the like before.

With the cacophony of support for both contestants ringing in her ears, Clemency watched Logan fisting the air and flexing his bulging biceps, while he paced his end of the ring. All the while glaring at Abe, Logan kept throwing back his head and stamping his feet, like a warring stag. Clemency thought Abe was brave for standing up to her brother and getting the mine girl out of his clutches. Sadly, although he looked confident while sizing up Logan, he was in for a fierce battering. Logan was capable of winning a fair fight but he'd not shy away from dirty tricks. Clemency hated being crammed among so many sweaty bodies and the constant jostling. The women were crying out like banshees. Lizzy the serving-maid, who earned well by servicing Logan's carnal needs – to Clemency's disgust, she had overheard Logan bragging about it – was pushing up the fat breasts almost hanging out of her bodice with her hands, the slut.

Glimpsing Clemency, Abe winked at her.

'Good luck,' she mouthed to him.

Intent on preening and prancing, Logan didn't notice. If he had, he'd have demanded later why she had been familiar with his opponent.

'You boys ready?' Dilly cried. 'Right then, I'll intervene only in the event of fear of crippling injury or loss of life. Match is over when one of you yells "Submit" or raises a hand in submission. On my count of three, begin.'

'Troublemaker!' a female screamed at Logan, fearing for Abe. If he were hurt too badly to work, he wouldn't be able to earn his keep.

'Go on, Logan, crush the little swine t'dust!'

'Silence!' Dilly boomed. The jostling halted and an expectant hush swept over the crowd. 'One, two . . .' a long dramatic pause, in which the opponents' and spectators' nerves were stretched taut, '. . . three!'

A cheer went up loud enough to topple the houses off the hills. Feet apart and knees bent, the adversaries locked eyes. There was no sneering now on Logan's face and no good humour in Abe's. They were deadly serious, shutting out those around them, intent only on what it took to win. Logan was looking for another victory to retain his crown of invincibility; Abe wanted to topple this bully and make him eat dust.

Clemency tensed her fists. She felt no disloyalty at wanting Abe to win, to beat the tyranny out of her brother. The village women had the right to walk the streets unmolested. The coarse, dirty and lazy, and the hard-working and decent, figured in roughly equal numbers among the mining community in Meryen. Since the squire had sold up, his charities had stopped altogether, including free schooling for the children, and the uncivilized were beginning to gain prominence. Clemency hated the small-mindedness in Logan and her father that made them a part of it. It was one thing to be tough but there was no pride in being a ruffian.

Uncle Cary had been telling her about plans among the Kivell brethren here, who wanted a safer and cleaner environment to live in. They were keen to pay for a miner's institute to encourage the men to forsake the public houses, and to set up a fund to offer financial aid to the needy. The Kivell Charity Fund would remind the lower orders where their gratitude should lie, and keep them in line. A teacher would be hired for the school and lessons resumed. It had been a pity the children's education had been brought to a halt; the brightest boys had been sent on to Camborne to learn to become mining engineers. Clemency had offered to do some teaching. Why not give these poorer children the benefit of her bright mind?

'You're worth more than that, Clemmie.' Uncle Cary had shaken his head and to him that was the end of the matter. He had been one of those who had offended her father. Seth had no time for the villagers and would have forbidden it anyway. She would have to think of something else to do that suited her. Starting up her own business appealed to her more and more. She was a person in her own right and not destined merely to become some man's attachment.

She was still reeling from her father's fury at her arriving home late from her ride that day. He had all but pulled her down off her pony. 'Where the hell have you been? I was worried you'd had an accident.'

Riled, she had folded her arms and narrowed her eyes. 'If you must know, I've been to Poltraze.'

She'd stalked away, but Seth had grabbed her and yanked her back. 'Why? I told you to stay on the farmland. How dare you disobey me?'

'What's got into you, Father? You've never bothered where I've gone before. You've always trusted me to take care of myself.'

'That was before.'

'Before what, for goodness' sake?'

It had surprised her to see him suddenly looking lost. 'Get into the house. Your mother will talk to you.'

'All right, I'm going.' She wriggled to get free. 'Let go of me. I won't be dragged there.'

He had trudged along at her side. 'What made you go to Poltraze?'

'I was curious about the new people. I thought you would be too. You wanted to live there, remember?'

'Well,' he said gruffly, 'did they receive you?'

So he was curious about them. She told him about Hattie's fall. 'They were all very grateful to me.'

'So they should be.' Had there been an element of pride in her father's rough reply? 'Silly young bitch could have lain there all night and died of the cold.'

'I'm sure that wouldn't have happened. Her brother, Kingsley Faraday, would have found her fairly easily.'

'How many are there in the family? What are they like?'

'I didn't think you were interested in them, Father,' she'd teased.

'Well, I am! They're our neighbours. They buy our produce. And I need to know if they're any threat.'

'Believe me, Father, the Faradays won't be a threat to anyone. Hattie is the only one who is likely to be seen outside the Poltraze grounds. Mr Faraday is soon to return to London. The rest of the family is reclusive. They will be showing no interest in the local gentry, the village, or anything else.'

'Really?' Clemency saw her father fingering his beard in a thoughtful manner. 'In that case you may call there again.'

'Why? Why should you allow that?'

'The Faraday girl sounds like a suitable acquaintance for you, that's why. She's a young lady and so are you. Never forget it. But,' he wagged a finger at her, 'be sure you tell your mother or me where and when you're going from now on.'

Later, her mother had explained that now she was a young woman her parents were concerned about her falling prey to inappropriate or predatory behaviour from a man. She had made it clear that if they felt it necessary, Clemency would be forbidden to travel anywhere without a chaperone.

'As if I would be that foolish, Mother. I thought you and Father would have credited me with more sense.' She had shaken her head, greatly amused, not taking it as a serious warning. 'But I'll keep you informed of my movements if it puts your minds at rest.' Well, nearly all her movements.

Abe had witnessed Logan fighting before and he knew how he made his first move. He rushed an opponent, seeming about to punch his face, then hammering his fists into his guts, or vice versa. Abe kept a steady stance, one foot planted in front of the other, his fists up to protect his face, trying to work out which way Logan would approach him.

Logan went at Abe with his fists aimed at his belly. Abe knew that the instant he dropped the defence of his face, Logan would turn his nose into splintered bone and pulp. The crowd hollered and cajoled, men enacting blows with their own fists, unsteadying the crowd. Cary Kivell moved behind Clemency to protect her.

Abe waited until he was sure of Logan's intention .At the very last instant, he whipped to the side. As Logan's fists worked like pistons in thin air, Abe got a firm purchase on his opponent's belt, hooked his leg round Logan's ankle, swung the heavier man over his shoulder and dumped him on the ground.

'Aargh!'

The look of shock on Logan's face would be talked about in Meryen for years.

Yells of disappointment mixed with some cries of 'Well done, Abe!' and loud applause blared out round the ring. Clemency had hardly been able to believe her eyes at the sight of Logan sailing through the air like salt thrown to avert bad luck, then cast down like a sack of rubbish. He was already regaining his feet but his cheeks were aflame.

'You can do it, Abe!' someone bawled.

'Get him, Logan!' from another.

To save face Logan went straight back in to the attack. Abe was poised but Logan got a blow to his head, which sent him staggering backwards, then Logan landed a punch on his jaw.

Logan was carried along on grit and fury. He wanted to kill the youth who had humiliated him. It made him careless. He didn't see the iron fist coming and his guts exploded with pain. He punched out wildly. His fist caught the youth's side but made small impact. He must control himself. He was getting nowhere.

Seeming to aim his raised knuckles for Logan's jaw, Abe changed swiftly to a wrestling hitch. He planted one leg across Logan's front, thrust his hip against the other man's middle then, hooking his shoulder in the crook of Logan's elbow, he pivoted round and with a mighty heave that pushed the air out of his lungs, he lifted the heavy weight of Logan's body over his hip and once more decked Logan on the straw. Logan blasphemed so fiercely that some in the hubbub winced. Flinging himself down on one knee, Abe clutched Logan's arm and twisted it out wide.

Stunned again, his yanked arm burning in pain, Logan delayed a moment in thrusting his torso round to get his free hand on Abe. Abe, still on one knee, kept his distance, leaving Logan floundering with his legs to try to kick him away. 'Submit, Kivell,' Abe snarled.

Logan swore profanely, clawing the air as he tried to seize the youth tormenting him.

Abe got to his feet and, using both hands, keeping Logan's arm twisted, he dragged him round the ring, hopping out of Logan's desperate reach.

Her eyes the size of planets, hands to her open mouth, Clemency was astounded to see Abe reducing Logan from top dog to runt of the litter. She was beginning to feel sorry for Logan. If this went on and Abe was victorious, Logan would never be able to show his face in Meryen again. The family would be ashamed of him.

Logan flung himself on to his front, straw mixing with the saliva on his lips. Pulling back on the arm being hauled, enduring the agony, he shuffled on to his knees and issued a bellow louder than cannon fire. With the greatest effort of his life he yanked and tugged until his hand was free.

'Give it up, Kivell,' Mr Treneer cried. 'You're no match for a real man.'

''Tis David and Goliath all over again!' the man next to him roared.

Laughter swept round, as well as much disgruntled murmuring. Money didn't seem likely to be made now. Clemency felt her heart clench for Logan, now kneeling with his head bowed and panting like an old nag.

Logan looked up. He had said no rules. The young miner was coming at him to finish him off. Logan panted harder, putting a hand to his throat as if too out of breath to resist the next onslaught. He saw Abe's ploy. He was going to skirt round him, get a stranglehold on his neck or grab both his arms. Logan waited. The second Abe had swerved round and was behind him Logan swivelled on his knees and butted Abe viciously in the guts.

'Uhh!' As Abe buckled over, Logan took the youth's body over his broad shoulders and staggered up on to his feet. He swung Abe round and round as if playing a cruel game with an infant. The crowd went wild, screaming the men's names, issuing instructions, some desperate, some cruel. Abe kicked and struggled and beat on Logan's arms to take both of them down. He was about to be thrown, heaved yards away, and would be badly injured.

Logan stopped spinning. The crowd hushed. Clemency bit her lip, not wanting to look. Any moment now some of Abe's bones would be broken on the straw-strewn court. Pray God he didn't land on his head. Logan raised Abe up above his own head. Every mouth opened in a gasp. Then Logan swung Abe down on to his feet in from of him and butted him in the mouth. Blood sprayed from Abe's split lips over Logan's brow. Both men were rocking, unsteady from the previous assaults and the circling. Clenching his teeth, Logan pulled back his fist and punched into Abe's jaw. Abe was thrown off his feet and went down with a sickening wallop. Clemency was among those who screamed in horror.

Dilly Trewin stepped into the arena and began the count. Swaying, panting, wiping blood and sweat off his face with the back of his bruised hand, Logan kept slitted eyes on the youth he had felled.

Dazed but not out of it, his head spinning, Abe scrabbled to heave himself up. He got on to one hand and knee. His followers yelled frantically, willing him all the way up off the ground. Clemency had her fingers pressed in hard against her cheeks. *Get up, Abe.* He was like a newborn foal, up on both knees, back down on one knee, looking up at the sky as if trying to gain strength from a higher power.

'Six, seven . . .'

Clemency's eyes darted between Abe and Dilly Trewin. 'Abe, get up.'

Bent over, Abe had only one hand to lift up. The landlord's thick nicotine-stained finger kept slamming down relentlessly on the palm of his hairy paw. Wobbling, Abe got the hand up but his knee sank down.

'. . . eight, nine, ten. Out! The winner is Logan Kivell!' The landlord was much relieved. A different outcome would likely have meant his establishment being ripped apart in an ugly drunken brawl.

Tremendous cheers went up in the Kivell camp. Cary Kivell nearly deafened Clemency. He had a long way to go before he left behind the wilder family traits.

Usually there was a rush forward to congratulate, commiserate and to pick up the loser. No one stirred and the excitement died away. On slow steps Logan was advancing on the youth he had beaten to the ground.

'No, Logan, don't hurt him again!' Clemency cried. She would never forgive her brother for such savage behaviour.

The man reached the youth. No one dared breathe. Abe was sitting cross-legged, muggy in the head, blood spattered on his chin, neck and chest, watching this Goliath who had rewritten the Biblical account of clever thoughtfulness over-coming brute force. Abe was on the alert, ready to defend himself.

Logan held out his hand towards Abe. 'Well done, you did well.' In one heave he brought the worthy David, although the loser, to his feet and slapped his shoulder. Abe tottered, but Mr Treneer was there to grab him.

The acknowledgement brought on a rousing chorus of approval from both camps. It was considered the best-fought fight in ages. It would go down in village history, particularly with the quarrelsome Logan Kivell having been taken down a peg or two. Clemency was proud of her brother.

Raising his arms with balled fists in the air Logan trod out a victory circle and howled his triumph. Applause and thrilled talk filled the air. It was almost as if Meryen and the Kivells as a whole had been brought closer together over the incident.

Logan felt elated. He had won the day and avoided looking a fool. There would have been nothing worse than to be beaten by a lesser man. Light-hearted, aching and hurting in places, he turned for one last lap, and fell over his own feet. 'Wha—' He was falling. He flailed his arms like a swimmer drowning but the straw was coming up to meet him. He plummeted down on his side. Clemency watched with horror as his elbow struck the ground first and she shrieked at the gut-churning sound of Logan's joint splintering and breaking.

'Logan!'

'Owyah! Oh, my God! Ow! Ow!' Logan screamed again and again, rolling about in the worst agony of his life.

Clemency ran to him and fell down on her knees. 'Lay your head on my lap, Logan. Uncle Cary, fetch Uncle Henry!' Henry Cardell had married a Kivell woman and was the local apothecary and an accomplished bone-setter. 'Someone fetch water!'

She was met with shocked faces. Up on his feet now, Abe went to her. 'Logan, it'll be all right.'

Someone pushed through the mêlée. Blythe Knuckey was now staring down on the fallen anti-hero. With hands on her thick hips, she ran her avid eyes round the gathering. 'Don't look so big-headed now, does he? Not so indestructible now. Now he knows what it's like to be on the receiving end of something undeserved. God don't pay His debts with money.'

Logan groaned and Clemency turned his head so that he could vomit on the ground. He whimpered when he was finished.

'See how the mighty are fallen.' Mr Treneer smirked. 'Serve him right for harassing my poor daughter and the other young maids. Perhaps the village women will have one less thing to fear from now on.'

As others remembered past hurts, both their own and those of their loved ones or friends, mutters of agreement rang out, then insults. Mr Treneer, resting a hand on a kindly shoulder to take the weight off one of his throbbing legs, threw back his head and laughed and laughed. Others too let rip with their lungs, allowing tears of sarcastic hilarity to flow down their cheeks unchecked.

Clemency wanted to shout at them to stop, but knew they would deride Logan even more for needing a girl to take up his cause. Groaning, Logan turned his face towards her. He was trembling from pain and shock, but Clemency had the dreadful feeling that at this moment her brother wished only to die of shame.

Seven

Hattie's trunks were packed for London. She and Kingsley had sat down to their last evening meal with their parents, and Jane and Adela. Now she was creeping down the long, dark first-floor corridor of the previously little-used east wing. After dark, something about the old house made her feel she should steal about quietly. She didn't want to make a disturbance, to cause the ancient timbers to heave and groan more than they usually did. She felt a sense that the house aged even more as the sunlight dwindled and she was keen to show her respect. She was on her way to Matthew's study to bid him goodbye. He would not join the line-up tomorrow morning to see her and Kingsley off. He lived as if he were their next-door neighbour, rather than a member of the family, but he always extended a welcome to any of them.

Once seated on a plush stool close beside her brother, in front of the nondescript grey-stone hearth, she announced a trifle petulantly, 'I didn't want to leave here just yet. I so wanted to see more of my new friend, Miss Clemency Kivell. I've written to her. I'm hoping she may be able to slip over in time to say goodbye to me.'

The only light came from the leaping flames in the antiquated brass grate and Matthew was partly in shadow. After being robbed of most of his sight five years ago in a terrible tragedy while serving in the Life Guards, he had learned to move expertly about with the use of his remaining senses, and never required the servants to light lanterns or candles. His rooms were furnished thinly. The fashionable clutter of the day was inappropriate for him, but Matthew put no value on possessions anyway. The firelight disguised the scarring to the right side of his face and neck. Thankfully, his eyes were intact. Before the accident they had been a calm dove grey; now, as if in compensation, they were strangely beautiful, like softly glittering orbs. Hattie fancied he looked like a story-book hero. He was a real-life hero; he had been decorated for his bravery in saving so many fellow officers in the mess fire. Sadly, the fire had taken a life – and, in doing so, made Jane a widow. The family had thanked God that Kingsley, who had been there visiting, had come through unscathed.

'Kingsley is doing the right thing for you, Hattie.' Matthew Faraday's voice was slow and husky, sometimes whispery, which made it necessary to concentrate while conversing with him. 'You mustn't become part of this, of the rest of us.'

'What do you mean?' Hattie wished he would sit well. He had good posture but was inclined to slouch, as if wanting to wind himself in from everything. On his lap was a portable writing desk. He wrote reams of poetry, poignant stuff, but some surprisingly comical, and the papers were in danger of slipping to the floor. Despite his impaired eyesight, he was able to write in surprisingly straight lines. He published his work under the pseudonym 'M. R. Dayton' and it had received much praise. Matthew also had the habit of holding his face away from other people, making communication even harder. His thoughts and moods were generally known only to himself; even his manservant, the former corporal in his service, was kept guessing.

'It has to be said, Hattie dear, some would call us here a freak show.' Matthew delivered this judgement with passive resignation. He did not mind for himself, his parents or Jane, but he was passionate that Hattie and Kingsley should live a full and normal life.

'Don't say that, Matthew! I can't bear it. Yes, Mama and Papa have always been like perpetual children, and Jane has chosen to hide herself away and make herself a martyr to grief. But you, you didn't deserve what happened to you.' Her voice softened. 'It's not so bad, you know, your face. You're not so badly scarred that society would be offended at the sight. Rather it makes you dashing. Your heroism would ensure that you'd be greatly sought after to attend the most important drawing-rooms. Members of your old regiment would be thrilled to see you. The ladies would adore you, I'm sure. They would fall over themselves to become your wife. You could have a family, Matthew. Don't you want that? Oh, do say you'll come with us. Kingsley looks up to you. He needs you, I think. He will hate leaving you behind.'

'Perhaps some of what you say is true, but it isn't what I want. Besides, Mama, Papa and Jane mustn't be deserted altogether. This house is mine, not Kingsley's. It was my decision to come here, to bring all the family with me, except for you, to protect them from ridicule, from the things that would frighten them. I didn't want you to come down here, Hattie. I wouldn't have given in to your pleas, as Kingsley did. You'll find no adventure here. Go to London and do well. Do it for all of us, so we can be proud of you.'

Hattie jumped up and hugged his neck, squeezing him with intense emotion. It broke her heart that his once strong build was fading. He ate so little and was becoming thin. 'I'll come back to see you. I will, I promise. Don't forbid me to come. I love you, Matthew. You're so very dear to me.'

Matthew lifted a hand to stroke her hair but otherwise remained motionless.

Hattie kept her display of affection brief. Matthew didn't like to be touched or to have people too close to him.

'Go now,' Matthew said. 'I love you too, Hattie. God be with you.'

Hattie closed the door behind her softly. Where did Matthew go in his thoughts when he was alone, which was almost all the time? He instructed Barker, his manservant, to bring his meals to the wing. He didn't appear to be lonely but he had to be. It was a dreadful thing to shut yourself off from all contact; not to want people to know you existed. Matthew would shrivel and dry up. He might go mad, end up a rambling old man, needing to be shut away for ever. Hot tears stung Hattie's eyes. It wasn't fair. Matthew wouldn't harm a living thing. It wasn't right he should suffer like this, going through all kinds of private agonies that made him shun the whole world. He used to have so many interests. He had planned a military career. Now he was going to whittle himself away, gradually turn into a bewildered nothing.

It must not be allowed. She could not possibly live a happy life knowing she had left here without doing something about it. Matthew would not listen to her; her parents were incapable of reasoning with him; Jane was too selfish to care about anyone except herself. Kingsley must do something.

She darted along to the end of the corridor and made for the stairs. By now she was sobbing like a child – not the best way to approach Kingsley, but she must impress upon him how much she feared for Matthew. She started down the stairs. On the third stair her heel caught in her petticoats and she fell to the bottom, screaming all the way.

Clemency made an early-morning arrival at Poltraze. The Faraday spaniels were tearing about at the end of the gently sloping lawn and barked at her. She expected them to race up and greet her, perhaps be suspicious of her, but they carried on with their play. Then she saw that their master and mistress were with them, two figures with their staffs, like peculiar trees in shawl-collared, ankle-length, fur-trimmed cloaks. Mr Faraday wore dark green, with a blue and red scarf dangling almost to his feet, and Mrs Faraday was in light blue, one hand inside a large fur muff. Her bonnet was twice the size necessary to frame her face and was besieged by orange-tinted plumes. Clemency had the impression that someone had dressed them like this so that they could be easily spotted if they got lost. The couple had seemed scatterbrained to her and, from the opinion she had formed of them, not unlikely to lose their way in the grounds.

A stable boy appeared but instead of taking Clemency's pony he stood to attention. He must be waiting to see if she was to be admitted, Clemency decided. All visitors would, no doubt, receive this treatment since the Faradays seemed to want to keep their distance. She did not need to use the bell-pull. The housekeeper unbolted the door to her.

'Good morning, Miss Kivell.' Mrs Secombe's tone was sombre. 'Please come in. Miss Faraday has told me she invited you to see her off to London. As it happens, she won't be travelling today. Yesterday she took a fall down the stairs. It was such a to-do. If you'll follow me, I'll show you up to her room.'

'A fall? How awful. Was Miss Faraday badly hurt?' Clemency handed over her hat and gloves.

'It could have been a lot worse.' Mrs Secombe's double chin wobbled and she said no more, simply adjusted her spectacles and mounted the stairs; discreet and unassuming, the best of all servants.

Clemency wondered why Hattie had the master bedroom at the front of the house, and not her parents. Mrs Secombe raised a respectful hand to bid Clemency to wait then she entered.

'What is it, Mrs Secombe?' Hattie groaned from the four-poster bed.

'Miss Kivell is here, Miss Hattie. Shall I—?'

'Oh, send her in! I'm so bored. It will be wonderful to have her company.'

Clemency grinned, glad that her friend's mishap had not sapped her energy.

'Please don't tire her, Miss Kivell,' Mrs Secombe said kindly before she withdrew. 'It's been a devil of a job to get her to stay in bed.'

The room was pleasantly changed from Clemency's last trespass inside it. The heavy damask drapes had been replaced by lace, silks and muslin, more suitable to a young woman like Hattie. Tucked up in bedding and shawls, with a small linen bandage covering the corner of her brow, Hattie was propped up dejectedly in the vast bed, looking like a delicate, slightly damaged porcelain doll.

'I was expecting to see luggage on the front steps and a carriage waiting. What rotten luck to have had an accident, and a serious one by all account.'

'Mrs Secombe hinted it was a near-disaster, did she?' Hattie pushed at the bedcovers and rested her arms on top of them.

Clemency stared, her lower lip drooping. Hattie's arm was in a sling – the left arm, the same one that Logan had injured.

'I was so shocked to be suddenly tumbling down, I screamed from top to bottom. Kingsley expected to find me dead. Now this has delayed our departure and he is not in the best of tempers. Clemency, what is it? Is the sight of me distressing to you?'

'It is on your account, Hattie. And here's a strange co-incidence.' She told her friend about Logan's broken arm and the agony he was still in, and the reason behind the fight.

'Well, thankfully, I've only suffered a sprained wrist and a bump on the head. Kingsley sent for the doctor at St Day, and he said I must rest for a month before I travel. It's quite un-necessary to delay that long. I shall be quite recovered in a day or two. But I'm rather thrilled it will give me the chance to get to know you better. I'd quite like to meet Abe again too. He must be nursing more aches and pains than I this morning. Kingsley and Jane would be horrified at my opinion but I think it's somehow natural for men to wage war.'

Clemency made a wry face. 'It's as natural as breathing to my menfolk. Mr Faraday didn't send for Meryen's doctor? I can assure you he is trustworthy and honest. He's getting on in years but fully capable.' It had scandalized the village two years ago, when the young village doctor of the day, cleverly hiding his sadistic nature, had been the abductor of Squire Nankervis's young son. Clemency was one of only two people who knew that the married doctor had been the lover of her cousin Rachel, sister to Jowan, the carpenter. It had taken a while for the new doctor to prove to the locals he was trustworthy.

'You must have noticed my family is not interested in the village.' A light flush washed Hattie's face. It was hard not to tell Clemency the reason why. She hoped Clemency would ask no more questions on the subject. She went on brightly, 'But I'd like to take a peek at it, although not to venture actually inside it. Tell me, how is your brother faring? He must surely be laid up even worse than I am.'

'It's the first time I've known him to be bound to his bed. He's going to be a very irritable patient.' Clemency found it hard to talk about the accident.

Logan had yelped and groaned in pain all the way home in Cary Kivell's carriage. On the farmhouse kitchen table, he had yelled throughout as Henry Cardell had applied an alcohol-based antiseptic to clean his misshapen, bleeding arm, which was hanging limp from the elbow like a ship's destroyed mast. Then Cardell had cut into the arm in three places to remove tiny splinters of bone.

'Am I going to lose my arm?' Logan had screamed again and again, at one point clutching his apothecary uncle by the shirt collar, almost choking him.

'Not if I've anything to do with it, you won't.' Henry Cardell, a man of stout stature, had forced him to lie down again. It had taken Clemency's father and her brothers' combined strength to hold Logan still while Henry Cardell, after some careful deliberation, had deftly, almost cruelly, crooked the elbow joint and the other broken bones back into place. Logan had howled like an animal skinned alive. He had slipped into semi-consciousness for an instant, and then whimpered while his arm was finally sewn up, his wounds dressed and splints tied on. The appalling echoes of Logan's anguish still brought chills to Clemency. With his arm finally in a sling, Logan had fully passed out. Now there was the worry, over the next few days, of infection setting in. Added to this fear was the knowledge that Logan's arm would never again have the same strength, and that it would be scarred and pitted and perhaps shorter than his other arm. There would be no more fighting and daring deeds for him. The result of his shameful behaviour towards the three village girls, and then his conceit, was that he was now a cripple. Meryen would see it as a just reward.

Clemency had given up her bed for Logan – he couldn't be nursed on the settee – and she had wanted to take a turn tending him, but her mother had refused to leave his side. 'Why don't you go out somewhere, Clemency?' Verena had suggested. 'Your sisters-in-law are eager to get the children settled and the servants will see to everything else. Now you have no room to retire to you will be at a loose end. Just be sure to be home before it gets dark.' So Clemency had come to Poltraze.

'I'd like to meet your family, especially Logan. He sounds fascinating,' Hattie said, with a wistful sigh. She had a picture of a darkly handsome, sad-eyed man reclining bravely in bandages, waiting for a maiden to put a goblet of healing nectar to his lips. Logan was like Matthew. No, Matthew wasn't like that at all. Matthew was not a confrontational ne'er-do-well. Clemency had not hidden the fact that her brother had been bothering three village girls and had challenged Abe after Abe had bravely gone to their defence. Matthew was brave beyond measure. And, to Hattie's grief, he wasn't waiting for anyone to do anything for him.

'Fascinating? Logan's hardly that,' Clemency said grimly. Hattie's sheltered existence would never prepare her for facing men like Logan.

Her mood having taken a dip, Hattie reached for the silver bell on the bedside cabinet stand. 'I can't lie here like this. Kingsley won't hear of me going downstairs, but I will take to the couch.'

'Would you like me to leave?' Clemency asked, noting

Hattie's sudden loss of spirits, probably from the shock of the accident. She didn't want to return home yet; she would prefer to linger here with her friend. At home her father was clumping about like a sore-headed bear. Logan had scared and offended three highly moral young women. In addition, his insults to Abe would be taken to include the whole mining community. Neither could any pride be salvaged from the humiliation of Logan's clumsy accident. The spectators at the fight would not deem his uncharacteristic congratulation to Abe as admirable. The family members who'd watched the fight considered Logan had wantonly let down the Kivell name. None had been to Trenbarvear to enquire after him. Family feelings were running against those who had taken themselves off to the former Poltraze Farm. Clemency was experiencing something she had never suffered before – being shut out by her family. Were the Faradays in some sort of exile too, she wondered? She wanted to stay here and see what she could discover about them.

'Oh, no, don't go!' Hattie cried in alarm. 'Please don't think I meant you should leave. You're my friend, the only one I have here. We must find something diverting to do. I know – I have a lot of old magazines. We could cut out pictures to make scrapbooks. I love doing that, don't you? I'm sure you have an artistic eye, Clemency. I'll take a little rest whenever it is necessary. We could have luncheon together in here. Please don't say you have to go.'

'I don't. I'd be happy to spend the day with you.'

'Oh, that's wonderful.' Hattie laughed delightedly.

Hattie's maid, slim and as neat as a new dressmaking pin, listened to her demands while smiling indulgently. Clemency wasn't surprised the servant was so kind and understanding towards her young mistress. It was plain to see why people should seek to nurture Hattie; she was utterly charming, without an unkind bone in her body. 'If that's what you wish to do, Miss Hattie, I'll set up the things on the tea table. I'm pleased the young lady is here to distract you after your ordeal, but I recommend you return to bed in twenty minutes.'

'I'd prefer to rest on the couch if I tire. I promise to be sensible, Bridie. Do not fear. Miss Kivell will take good care of me and will call for you if you're needed.'

'As you please then, Miss Hattie.'

Bridie prepared the striped silk Georgian couch with pillows and cushions and, once Hattie was settled on it, covered her legs with a soft blanket. Then she fetched the things needed for making the scrapbook. After she had left the room, Hattie explained to Clemency that 'Bridie' was the nickname of the treasured Bridlington, who was also Mrs Faraday's personal maid.

Clemency slid a buttoned slipper chair over to the couch and Hattie smiled contentedly at her. A pleasantly peaceful half-hour passed in which the girls cut out painted pictures of cherubic children, some in white wigs, as well as angels, flowers, birds, animals and country scenes. They created a happy mess, scattering snips of paper on their laps, the tea table and the floor. They talked of nothing except how they would arrange the cuttings on the scrapbook pages, both glad to forget their troublesome families for a while.

Presently, Hattie suppressed a yawn. 'It's time for morning tea,' she said. 'I confess I am a little tired. I'll watch while you do the pasting, if I may, Clemency. I've so enjoyed doing this with you.'

'And I have with you, Hattie. I do wish I had a sister,' Clemency said, as they tidied up to receive the refreshment. It was strange, she had never wished that before.

'Well, I have a sister but I might as well not.' Hattie made a face. 'Jane is eight years older than I and has never taken the slightest interest in me. She makes it obvious she dislikes me. The feeling is mutual. She's bossy and condescending. She's quite horrid to the servants and persists in patronizing dear Mama and Papa. She married a lieutenant in my brother's regiment and when he was killed she was inconsolable for months. I felt sorry for her, of course, but she has turned her widowhood into a passion. She returned to live with us and turned her room into a shrine to Hugh. She's done the same to the west wing here. It's unhealthy. It positively gives me the creeps. A meeting with her would not be at all edifying for you.'

This made Clemency hope she would meet Jane Hartley very soon. She enjoyed meeting new people and forming opinions of them, keen to see if her own opinions coincided with those of others. 'I didn't take the younger Mr Faraday for a military man. Was he a close friend of your late brother-in-law?'

'No, not close, but he had great admiration for Hugh.' Hattie looked down. It was Matthew who had been Hugh's friend. Now Clemency was her friend it seemed a snub not to confide in her about Matthew's existence, but it was his firm request that the locals were not told about him. She would never break Matthew's trust.

The door opened and a young parlourmaid came in, expertly balancing a large tea tray.

'Ah, Patience, has Cook put on any sweetmeats for us?' Hattie asked eagerly. She beamed at Clemency. 'Cook always spoils me when I'm unwell.'

'And rightly so. It's ginger snaps today,' Kingsley's strong voice answered, as he followed in after the maid.

Clemency noticed three cups on the mahogany tray. Mr Faraday had invited himself to join them. His manner was bright but underneath it she thought he seemed harassed.

'It's a pleasure to meet you again, Miss Kivell,' Kingsley said sincerely, almost stopping in his tracks, so breathtakingly beautiful he found her. Her presence helped lift the shock and horror that still affected him after believing, if only for a short time last night, that Hattie had fallen to her death. Once this fear had abated, he had been annoyed at having to delay his journey to London. However, the aggravation was worth it just to see this young beauty again. How could her father let her out of his sight? She was a desirable prize to men and should be guarded and shielded for the precious soul she was. In London society, even dressed as she was now in her provincial clothes and with a simple hairstyle, she would cause a stir.

'You're joining us, Kingsley?' Hattie muttered ungraciously. It wasn't unknown for her sociable brother to join her and her visitors while in London, but Clemency was her only friend down here and she wanted to keep her all to herself.

'For a minute or two, if I may.' He edged an apologetic look at Hattie and turned towards the door. 'Jane and Adela are here to see you too.'

Oh, no. Hattie groaned inwardly. Selfish Jane had not bothered to come to her immediately after her accident, so why now, of all the inconvenient times?

Clemency's stare shot to the door. The widow and her companion were taking their time. Did they intend to make a grand entrance?

Two women in black, their heads slightly bowed, crept into the room wringing sorrowful, lace-mittened hands. Quite a performance, Clemency thought.

'Oh, Harriet, dear, what a terrible thing to befall you,' Jane declared, in the tone of someone sympathizing with the recently bereaved.

Hattie formed her lips into an impatient moue at her sister's turn of phrase. Jane always insisted on morbid drama. She decided she would return some. 'I thought I was falling to my death,' she said, feigning a traumatized whimper. 'Let me introduce you to my particular friend, Miss Clemency Kivell. Her family owns land hereabouts. Clemency, this is my sister, Mrs Hartley, and her companion, Miss Miniver.'

'Miss Kivell.' Jane allowed Clemency a brief nod, and a thinly veiled scowl of disapproval.

'I'm very pleased to meet you both,' Clemency replied, thinking she had never before met such pale and lifeless creatures. Mrs Hartley's opinion of her was obvious: it was plain she thought Clemency shouldn't have been admitted past the kitchens. Clemency summed her up as a pathetic fraud. True and lasting grief was a solitary affair. She had probably been left with no means and was leeching off her brother. At that moment she felt sympathy for Kingsley Faraday. It was he who owned Poltraze, not his parents. Doubtless the old couple had long been incapable of administering monetary matters and now relied on their son's duty and fondness.

'Oh, you are all about to take tea,' Jane muttered mournfully, as if she had been deliberately left out. 'Miss Miniver and I will depart. We wish you all good morning.' Jane turned slowly, like an infirm old woman, and trailed out as if she barely had an ounce of strength.

The only acknowledgement from Miss Miniver was a humble curtsy to no one in particular, as if the woman had no rights. She followed in the widow's wake as if walking on sheets of hazardous ice, then closed the door with a careful click.

They're both deplorable, Clemency thought, but supposed the mouse-like Miss Miniver, doubtless destitute, had no choice but to cleave to the widow's every whim. Clemency had no wish ever to set eyes on them again.

She caught Kingsley gazing at her with a glint of amusement.

Her expression had revealed her disparaging opinion of the perpetual gravesiders. So be it. She ignored him.

'You can pour the tea, Patience,' Hattie said, waving her hand in front of her face. 'I swear Jane and that woman bring the stink of the grave with them.'

'Now, Hattie, that was unkind of you.' Kingsley seated himself where he would gain a direct view of Clemency. The shrivelled and wilting Jane had been jealous of Clemency's supreme beauty. He focused on her full red lips. It would be bliss to kiss them, but he didn't want to be her lover. She should stay untouched. At every age her innocence and self-containment would remain a fascinating enticement. He drank her in, dwelling on her every matchless feature. The thought of her would enthral him when he could at last return to London. It would be the greatest pleasure to him if she'd allow him to commission a painting of her. He would hang it in his study and feast on it every day. She would be captured as a young goddess. Her heaven-inspired looks would be an eternal object of rapturous fantasy; something he could cherish and adore for ever.

Clemency sipped from her bone china cup, fully aware of his scrutiny. She wasn't concerned by it. Men had stared at her for years, curious, she supposed, as to why she was permitted to roam at will, perhaps taken aback by her single-mindedness.

Hattie was applying herself to the refreshments. 'Mmm, these ginger snaps are delicious as usual. Eat up, Clemency,' she urged.

Kingsley glanced at the neat piles of magazine cuttings. 'Miss Kivell's company has animated you, Hattie. But I caution against overexerting yourself.'

'I'm sure Clemency wouldn't mind if I happened to doze off, would you, Clemency?'

'I'd be happy to continue quietly with our project, Hattie,' Clemency replied, relishing the taste of the ginger on her tongue. Kivell women were renowned for their culinary expertise but she had not tasted this delicacy before.

Impatient with her brother's intrusion, Hattie blurted out, 'Kingsley, why don't you go on to London as planned? You're making me feel guilty about delaying you. You're not needed here any more. You can send someone down to accompany me there when I am recovered.'

Kingsley studied her for a moment. It was a tempting proposition. The family was settled into the house and he was stagnating here. 'Do you know, I might very well do that?' He eyed her sternly. 'But only if I have your solemn promise you will do nothing foolhardy.'

'I wasn't doing anything foolhardy when I fell down the stairs. It was purely an accident. But, yes, you have my promise, Kingsley. Go. It's easy to see you are eager to get back to your usual life.'

He was on his feet. 'Then I shall leave today after all. I'll get a later train on reaching Plymouth. I need to go and stop my trunk being unpacked and to say goodbye to the others. I shall return before I take my leave. Enjoy the rest of your time here today, Miss Kivell.'

'Thank you, Mr Faraday, I wish you a safe journey.' She inclined her head to him.

Soon after the carriage had clattered away, Hattie drifted off into a motionless sleep. Clemency sat at a higher table and finished gluing the pictures in the scrapbook. Every so often she paused to listen. The only sound was the restful ticking of the carriage clock on the mantelpiece. On the quarter hour the bolder clocks in the house chimed melodiously and the hour was heralded with muted clangs. She could almost believe she was alone in the house, as on the days when she had broken in and wandered the building undisturbed. She would find no such soothing calm at her new home.

At the thought of home, dread made her heart lurch and her fingers tremble round the glue brush. Tension hovered thickly in the air at Trenbarvear. Resentment and recriminations were building up and she feared that Logan's suffering was only the beginning. Regret and anger would fester like a raw and open wound that could never be healed. Her mother knew it in her own heart, and one by one her brothers would come to admit that they did not belong there. Her father had selfishly uprooted them, needlessly taking away their security, and unfeelingly turning against some of their own flesh and blood. Already it was too late for forgiveness in certain quarters. How long would it be before the first of her father's nearest kin turned against him for good?

Eight

Her face was an expression of saintliness but her mind a hive of spiteful intent when Blythe burst into the crib-house. Her beady eyes homed in on Serenity and Betsy. 'So, after all the trouble you pair caused giving Logan Kivell the eye again yesterday, you've dared to show your faces.'

The girls and the rest of the company were ready for her. Laughter broke out, drowning most of Blythe's venom. Then came a rousing country song about a gossiping old woman who'd had her troublemaking tongue sewn up by a good fairy.

Blythe flounced out and banged the door to, seeming fully capable of spitting out rivets as she clumped into the bath-house. She swooped on Jenny Clymo who was picking up the dirty laundry of the three mine managers who had not long washed themselves down after their daily tour underground. 'Haven't you finished that yet? Lazy whelp. You're as slow as a dead snail. You'd better've polished their boots properly or I'll lam one on 'ee.' She raised the back of her knuckly hand in threat, then waved a hand in front her wrinkled nose. 'Gah, they don't smell any better even with the help of the soap ball. People are too dirty. The whole of Meryen's filthy with all these newcomers constantly drifting in. The middens are overrunning, the privies aren't emptied nearly enough. We've had scarlet fever and diphtheria in the last two years. Us clean and decent folk could go down with anything at any moment because others are so ruddy beastly. I've noticed your mother's not at all particular about the hygiene of your house, Jenny Clymo.'

Keeping her head averted, Jenny clutched the bundle of towels, the white duck coats, flannel shirts and drawers and long woollen socks. 'That's not true, Mrs Knuckey.' Jenny was near to tears. The bitter old shrew had harped on at her all morning, accusing her in front of the managers of being slow and lazy and useless at her work. Mrs Knuckey was out to get her dismissed. On her first day at the job the old woman had taken a swipe at her ears. Other times Jenny had been pushed about or cruelly prodded.

Yesterday, in chapel, instead of offering up prayer and supplication to the Lord, Mrs Knuckey had spread evil lies down the pews to those who'd listen: 'That seemingly innocent young Jenny Clymo is as wanton as the Treneer and Angove maids. They're all no better than streetwalkers. They was flirting in an unseemly manner with that devil Logan Kivell. They were the cause of that disgusting brawl 'tween he and Abe Deveril.' No one actually believed her, thank God, and Blythe Knuckey knew it. But she had basked in the glory of knowing that the taint of shame would be felt by the three girls. Jenny and her friends already felt guilty, knowing that Abe's beating meant he'd be unable to work under grass for the next two or three days.

Jenny did not know Blythe was jealous of her because Jeroboam Hearne, the senior mine manager, seemed taken with Jenny. He had been eager to give her the job, and he always made a point of speaking to her kindly, while he was stern with others, and often downright rude to Blythe.

'Gah, there's flies all round your place. Hang those safety hats up straight, maid. Must I tell you every darn day? My, you're as much use as a cow with wooden udders. Hurry up and get those foot bowls emptied. Be sure to scrub 'em really well. And make sure you wash your hands thoroughly after everything you do. Don't want no diseases brought round here.'

'Mrs Knuckey!' Jenny wailed.

'Shut your jaw or I'll go tell Mr Hearne you're forever slacking and you'll be thrown out. God knows I deserve better help than you.' With a sneering shake of her head Blythe sailed out.

Jenny couldn't hold back the tears and she ran all the way to the washhouse. Blinded by her weeping, she collided with someone and the laundry was sent flying all over the muddy ground. 'Oh!' When she saw who it was, her tears were checked abruptly and her whole body shook. 'Mr Hearne! I'm so sorry. I . . . I . . .' She was in trouble now. The senior mine manager was insistent that all tasks should be done to the highest standard. Mrs Knuckey never allowed Jenny to clean his office or take meals to him. 'Mr Hearne is nearly a gentleman. You'd soon make a fool of yourself in front of him and get on his gidge, and out you'd go,' she'd threatened more than once.

'I'm not concerned about the bump, Jenny. You're crying. Why's that?' Mr Hearne was portly, with the face of a merry monk, although he wasn't known for conviviality. A heaving spread of whiskers circled his fleshy chin. His deep bass voice could echo like the ear-splitting boom, rattle and thump of the works. At the moment it was as gentle as the tranquil sound of the water flowing down the many leats.

Jenny's tensed shoulders sagged with relief. Mr Hearne didn't seem angry with her. She wasn't to get a dressing-down. 'It – it's nothing, sir.'

Mr Hearne jiggled the silver watch chain that dangled importantly from his plaid waistcoat. His job brought in good money and he was proud of his fine acquisitions. 'It must be something or you wouldn't be in a state. Are you hurt? Has someone upset you? Tell me.' His hooded eyes probed her.

'I . . .' Jenny's eyes scuttled left and right. She was itching to gather up the laundry. If she didn't soon return to the bath-house and render it neat and spotless it would be Mrs Knuckey who'd be telling Mr Hearne something about her. Thank God she and Mr Hearne didn't generally see that much of each other. This was mortifying.

'You don't want to say, is that it?'

'Not really, sir.'

'You don't have to be afraid, Jenny, especially of me, you know. I like you, you remind me of someone. Come along with me now and tell me everything.'

The next moment Jenny was recoiling from him, her freckled cheeks turning scarlet, for Mr Hearne had crooked a finger under her chin. No man had ever touched her before. What did he mean by all this? If Mrs Knuckey spied them she'd muddy her name worse than she had already tried to do. Fresh tears pricked Jenny's eyelids. She seemed to be in for some-thing worse than the loss of her job. Mr Hearne was her master and she was powerless to go against him.

A short time later Mr Hearne wore an expression of smug satisfaction. He sent for Blythe Knuckey to come at once to the office, where he let rip fierce words of condemnation over her bullying manner towards her young assistant.

Blythe resorted to a great deal of fawning and promises of repentance. But the blood thundered through her heart with malice. Make fun of her, would they, those two young bitches in the crib-house? And the third little slattern had dared to run and tell tales about her in the hope of getting her dismissed? Well, those three Meryen maids had made the worse mistake of their lives in making an enemy of her. By the time she had finished with them they'd curse the day they were born.

Nine

It was the first time he had not saddled his horse himself. Proud of his black stallion, Logan had given his exclusive attention to the headstrong Spartacus. Now he was unable to swing up on to the saddle and would have to use the mounting block. His mother had helped him into his riding coat, draping it carefully around his sling. She had placed his hat firmly on his head. And then he had suffered the indignity of her winding a muffler around his neck and imploring him to wear gloves. His hands did not feel the cold – although he had yet to discover if his injured arm would soon do so. His fingers were as thick and tough as those of a labourer's, another thing he was proud of. He had no desire for the pale-skinned hands and well-trimmed nails that fluttered about drawing rooms or in boardrooms.

'I'll be all right, Mother.' He had barely contained his temper. Damn everything to Hell! He had an audience of worried-looking sisters-in-law, poised to help his mother to fuss over him, and peering young nephews and nieces. Thank God Clemency had already left for another of her regular visits to Poltraze. He would have hated enduring this in front of his strong-willed sister. He would never forget the comfort and protection Clemency had given him on the day of his accident. He would always protect her. God help any man who sought to sully her or break her heart. He might be left with a weak arm but the rest of him was iron and rock, or it soon would be again.

'I understand you wanting some fresh air and a different scene after being confined for two weeks, dear, but I do wish you had let Clemency drive you somewhere, as she offered.' Verena's head reached only to his chest and her arms were about his waist – her way of trying to hold him back. She appeared to be imploring her beloved son not to go to war for Queen and country, except that Logan's tired despair belied such a scene. 'Don't forget you were so ill with the infection. The wind is particularly harsh today and rain is a certainty fairly soon.'

'I'll be fine on Spartacus. I'm not going to fall off him. I've got my strength back,' he declared angrily. The lie scoured his soul. He had regained only a small portion of his former potency. 'I want some time alone! I can't stand all this fussing. If I don't get away from here for a while I'll go mad.'

'Very well dear, if you must.' Verena stroked his arm to calm him. She had endured her son's unreasonable attitude throughout his recovery with her customary patience. When she had read to him, he had complained that he couldn't take in the words. When she had played the flute to soothe him he had protested that it made his head ache. His bed had been uncomfortable, his food had not been right. He had got into a fury when she had refused to allow him to overindulge in brandy. He had suffered the terrible pain in his arm as if it didn't exist, but his embarrassment at having to accept personal care from others had turned his face puce. He had hardly breathed throughout, gritting his teeth and clenching his good fist. Logan was a proud young man publicly shamed. Verena feared he might sink into depression or become moodily dangerous.

'Where do you intend to go, Logan? Please do not stay out long or I shall worry.'

The stable boy brought the stallion to the mounting block. 'I'll return when I feel like it. Am I a free man no longer?' Bitterness and wrath burned in his grating tone.

'Oh, Logan,' Verena breathed, overcome with anxiety. The last two weeks had been difficult for her too and she was tired and low.

He turned his head and cast his gaunt eyes on her. 'Please, Mama.' He kissed her cheek. God, was his shame never to end? He had no right to be worrying his dearest mother.

The women and children stood back as he climbed the three stone steps of the mounting block. Anxious eyes beheld him as he took the reins from the stable boy and clambered clumsily on to the horse's broad back. Verena knew agony seared his arm with every movement and that he welcomed it. He could deal with physical pain.

Avoiding sight of the new house, well on the way towards completion without his help, Logan trotted off. Once he was well out of sight he let the reins fall and allowed Spartacus to walk on where he willed. Then, hugging his arm in the sling, he bowed his head and gave way to the enormous racking sobs that had been building up inside him since his own ridiculous actions had brought him down and shamed him in the eyes of men.

'This is such a hoot,' Hattie sang out.

Clemency was leading the way to Meryen along a narrow back lane that would take them past Burnt Oak. It was a route that had once been used by live-out servants at Poltraze. They were riding between the sheltering high hedgerows of Trenbarvear fields. The hedges were strewn with saturated plant life that had now died off, which made it necessary to ride mostly in single file to prevent a soaking. They were to call on a cousin of Clemency's, Rachel Retallack, the sister to Jowan. Hattie had dressed more plainly than usual in the hope that the villagers would assume she was a distant relative of the Kivells.

'It's such a romantic story, about your cousin marrying a former miner,' Hattie babbled on. 'And he the man who'd helped you save the squire's little baby. Does Mrs Retallack live near Abe Deveril?'

'I've no idea where Deveril lives,' Clemency replied curtly.

'No, of course, there's no reason why you should.' Hattie had gathered something of the fierce Kivell loyalty. Although it was Clemency's brother's disgraceful behaviour that had led to the conflict with Abe, and then Logan's own fault he had fallen over and been badly injured, Clemency viewed Abe as partly responsible for Logan's downfall.

'I can't wait to see the village, and Mrs Retallack's child. I'd like to stop off somewhere and purchase a little gift for him. You'll have to advise me. I haven't a clue what to present to a newborn baby. Oh, something silver, isn't it?'

'I don't think we should venture anywhere except to Rachel's cottage, and only for a few minutes,' Clemency cautioned, her usual friendly self again. 'Rain is not too far off. Mrs Secombe made a fuss about you going out at all.'

'Oh, I do wish I had come down here in the summer,' Hattie said with a sigh. 'And I wish it was market day. There probably won't be another opportunity to see all the things that go on in the village. I'm to leave for London in a week's time. I wish you could come with me, Clemency. What fun we would have.'

Clemency made no reply. She couldn't think of anything worse than being in a big, smelly city, where silly rules of etiquette reigned supreme. She liked Hattie immensely but she was dizzy and naïve. Contacts of her age would, no doubt, be likewise, or condescending towards her, and the young men milksops or prigs. She paid no heed as Hattie prattled on, for just ahead behind the hedge on Hattie's side someone was lurking.

Clemency pulled in front of Hattie, startling her, and reined in. She never went anywhere without a small firearm for protection and she was an excellent markswoman. 'I know there's someone there,' she cried, brandishing her weapon. 'I have a gun. Show yourself or you may be shot and killed.'

'Hold there!' said a familiar voice.

'Abe?' Hattie's heart was thudding from the sudden excitement and Clemency's fierce readiness to defend her.

'Come out, show yourself.' Although Clemency had recognized Abe's voice she did not lower the gun. She knew he had already left his place. The next moment he appeared, having scaled the hedge a few feet further down. He jumped down on to the muddy, pitted ground and put his hands up in play. 'Don't shoot, I beg you.'

Hattie laughed with relief and pleasure. 'We were hoping to happen upon you sometime, Mr Deveril,' she simpered.

Clemency's stony glare conveyed a cooler message, but Abe didn't care. Men spoke of Clemency Kivell as being a challenge in every way. 'It's a pleasure to meet with you again, ladies,' he said, brazenly straightening the heavy bag on his shoulder.

'So you see fit to poach on my father's land now, do you?' Clemency nudged her pony straight at him, making him fall back into the hedge.

'Clemency, have a care!' Hattie cried. 'Mr Deveril was forced to take a few days off from work due to his injuries from the altercation with your brother. A couple of rabbits or whatever he has taken isn't going to make your family go without.'

After a stark silence, Clemency said, 'I suppose not.' It was well to make sure this individual knew who had the upper hand. However, she should remember that Logan's actions must have caused Abe and his family some hardship. She put the gun away and allowed Abe the space to stand up straight and put his hat back on. 'You have returned to work now?'

Rubbing his neck where it had been scratched by blackthorns, he merely nodded, not deigning to speak to this supercilious madam. She was no better than he was. Her surname meant nothing special to him, no more than her brother's had on the day he'd squared up to Logan.

'Oh, please, no more of this,' Hattie begged, getting exasperated. 'I thought we were all friends. Do make up your differences. Or at least be civil.'

Up on high ground, Logan had wept himself dry He was left numb and suffering the warning signs of faintness. He should go home while he was able. Then he spied his sister with two others. He would be interested to meet the young lady from the big house, but why were Clemency and Miss Harriet Faraday talking to Abe Deveril? The miner didn't seem to be bothering them, but Logan was curious to investigate. Ignoring his weariness and discomfort and the pains stabbing like hot rods all through his arm, he cantered towards them.

The three in the lane saw the rider coming down the valley. 'It's Logan,' Clemency told Hattie. She swept her eyes towards Abe. He stood his ground, unconcerned about the newcomer's identity, but showed no sign of any enmity or mocking. She remembered how Abe had spoken reassuringly to Logan after his fall.

Logan jumped a stile and was with them within a few moments. Tension lay thick in the air. The mood and outcome of the meeting were entirely in Logan's hands.

'What's going on here?' Logan's voice was grave and edged with exhaustion. The ride had sapped a lot of his meagre strength, the unwise jump over the stile had jolted his hurt arm unbearably, and he was unable to sit proudly in the saddle. He knew he was going to suffer for this outing for the next two or three days.

'Miss Faraday and I were passing the time of day with Abe,' Clemency said. 'We've all met before.' She explained Abe's part in aiding Hattie after her plunge from her pony.

'I'm pleased to see you are well enough to be out and about, Mr Kivell.' Hattie had lifted her tiny net veil. Logan Kivell was just like her girlish romantic imaginings, brooding and gaunt, a trifle fierce and very darkly handsome.

'Thank you, Miss Faraday,' he replied, surprising Clemency, for he spoke as politely as if ushered into a genteel drawing room.

'I'm pleased too that you're recovering,' Abe said.

'Why?' Logan was suspicious. 'Surely my name is mocked all over Meryen? People must be glad about my misfortune, saying I deserved it.'

Abe shrugged. 'You won our match fair and square and congratulated me for my performance. People's views are their own affair. Of course, you're still ill thought of over your treatment towards the three girls.'

'Perhaps I should apologize to them.' Logan's remark was superior and sarcastic but the instant he'd uttered it he saw how mean-spirited and unmanly it had been for him to torment a bunch of lowly, innocent girls.

Clemency knew he would not follow through his suggestion. Meekness and mildness would never run through Logan's veins. 'Miss Faraday and I are on our way to Meryen, to see Rachel. Will you join us, Logan? Perhaps Abe could ride with you.' Let the villagers make what they would of that. She was amused at her proposal, but it wouldn't happen. Logan would be appalled at the notion and Abe would decline.

'I'll walk. I advise you not to go near Chapel Place in the village,' Abe said grimly. 'There's a case of cholera. A child is dangerously ill.'

'Then I think I shall give the visit a miss,' Hattie said at once. She would not place herself at such a risk. Disease was bad anywhere but among the lower classes it tended to turn more swiftly into an epidemic, its outcome more deadly.

'I'll go home too,' Logan said. The last of his reserves was waning and he longed for sleep.

'If you ride with us to the Poltraze gates,' Clemency said, concerned that he was clearly weakening, 'I'll ensure you get home safely.'

Logan did not protest, and he had no care about Hattie Faraday's obvious disappointment to be so soon losing his sister's company. She had pleasant features but in his view as much substance as thistledown. She and Clemency might be friends but in the way that opposites attract.

The gathering broke up. Abe went off down the lane whistling cheerfully, happy about the three rabbits tucked inside his bag.

When Clemency and Logan were alone and trotting towards Trenbarvear, she keeping a close eye on him, fearing he might pass out and fall to the ground, Logan asked, 'What do you see in her?'

'Hattie's fun.'

'She'd soon annoy me. I think you bother with her because it's something to do.'

'I suppose that is partly true.' She sighed. 'But the Faradays are an intriguing lot.'

'Really? Perhaps I'll turn up at Poltraze one day to see for myself.'

Clemency hoped he would not. From the way Hattie had been gazing winsomely at Logan she feared her friend might become infatuated with him. Females were often drawn to men who were wicked and wild. 'Logan, what do you think of life at the farm?'

'I hate it.' His tone was barbed with bitterness and resentment. 'Father's ruined everything. We'll never belong there. It's split the family apart. I agreed to go because I thought the old loyalties would resurface, but they never will. At Burnt Oak we had everything we could ever want. As soon as I'm well I'm moving out. Don't say anything about it, Clemmie. I'll do it myself. Do you blame me?'

'No not at all.' Her heart was grieved. How much more splintering of the family was there to be? It was her mother who would suffer most. 'What will you do?'

'I don't know yet. I only made up my mind a short while ago. You're welcome to come with me.'

'Thank you, but I'm not ready to branch out yet and there's Mother to think of.'

As they closed in on Trenbarvear, the whole place cold and uninviting to Clemency, she thought over her statement. Her greatest wish would be to return to Burnt Oak but her father would see it as a personal insult and never forgive her if she did. She had the means to buy a home of her own and set up a business. It was silly to mull over the prospect, she could do nothing of the kind until she was twenty-one, and she knew what her father would say if she mentioned it: '*Over my dead body!*'

Ten

She knew she shouldn't do it. She could be dismissed from her job and end up destitute. Sitting behind the Clymo family in the Methodist chapel – the first of the two of that denomination to be built in Meryen by the miners themselves – Blythe was itching to give way to temptation. If she did speak up it would be the little wasp Jenny Clymo who would be thrown out of work. And, Blythe reasoned, it was her Christian duty to save young Jenny from the evil clutches of Jeroboam Hearne. The mine manager, presently spouting hymns and prayers in the Anglican church – the hypocrite – was using the maid, bringing her to odious sin almost every day as he committed adultery with her. And the girl enjoyed his attentions. She had even gone to his house more than once. Today, Blythe had noticed, Jenny was hiding a little filigree-framed floral brooch under her shawl. Her parents couldn't afford to give her such a piece. Shameless little slut!

The long service ended, after much prayer for the souls of the unfortunate boy and his younger brother, who had succumbed to cholera at Chapel Place, a short dead-end lane behind the chapel. The congregation was sparse today, only the hardiest and the most faithful attending, but still fearful of infection. Fervent prayer had been said for God's mercy and protection in stamping out the devil's desire to spread disease. Fear and tension were stalking Meryen, with people constantly asking about each other's health.

The circuit preacher, a hell and damnation devotee, a tinner from St Day, had toned down his presentation a little in respect of the village's sorrow. The congregation was eager to return safely home, and he dispensed with his usual long shaking of hands at the chapel doors. Blythe knew she must not tarry if she was to obtain a fair-sized audience when she did her duty by informing Thomas Clymo of his daughter's wickedness. Her sharp nose twitching like a hunting dog's, she levered her way through the departing worshippers to snare Mr Clymo. He was standing outside on the cobbled court, inches from the preacher, putting on his cap. With him were his frail wife and brood of five. Jenny was pulling her younger siblings' inadequate hand-me-down clothing more warmly about their scrappy bodies. All the little ones wore makeshift shoes. To Blythe's pleasure, Serenity Treneer and Betsy Angove and their families were close by.

'A word with you, if you please, Mr Clymo,' she boomed, drawing, as she intended, the attention of all those who were about to leave the court or still filing out of the chapel.

'What is it, Mrs Knuckey?' Thomas Clymo was a frail, bent figure. He was breathing heavily as he gazed suspiciously at Blythe. The most loathed person in Meryen would not have hailed him to make kind enquiries about his health.

'I'm sorry to keep you, I'm sure.' Blythe steepled her gloved hands together in prayer fashion and arranged her ugly features into an expression of pained saintliness. 'Goodness knows I've been agonizing over this for many a week, but I can't keep silent no longer.'

'With the Lord's help you will surely succeed.' Thomas Clymo dismissed her cuttingly. He was offended at the woman's spiteful rumours about Jenny, the mainstay of his family; as good and innocent a daughter as any father could hope for. He waved his family onwards. 'Come along now. Home.'

Pinched to indignation – how dare this man, a slacker in Blythe's opinion, try to make a fool of her – Blythe shouted,

'You would not take such a disrespectful stance with me, Thomas Clymo, if you knew that your daughter Jenny is conducting an intimate affair with Mr Jeroboam Hearne. There, you have it. What do you say now?'

The jaws of just about everyone dropped in unison. Eyes broadened to the size of pot lids. Mrs Clymo, of fragile nerves, and frail from constant childbearing, collapsed with a horrified sigh. As her father caught her mother, Jenny slammed her hands to her face and screamed, 'I am not!'

'Liar!' Thomas Clymo snarled at Blythe, and then disintegrated into a fit of painful coughing.

'Your maid is a menace to men – from the ungodly like Logan Kivell to decent married men, her betters,' Blythe retorted, chin thrust up, revelling in her mischief. 'She should be horsewhipped. If I am lying then, pray. where did she get that brooch she is taking pains to conceal from you? The fine piece now lying on her breast?'

Jenny clutched her hands to her bosom and backed away with scorched cheeks. Shocked eyes were turned accusingly upon her.

'Jenny wouldn't do no such thing!' Serenity exclaimed angrily. 'The old witch is just out to make trouble.' Her own troubled father forbade her to speak again.

The preacher eased the ailing Mrs Clymo clear of her husband so that Thomas could better answer the charge. After beating his chest hard to win a little frothy breath, and trembling like the last leaf on a storm-lashed twig, he pointed at Jenny. 'Is this the – the truth?'

'I . . . I . . .' Ashamed, Jenny could say no more. Her tongue was like a lead weight in her mouth. She was in a living nightmare. She should have hidden the brooch in a secret place.

'Go on!' Blythe flew at her. 'Show your father and the preacher and all the good people here the evidence of your sin.'

As though anchored by some invisible force, Jenny was incapable of moving a muscle, other than to sob burning tears of horror.

Blythe whipped open Jenny's shawl and pointed in malicious triumph. 'There! See, everyone? This maid is no better than a common trollop.'

'I've done nothing wrong!' Jenny wailed. 'It's not what—'

More swiftly than he had moved in many years, Thomas Clymo lurched forward and slapped Jenny across the face. Spittle ran down from the corners of his thin, bloodless lips and his breathing was a laboured wheeze. 'I'll have no Jezebel living under my roof! Go. Get your things out of my house before I return there or I'll take the kindling axe to you!'

'Father, let me explain,' Jenny pleaded, cradling her bruised cheek.

He roared in fury, which made him gag and choke. He was fighting for breath but raised his hand to strike her again.

Crying hysterically, Jenny tore off.

She left behind a Babel of astonishment and outrage, Among the onlookers were her mother, her brothers and her sisters, all sobbing in despair. Not only were they flung down in disgrace, they had also just lost the main breadwinner in the family, their security, their beloved Jenny.

Serenity pulled Betsy aside. 'I can't believe Jenny would ever do such a thing. She'd never willingly go with a man of Mr Hearne's age, especially a married man, and if he'd been forcing her she'd have become distressed and withdrawn. She's been the exact opposite lately. She wouldn't have stolen the brooch either. We must go up to the church and tell Mr Hearne what's happened before someone else does. Hopefully, he'll put it all to rights.'

In the event, the girls had no need to go to the church. Jeroboam Hearne and his wife were about to travel past in their trap on their way home. They both flinched as a stream of catcalls and accusations was launched at the senior mine manager. Grabbing Betsy's arm, Serenity pulled her through the throng to face the trap. Blythe carefully crept to the back of the group of people and said nothing. Her work was finished. Jenny Clymo had been exiled and Jeroboam Hearne would have to resign his position. Served them both right.

Hearne pulled on the reins and the pony stopped. Then the mine manager stood up on the trap and glared down at the Methodists. 'What is the meaning of this? How dare any of you accuse me of such behaviour! I'll have the law on you.'

'Don't lie to us.' The preacher strode forward. He considered Anglicans to have looser morals than backsliders of his own belief. 'You deflowered an innocent young girl and gave her a gift to entice her in deeper.'

'I did nothing of the sort.' Hearne hefted his weighty self down to the ground.

'We don't believe what they're saying, Mr Hearne, not me and Betsy,' Serenity pitched in.

'Hold your tongue, girl,' Mr Treneer cried.

'Let me speak.' Mrs Hearne's cool voice cut through the tension. She sat, straight and dignified, up on the trap, her tight, glossy ringlets covered by a fur-trimmed bonnet that was the envy of every woman in the village. Only a slight pinkness of the cheeks betrayed her emotion; otherwise she appeared calm and composed.

Why wasn't she heartbroken and humiliated over her husband's adultery, the villagers wondered.

'Someone mentioned a brooch that Jenny was wearing. It was I who gave her the brooch.' She paused to allow the gasps of surprise to pass among her husband's accusers. 'Mr Hearne had mentioned to me that Jenny was upset at being bullied by Blythe Knuckey. It struck a chord with him, for a reason. We are not born and bred villagers and everyone here has assumed we have always been childless. In fact we did have a daughter – a quiet, pretty little red-haired girl. She died when she was three years old. Jenny reminded Mr Hearne of our daughter. If she had lived she would have been Jenny's age now. Jenny was twice invited to our house to earn extra money for her family when our kitchen maid fell ill. I was drawn to her for the same reason as my husband. I gave Jenny the brooch. It is not valuable. It was something that caught my eye on a market stall and I bought it. I would not have dreamt of embarrassing Jenny by offering her something fine.'

'She hid it from me,' Thomas Clymo rasped, badly in need of a seat. His head drooped in guilt and shame. He had struck Jenny and ordered her out of her home on a false accusation from a notorious gossip and troublemaker.

'She told me of her intention to do so,' Mrs Hearne said. 'Jenny is a kind girl. She asked me if I'd mind if she gave the brooch to her mother as a Christmas gift. I suppose she wanted to wear it herself just once. Both my husband and Jenny have been grossly slandered. The relationship between them is as superior and worker only. It has always been entirely innocent.' She delivered her final words acidly: 'I doubt if I will have to look far to discover the perpetrator of these evil lies.'

All eyes searched the crowd for Blythe Knuckey. Before she could skulk away the counthouse woman found herself surrounded by a sea of livid faces. 'I – I—' Blythe blustered, her fingers picking at her drawstring cloth bag. 'I was so sure I was right,' she ended lamely.

'You are dismissed from your employment, Mrs Knuckey.' Hearne's voice was hard and cold. 'I will send you the wages you're due. If you ever set foot on Wheal Verity property again I'll have you jailed for trespass. Now, someone tell me where poor Jenny is.'

'She ran off,' Serenity said, glaring first at Blythe Knuckey and then at Thomas Clymo. 'Betsy and I will go and find her. She'll take comfort from us better'n anyone else.'

As stern as a judge, the preacher confronted Blythe. 'Take yourself home, woman, and fall on your knees and beg the Lord's forgiveness for what you've done this sorry day, as I must also do for believing your cruel lies. Before you think to step inside the chapel again you must prove to the brethren that you are fully repentant, and you must make recompense to those you tried to defile. Start praying, woman, for Jenny's safe return.'

This house would do him well. A short time ago, Logan had told the Cardells, one uncle and aunt who had kept faith in him, of his intention to move out of Trenbarvear. 'I've lined my pockets thickly here and there, succeeded in many a productive undertaking.' He'd tapped the side of his nose to convey that those undertakings had not been law-abiding. 'I intend to buy a house and start up a business, right here in Meryen. The villagers and everyone else' – he had dropped his voice in grim prophecy – 'will learn that they can laugh at me only once.'

The apothecary and his wife had exchanged delighted smiles. 'I'm glad you approve.'

'Oh, we think we can offer you more than approval, m'boy.' Henry Cardell had beamed at his nephew. 'We knew you'd break free from Seth's iron will one day and seek your own success.'

So here he was, out on the narrow pavement beyond the walls and high iron gates of a fine but somewhat neglected late-Georgian house – his house. He had bought it from his uncle, who had purchased it twenty-four hours ago, to rent, from the long-widowed Mrs Alice Brookson. The widow, currently packing up to leave, had lived on her late husband's holdings in East India until they had failed a month ago. Her servants, except for one faithful maid, had deserted her.

It didn't matter to Logan if the house suited him perfectly or not; it would be somewhere to return to between his travels, where he could be close to his family.

He could no longer bear it at the farm; the noise and bustle, the women clacking about women's concerns – speculation about when his pregnant sister-in-law would go into labour, lurid details of childbirth. He had been forced to listen to it all during his recovery. It wasn't for men to know about such things; the women should have taken account of his presence in the farmhouse.

He was sick of his father, too, whose irritability and bitterness were directed at almost everyone else in the world. He was becoming more and more unreasonable and complained about the most trivial occurrences. Every now and again he glared at Logan, still resenting him for making a fool of himself in the village. Seated at the crowded breakfast table this morning, his father had started on Clemency.

'I suppose you're slinking off to Poltraze again today.' It was both a condemnation and a protest.

'No.' Clemency had sighed over his ill humour. 'I'm going to help Mother make plans for Christmas.'

'I should bleddy well think so too! You leave your mother far too often with a heavy load.' Seth had stuffed a huge forkful of bacon and eggs into his mouth, then went on, spitting out crumbs, 'She's got enough to do, nursing your brother. He's a worry to her.'

Logan had seethed. 'I am not. I manage to do very well for myself now.' With unending determination, through all the pain and awkwardness, he had become adept to using one hand. 'If you don't want me here you only have to say so.'

'Your father didn't mean anything like that, dear,' Verena had said, massaging her forehead. The tension was getting to his usually unflappable mother. Yesterday she had snapped at the children and ordered them to be silent.

'If that's the way he bleddy feels …' Seth had muttered darkly, carrying on munching and spilling food.

It hit Logan then that since his accident his father didn't

often speak to him directly. He recalled that Seth used to tell him he was his favourite son, the one most like him, hard and fearless. Now it seemed to Logan he had lost that affection for good and was even an embarrassment to his father.

'Tell me more about your fancy friends at Poltraze, Clemency.' Seth had pointed his eggy fork at her. 'The farm boys who deliver to the house see only some stiff servants. Can't see what the continuing attraction is for you there.'

'I've told you, Father, Miss Hattie and I have a lot in common.' Once, Clemency would have replied either gaily or as one irritated by a fussy child, but these days she was careful in her speech. It was no wonder she went to Poltraze as often as she could.

'Time I went over there for a visit myself.' Seth had issued the remark like a threat. 'You've buttered 'em up. I'll see if they're likely to sell up. If not, I'll tell them a tale or two – something to see them wanting to put a distance between themselves and Poltraze.'

'It wouldn't work, nothing would,' Clemency stressed, horrified at Seth's intention. 'Except for Miss Hattie, the Faradays are eccentrics. They have come here for the isolation and will not be moved.'

'Sounds to me as if they have secrets.' Seth was thoughtful.

'They have not!'

He'd waved his knife at her, leaning in her direction like a hawk latched on to its prey. 'There's something though, isn't there? If the truth was brought out maybe the Faradays would be willing to sell up cheap. What's going on there? And don't you dare say nothing.'

Clemency had slammed down her cutlery, making Verena wince and bring a hand up to her heart. 'I just want to go somewhere without any family being there. We're all getting on top of each other. One new house might be nearly ready to move into but there'll still be a terrible crush here. We're all getting fed up. We will be at one another's throats soon. There could even be murder!'

Seth had leapt up, thrusting his chair away. Darting round from the head of the table he'd clutched Clemency by the arms and shaken her like a madman. 'Murder, you say? There'll be murder in this house if you don't learn some respect towards me quick!'

'Let go of me,' Clemency had snarled, struggling.

'Seth, please!' Verena was on her feet, looking about to scream in frustration.

Jowan, who had spent the night at the farm, had stepped in. 'Please, Uncle Seth, let Clemency go. I don't think she meant to be disrespectful.'

Seth was in no mood to listen. Scowling into Clemency's glittering, defiant eyes, he kept an unbreakable grip on her.

Logan couldn't stand it. Reaching Clemency's side, he'd pushed hard against his father's bulging shoulder. 'For God's sake, let her go! Are you going to start being a brute to your own daughter? Think of Mother. All this is making her ill.'

Something in his words reached the small reasonable part of Seth's brain. He glanced at Verena. She was holding both her hands to her head, pale and trembling. He released Clemency, but still angry with her, pushed her away.

'Uncle Seth, don't,' Jowan protested. Easing between Logan and Clemency, he laid protective hands on her. Clemency looked up at him gratefully.

Seth had remained silent for a moment then had given an unexpected satisfied grin. 'Well, I can see what lies here. The pair of you has a fondness for each other. I give you my blessing. What could make a better match, this wayward daughter of mine to a strong kinsman of good standing? Consider it a betrothal.'

Stunned, Clemency and Jowan gasped simultaneously, 'What?'

'So glad you're both delighted.' Seth had chuckled. 'Verena, my darling, isn't this good news? We won't have to worry about our daughter again. It will be a long betrothal so you'll not lose her while you're in most need of her. Clemency, take your mother upstairs and see that she rests.'

While his two brothers stayed prudently quiet to avoid further unpleasantness, Logan eyed Seth coldly. 'You know damned well there's nothing like that between Clemency and Jowan. You're losing all reason. I'm not staying in this miserable place.'

'Do as you damned well please,' Seth had hissed, and turned his back on Logan.

The bag Logan had packed was in the Cardell guest room. As soon as Mrs Brookson had taken her unfortunate departure from Meryen, it would be unpacked in the house before him. His own house. It felt good. He was sorry that his mother was upset at the way he had moved out of Trenbarvear, but she and Clemency could live here with him if things ever got too much for them.

Suddenly he was struck with a tremendous force and almost upended. He yelped as a pain slashed through his slowly mending arm. For one horrible moment he thought his arm had been shredded to bits. He cradled the sling for extra support and gazed down at a slight, red-haired girl who was sprawled on the pavement, in floods of tears and clearly in despair. Her shawl was dragging from one arm and her bonnet barely hanging from its strings. It was one of the mine girls he had taunted outside the Nankervis Arms.

'I'm sorry . . .' she began, unmistakably afraid of him. 'S–sorry, I . . .'

'Jenny! Jenny! Wait for us!'

Logan recognized Serenity Treneer's voice, and the sound of running feet. 'Don't worry, I'm not angry with you,' he told the stricken girl. 'Your friends are coming. Whatever the matter is, they will look after you.'

'No! I don't want to see them,' Jenny wailed. She couldn't bear the thought of facing even her closest friends. She wanted to hide away somewhere and die, to end her public humiliation. After her father's cruel dismissal, she had diverted off High Street and run along George Road, a better part of Meryen, to avoid those who knew her, never intending to go home. She had scant belongings to take with her and couldn't bear a last look at the place where she had known her only security, where she had loved and cared for her little brothers and sisters. Who would care for them now?

Logan acted quickly. 'All right, if you don't want to see them, hide in there.' He opened the iron gates, swept the girl up and set her down behind the wall.

Jenny fell down to a crouch and wrapped her shaking hands over her mouth to smother her sobs.

Serenity and Betsy Angove appeared, running past the end of the road. Serenity brought her feet to a staggering halt. Logan Kivell was gazing down from the top end of George Road. She could ask him if he had seen a girl running. Even in her agitation she appreciated the sight of him, tall and broad-shouldered, his black hair nestling luxuriantly about his handsome, rugged face.

'Come on!' Betsy pulled her by the arm. 'Jenny won't have gone that way.'

Logan watched as the mine girls disappeared on their fool's errand. He stepped inside the gate. He didn't care to find out yet what was wrong with the girl, Jenny, cowering by the wall. She was distraught and needed urgent protection; probably even from herself, judging by the state she was in. He owed her something for the occasion when he'd tormented her and he took it into his mind to help her in any way he could. Hauling up her shivering little body, he guided her to the front door and yanked at the bell-pull. There was a loud jangle somewhere inside the house.

After a time the one remaining maid opened the door cautiously. 'Yes, sir, what is it?'

'Let us through,' Logan demanded, crossing the threshold into the paved porch. 'I am here to see your mistress, and this poor girl needs shelter.'

Mrs Alice Brookson studied him curiously. 'I can see by your countenance, sir, that you are unmistakably Mr Kivell. What ails the child?' Her voice was dignified yet compassionate. The lady who, like her maid, was wearing an apron, was packing away bric-a-brac from the hall side table. Logan gazed at her in surprise. Although long past the prime of life, she was as handsome and regal as any renowned beauty half her age.

Logan had a sudden impulse towards philanthropy. 'Mrs Brookson,' he bowed his head to her, 'I believe I am right in thinking that you have no real desire to leave this house?'

'Indeed I do not, Mr Kivell. I have lived here, with Maudie' – she indicated the maid – 'in my service, for over thirty contented years. We really do not have anywhere else to go.'

'Then you need not leave. I now own this house and, if you wish to remain, I'm sure we could live here together quite amicably. You may unpack your belongings. I shall engage new staff on the morrow.'

He was still supporting Jenny, who was so weak she seemed about to sink to the floor. She was clutching her shawl about her face, so that only her frightened eyes were visible. 'Now let us see what we can do for this poor desperate girl.'

Eleven

Clemency was in Hattie's room, waiting while she and Mrs Secombe dealt with a staff matter downstairs. If Clemency were any other girl she would be excited and impatient to pass on the news that she had just become engaged, but she had not taken her father's sudden matchmaking seriously, and nor had Jowan. He'd merely given her a wry look. Marriage was something she had no intention of considering for a good many years. For the time being though she would appear to acquiesce to her father's wishes, in order to keep the peace. She hated the way Seth baited Logan. She and Logan had left the farm together, he taking an overnight bag, rumbling that he'd return home only when he chose to. Their mother had been saddened, but Clemency had seen in her eyes that she thought time away for Logan might ease the strain.

Hattie, on the other hand, was looking forward to becoming a wife. It was a matter of honour to her, as to all girls of her station, to gain a well-placed husband, and hopefully one who was also young and handsome. Clemency hoped that Hattie would succeed in her dream and that it would make her happy. She smiled as she heard the sound of the spaniels scurrying downstairs, with Clarry and Phee's piping voices calling affectionately after them. The couple had taken the room nearest to the stairs so that the dogs wouldn't disturb Hattie as they tore along the corridor. They doted on their children and took care to put their comforts first. Each time Clemency spoke to the couple they mentioned how much they missed Kingsley, and how they were dreading Hattie leaving Poltraze. Clemency thought it was a shame they would be left with just the morbid Jane.

'I hope you will continue to brighten us with your lovely presence, Clemency,' Clarry had said cajolingly. 'We like having young people about us.'

Clemency had promised to continue her visits to the house. Wandering to Hattie's reading table she picked up a small bound book entitled *Fantastical Journeys: Poems by M.R. Dayton*. She read the handwritten dedication, *To my dearest Hattie. A rose, a loving heart, a princess. With my warmest love, Matthew.* Was the book a gift from a beau? It was certainly from someone who held Hattie in great affection.

Sounds filtered through the door. One of the puppies had lingered behind and was searching in the wrong place for its master and mistress. She went out into the corridor to direct it down the stairs.

'Bridie, I've come to see Miss Hattie. Is she in her room? Oh – you're not Bridie. Who . . .?'

As the puppy scampered off in the right direction, Clemency walked towards the man who had mistaken her for the lady's maid. She studied every angle of his thin white face. Who on earth was this? He was not a servant. He had no feature common to a Faraday, but then none of them shared similar looks, and Hattie had not mentioned any other relatives. He must be a guest. He was bending his head forward and peering at her oddly out of the most extraordinary eyes. She fancied other worlds existed behind the hooded lids.

'Are you Hattie's friend?' he said at last, pulling his head back.

Clemency suspected that if he had had a shell on his back he would have withdrawn his entire self into it. 'You are correct, sir. My name is Clemency Kivell, but I dare say you know that already. Who am I addressing?'

Matthew sighed wearily. If only Hattie had left here with Kingsley, he wouldn't have been caught out by this girl. With his limited sight, as if looking down a tunnel, he saw that she was as beautiful and vivacious as her description. It was demeaning to be under her penetrating scrutiny, to suffer her curiosity. There was no point in lying to her. Coming from her tough, hardy background, she was bound to think of him as peculiar, or a coward, to lock himself away.

Clemency broke the silence. 'Well, sir, am I to know who you are?'

'I am Hattie's brother, Matthew Faraday. I live in the east wing.' He didn't know what else to say.

'Secretly,' Clemency stated, not sparing him. He was obviously not mentally ill. His reclusive way of life must therefore be of his own choosing. Why else had not Hattie, Kingsley or their parents mentioned him? Poor Hattie – to have two such strangely behaved siblings.

For the first time in years a blush stained Matthew's cheeks. Kingsley had spoken glowingly about this girl, adding that she could be sharp. 'Yes, I have my reasons.'

Bereavement, like Jane? Clemency wondered. Aloud, she said, 'Don't worry, I won't mention to a soul outside this house that I've met you. I'm not a gossip.' Her father might take it into his head to use the information to spread rumours that the Faradays were weird and might even be dangerous. The locals were already affronted by the Faradays' shunning of them; it was the poor who laid the food on the table of the rich, so they felt that the rich should at least spare them a few pennies. The mining community tended to be a suspicious breed. There were hard people among them, and the Kivell Charity Fund had not been accepted particularly well. The poor of Meryen were not happy about being beholden to the Kivells but since there was no help forthcoming from Poltraze, in cases of deprivation they had no choice. The Faradays were therefore unpopular and could easily end up being hounded.

'I thank you for your kind consideration,' Matthew replied, angling his head until he gained a reasonable view of her. It was plain that she didn't care for his perusal. 'Forgive me. I have problems with my sight.'

Realizing this for herself now and taking account of the scarring to the side of his face, Clemency was a little ashamed of her stony reaction. He must have had a terrible accident. Perhaps it had left him traumatized and made him seek isolation. She should not have thought so badly of him. 'I am sorry, Mr Faraday.'

'What are you sorry about, Clemency?' It was Hattie. Neither Clemency nor Matthew had heard her climb softly up the stairs and creep towards them. 'Matthew, what is going on?'

'Hattie! Good morning to you. I'd come along to tell you of some news from Kingsley.' It was Kingsley's custom to write to Matthew to try to keep him interested in life outside his own four walls. Sometimes he dropped a line or two to Hattie. He didn't bother to write to their parents. They sometimes took days to open their correspondence. 'I happened to meet Miss Kivell. I'm sorry to say that, of course, I took her by surprise.'

Hattie shot a look at Clemency and met raised brows. She would have to explain later why she had kept Matthew's existence a secret from her.

Clemency said, 'If it's family business I could return to Hattie's room.'

'It is nothing private, Miss Kivell,' Matthew said, feeling slightly more at ease. His secret was out but he was sure Clemency Kivell would keep her word to stay silent about him. Hattie need not be quite so embarrassed by the turn of events. 'Hattie, Kingsley has written to say a dear friend of his has suffered a grave illness and has gone to the country for what will be a long convalescence. Kingsley has gone to be at his side. He bids you your understanding and patience in waiting a month or two more to join him.' He kept back the fact that the 'dear friend' was actually Kingsley's six-year-old son, and that Kingsley had been distraught at the knowledge that he had nearly lost him. Now he wanted to spend some time with the boy and get to know him, and his younger sister, in a quiet setting that would be beneficial to the boy's health.

Hattie took the news well. 'Of course Kingsley must do his duty to his friend. I don't mind spending more time here at all. I shall be able to see more of Clemency.'

'I'm pleased that you've made a friend,' Matthew said. 'Now, please excuse me, ladies. It's been delightful to have met you, Miss Kivell.' He bowed his head to her, kissed Hattie and walked confidently along the dark corridor to a low, arched door adjoining his wing. It had only become apparent when he drew aside a thick tasselled curtain.

Clemency watched as he disappeared behind the curtain. She heard him open the door, walk through it, then close and lock it after him. 'Your brother makes sure he isn't disturbed, Hattie,' she said, not knowing what to make of the enigmatic Matthew Faraday.

'You don't know what Matthew's been through,' Hattie said defensively.

'No, I don't. I'm sorry if I sounded judgemental. I'm used to the men in my family pushing themselves forward and making demands. It was such a surprise to meet your brother in the way I did. You don't have to explain anything about him to me, Hattie. We need never speak of him again.'

'Thank you, Clemency, but now that you are aware of Matthew's existence, I will tell you one day about how brave he has been.' Hattie linked her arm through Clemency's. 'Let's go into my room. Now I'm to be here longer than anticipated we must come up with something really diverting to do. Matthew writes the most wonderful poetry, you know, under a pseudonym. Mama and I often read some to Papa of an evening. You must stay the night soon, if you can, and we shall entertain you.'

Clemency picked up the book she had looked at a few minutes earlier. 'Did Matthew write this?'

'Yes, and many other books.' Hattie clasped her hands in delight. 'He's so clever. He's almost blind, you know, but he manages well enough to put pen to paper. Oh, he has such a wonderful imagination. He makes up the most astonishing places, planets and islands, giving them the most breathtaking scenes and settings, and inventing truly fantastic creatures and people. Would you like to borrow the book? You might care to read out some of his poems yourself if you do stay the night with us.'

'I'd be very interested to become acquainted with Matthew's work. I shall take the greatest care with the book and show it to no one else. Hattie, I too would like to do something diverting, as you put it, but something that's also meaningful and worthwhile. I help my mother as much as she wants me to and I've sewed clothes for my brother's coming baby. But I want to do something that's a challenge. It's easy for men. They are so much more able to break out into the world and do as they please.' Just as Logan was about to do, she thought, burning with envy.

'Like Kingsley and Logan and even a labouring man like Abe,' Hattie mused, making unladylike faces. 'I'm not even supposed to show myself hereabouts, and you are restricted. Oh, Clemency, I haven't got any imagination. What can we do? You think of something.'

'What I'd really like is to see my family happy again,'

Clemency said wistfully. She had no idea how to make that happen.

'I would like to see my family leading a more open life,' Hattie said. 'When I was a girl Mama used to hold garden parties and take part in charitable events. She and Papa enjoyed meeting people. Sadly, they are not in a position to do fund-raising now, and they do get a little confused. Jane's self-centredness is so tedious; and then, of course, Kingsley and I won't be here very often. It's better that they keep themselves to themselves, but I can't help feeling so sad for them.'

Clemency thought of Matthew, whom she had promised not to mention to anyone else. Obviously he was another vulnerable member of the family. It was indeed a sad situation. It seemed that neither she nor Hattie would get their wish. She smiled warmly at her friend. 'We'll just have to take life as it comes, at least for the moment, and see what it brings us.'

Twelve

Serenity and Betsy left their next-door homes in Edge End ready for the walk to work. Two doors down was the Clymo house. Serenity knocked on the door, and the pair waited for the four forlorn little brothers and sisters of Jenny to join them for the trudge.

'Poor little mites,' Betsy said. 'None of 'em hardly had the strength to put one foot in front of the other yesterday. Both their parents are laid up and they're half starved. I've got a bit of barley bread for 'em for croust.'

'I've got some hevva cake.' Serenity intended to give the children most of her food; she would have some supper when she got home. Other neighbours had brought broth and eggs, whatever they could spare from their own meagre larders, for the Clymos. She frowned. 'Curtains haven't been drawn back yet. The littl'uns might have overslept.'

Betsy knocked again, louder. 'Do you think Jenny's dead? Most are saying it.'

'Seems likely.' Serenity shuddered. 'She's been gone more'n a week. Can't see she'd have gone far. I suppose someone will find her out on the downs one day. Poor Jenny, the only bit of pleasure she must have had was that stupid brooch. I could kill that old witch Blythe Knuckey for what she did to her. My mother says Mrs Clymo's taking it so bad she's gone into decline and not likely to last out the week. Mr Clymo will never forgive himself for hitting Jenny and sending her away. Doubt if he'll be long for this world either. It will be a terrible Christmas in this house. Someone ought to approach the Kivell Relief committee and ask for something for them. I'd go myself but Father would be furious.'

'Not many round here want to go cap in hand to that lot.'

'Needs must when the devil drives, and the devil in this case is Blythe Knuckey. Ooh, what I could do to her! Well, we can't go on waiting here. We'd better rouse the children.' Serenity tried the latch. 'It's locked. We'll have to go round the back.'

Betsy led the way down to the end of the terrace. Quickly, the girls rounded the garden wall at the very end and then made their way up the narrow grit path that ran alongside the back gardens. Each house had a privy, back to back with its neighbour, and its own individual gate knocked up from scraps of wood. They found the Clymos' gate open. 'Strange, seems they left by this way.'

Serenity pointed up the garden. 'The back door's open. We'll make sure.' A few steps along the ash path she stopped suddenly and cried out, 'My God! It's little Tommy, he's collapsed by the privy.'

The girls ran to the scrap of a boy. He was lying face down, wearing nothing but a threadbare cut-down nightshirt, which was fouled by watery excrement. He had vomited all the way from the doorstep. 'Cholera!' Serenity gasped. The disease was spread mainly by contaminated food and water, most often because sewage had not been cleared away. Without Jenny's protective hard work, her little brother had succumbed to one of life's evils. The girls knew that if they were careful they were unlikely to catch the disease merely by contact with a sufferer. Fearing for the boy, Serenity crept closer, with Betsy behind her. They soon stopped and clutched one another. 'It's too late. The poor mite's dead.'

Together they faced the house, dreading what they would find inside. 'Help us!' Serenity screamed. Betsy added her voice.

Abe – on the afternoon core that week – was the first to reach them. The evidence of his eyes told him what was wrong. Taking hold of the girls he pulled them back beyond the gate. 'Stay here! Mind you do. You've no need to see any more. Other men are on the way. We'll go inside.'

Serenity got through the day's work in a daze, crushing lumps of ore with a flat hammer, for once not feeling the inevitable aches and pains the continual labour brought with it. It was the same for Betsy. Sometimes they cried and other bal-maidens cried with them. Occasionally, someone would begin to sing the kind of hymn sung at a funeral and the girls would manage to find their voices to join in. Jeroboam Hearne turned up in the crib-shed. He had never come there before unless it had been to chastise a worker. This time he led the gathering in prayer for the souls of the whole dead Clymo family, and for Jenny.

At the end of the shift, as daylight was failing, Hearne collared Serenity and Betsy as they were changing out of their towser aprons into clean white ones and replacing their gooks with bonnets. 'Have you two any idea at all where Jenny might have run off to?'

'She had nowhere to go, Mr Hearne,' Serenity answered, sniffing sadly. 'She was mortified. She wouldn't have been able to face a soul again.'

He bowed his head. 'So she went off, lost and all alone, and is probably dead. Mrs Hearne is beside herself. She was thinking of offering Jenny a permanent post in our household. She found it eased her years of grief to have someone close by who reminded her of our little daughter.'

'There's only one person to blame for what happened,' Betsy said, turning as dark as storm clouds. 'She deserves to be punished!'

'Indeed she does.' Hearne thumped his fist into the palm of his hand. 'It should be she who is, dare I say the word, dead, and not those she made trouble for.'

Serenity ate her supper without tasting a morsel.

'At least they're all out of their suffering, and it was better for them all to go together,' her mother said, trying to offer some comfort, as they washed and dried the dishes. Her father was at the chapel for a meeting of men to discuss how the Clymo family might be buried.

'What a terrible way to go though. It's thought Mr and Mrs Clymo might have died before all the children did. Imagine their bewilderment, their suffering.'

'It would've been quite quick. Those littl'uns had nothing in them to stave it off. The people next door heard someone out in the garden through the night. If they'd known it was little Tommy, someone would've gone out to him, God rest his dear soul. Well, they're now altogether up there, safe with the Lord. No more hunger, hard slog and despair. Abe and the men have seen to the drains. Shouldn't be no risk to the rest of us, God willing.'

Putting the last dish away, Serenity said savagely, 'Bet that Knuckey witch is having a good laugh.'

'I doubt that.' Mrs Treneer settled at the hearth and picked up her knitting. 'I forgot to tell you, stones have been thrown at her windows and boys have been calling her names. She tried to tip her chamber pot on some of them but missed. Talk about spreading filth, the hypocrite. She can't have much to eat now she's not earning.'

'Serve her right if she starves to death.'

'Now maid, I don't hold with that sort of talk.' Mrs Treneer finished off a row of plain stitches. 'But I know what you mean.'

The sight of Jenny running away in tears and anguish was again in Serenity's mind. It never went away. There were a number of places a person could hide, but in the days since her disappearance they had all been checked. Abe had roamed over Poltraze and Trenbarvear land, and even inquired at Burnt Oak, but had come up with nothing. It tore at Serenity's heart to think of Jenny going mad with shame and despair, and her body cold and decomposing on the bleak moorland.

Remembering how she and Betsy had pursued Jenny, she thought of the moment when she had looked up George Road and seen Logan Kivell. There had been an interesting titbit of news about him. He had bought the Widow Brookson's house and moved into it, allowing her to stay on. Could he have seen Jenny that day? He might well have done if she had run past at the end of the road. No one had asked him. Someone should. Serenity hesitated. She didn't want to talk to the man. He was unlikely to be civil or interested in anything she had to say. He might make lewd suggestions to her again. But she felt she would be letting Jenny down if she did not do everything she possibly could to try to discover where she might have gone.

'I'm going out to see Betsy. I won't be long,' she told her mother.

Wrapped up warmly, she hurried through the village, hoping that Logan Kivell wasn't out carousing. He had apparently regained his standing and popularity in the Nankervis Arms by laying out lots of money for free drinks. When she reached the inn she paused to listen for Logan's voice. There was no laughter and little noise within its grimy walls. It was still early, so perhaps she might be in time to catch him before he left home – although the more she thought about it the more she dreaded seeing him. She feared he might do something to her – or, rather, she feared the effect he might have on her. He was an offensive brute yet she couldn't deny that he held some sort of attraction for her. She didn't understand what it was, except that she had heard that wicked men, especially handsome ones, had a way of beguiling the innocent. She told herself not to be so silly. She wasn't about to allow that to happen. She preferred Abe to any other man, and when the time felt right she would encourage him to look her way. The only reason she was out on this cold, windy night was to try to find out something about poor Jenny.

She would never dare enter the inn, of course. Before she went on to George Road, she glared across the street at Blythe Knuckey's cottage. Was the old mare spying on her? Serenity looked up and down the street. No one was about. She looked around for a sizeable stone, and then threw it with gusto at the troublemaker's door. 'I hope you rot in hell,' she muttered, twisting her hands in a strangling motion.

Determination filled her as she hastened towards the newly renamed Wingfield House. The moment she reached the end of George Road, the same spot she had run past two Sundays ago, she was unnerved to see a tall man striding along the pavement. In the lights coming from these superior dwellings, the distinctive fine build of Logan Kivell would be unmistakable even without his arm in a sling. Her feet faltered for a second but, swallowing hard and setting her expression firm, Serenity walked towards him.

Logan recognized her at once. Why, he wondered, should pretty young Serenity Treneer be coming this way, and at this time of day? He expected her to cross over to the opposite side of the road from him. It pleased and puzzled him that she did not and that she was in fact intending to speak to him; a pleasing mystery indeed. He waited until she had almost reached him before he stopped.

'Miss Treneer, what brings you this way?'

'M–Mr Kivell.' She cursed herself for stuttering. Then the words spilled nervously out of her. 'Forgive me for holding you up. The other day, I mean. It was on a Sunday, not the one just gone but the one before. You may have heard about a girl running away from outside the chapel, after there was some trouble there. Well, my friend Betsy and I ran after her but we couldn't catch up with her. No one has any idea where she went. It's feared she's dead – Jenny, that is. Jenny Clymo. She's small and ginger-haired and very shy. She was with Betsy and me that day . . . that day you had the fight with Abe Deveril.' If only he wouldn't keep such a steady gaze on her; it was off-putting. Her cheeks were burning hot, she was probably blushing as red as a poppy. 'You must be wondering why I'm telling you all this. Well, I saw you that day, when Jenny went missing, up this road, outside the house that's now yours. Did you happen to see a girl of that description? She would have been upset and crying, I expect. I'm really worried about her, desperate to know what's become of her. Something terrible has happened to her family, you see.'

Logan had listened to her breathless account, fully aware of Jenny's whereabouts. The last part troubled him though. 'What has happened to her family?'

'They're all dead.' She couldn't keep a sob out of her voice.

'Dead?' Logan exclaimed. 'How?'

'Cholera. They were struck down like lightning. Betsy and I, among others, had been looking out for the children – Jenny's younger brothers and sisters. We discovered the first of them dead. If poor Jenny was alive somewhere and got to hear of it, God only knows how she'd take it, all alone and—'

'Come with me, Serenity.' He reached out and took her arm.

Serenity tensed, still wary of him. 'What are you doing?'

'I'll take you to her.'

'Jenny's alive? You know where she is?'

'Yes, alive but heartbroken – I did see her that day.' He propelled Serenity along with him. 'She's been under my roof since then, being cared for by Mrs Brookson and by me. You are her friend; a good friend, loyal and reliable. She will have to be told this tragic news and it would be better coming from you.'

'You took Jenny in?' Her astonishment was plain.

'I did.' He wasn't ready yet to explain how or why. 'She's in a very fragile frame of mind after being thrown out on the streets for something she was completely innocent of. That Knuckey woman is evil to her wretched bones.' He would never forgive her for ridiculing him. 'I'd rather she was dead.'

'Me, too.' Serenity sighed. 'If only I'd known sooner where Jenny was. Minutes after she ran off from the chapel, the mine manager's wife cleared up all that dreadful business. She told Jenny's parents why Jenny was wearing a certain brooch. It was she who had given it to her, not Mr Hearne, as that evil old woman said. Mr Clymo was mortified at what he'd done to Jenny, throwing her out like that for nothing. He died not forgiving himself.'

'That is unfortunate, but he shouldn't have believed that witch's lies and he shouldn't have hit Jenny.' Once he'd decided to become Jenny's guardian, rather than merely her benefactor, Logan had warmed to the sorrowful, sweet-natured girl. Alice Brookson had agreed to take care of her, in return for being allowed to remain in her former home.

They had now reached the gates of his house. He unlatched them and led Serenity up to the front door. 'Perhaps, the fact that her parents and the village knew the truth may help her snap out of her depression, and then come to terms with all these deaths.'

'Mr Kivell, you're back already.' Maudie had hurried from

the kitchen to greet him. She stared at the girl he had brought in with him.

'This is Miss Treneer, a friend of Jenny's. She has important news for Jenny. Fetch her down from her room and bring her to the drawing room, Maudie. We'll join Mrs Brookson there.'

In awe of being in a gentry house, Serenity curtsied to the maid, then realized her mistake. She must remember she was only here for Jenny's sake. Poor Jenny, she might have been given a position here but she was in for more suffering.

Taking her by the elbow, Logan steered her into a large room grander than she could ever have imagined. There wasn't an inch of carpet visible; it was covered with tables, chairs, sofas, cabinets and stools, all lavished with beautiful embroidered cushions and tasselled runners. There were innumerable vases and ornamental figures and candlesticks and lamps – some as tall as Logan – with fringed shades. The walls were patterned – wallpaper! She had heard of it but had been able to believe that it really existed. How could anyone afford so much paper, painted with such strangely shaped yellow flowers? Serenity curtsied three times to Mrs Brookson to be sure to give the lady her due respect. She felt Mrs Brookson must be related to royalty for she was decked in diamonds and silks and had her feet, clad in polished buckled shoes, up on a stool. Two plump cats wearing collars dozed, one on a chair, the second in a blanket-lined basket. Serenity felt her shabby presence marred the splendid surroundings.

'I'm so glad you approached Mr Kivell, Serenity,' Alice Brookson said graciously. 'Do take a seat.'

Sit down? She was being invited to sit down on one of these lovely chairs? Mrs Brookson seemed kind. Jenny was fortunate to be working for her. Serenity took the plainest seat, an upright chair rather than an armchair. 'Thank you.' She reddened, realizing she had been staring.

Logan remained standing and took up a position by the mantelpiece. Serenity felt his eyes on her. He was a masterly presence. Her eyes shot open when Jenny, with her head hung down, came in with the maid. Her tragic little friend was wearing a made-to-measure cotton dress over petticoats, with a muslin shawl around her shoulders. Her hair was fixed in glossy ringlets. She had been taken in here, but not as a servant.

'Jenny is Mrs Brookson's companion and I am Jenny's guardian,' Logan explained with satisfaction.

'She is a welcome addition to the house.' Alice Brookson beckoned Jenny to sit near to her. 'Lift up your head, Jenny, dear.'

Obeying immediately, Jenny walked slowly towards the old lady with her back straight. Giving Serenity a transitory smile, she lowered herself carefully on to the end of a striped sofa. Her time here had begun to effect a transformation and Serenity was glad for her. If anyone deserved to go up in the world it was Jenny. Serenity felt a sneaking gratitude towards Logan.

'Thank you for coming here, Serenity. Maudie says you have news for me.' Jenny's voice was hoarse and it could only be guessed how much weeping she had done in the past few days.

'You will have to be brave, Jenny, dear,' Alice Brookson said.

Becoming aware of the sombre atmosphere, Maudie moved protectively behind Jenny.

Jenny glanced anxiously at the three women, then at Logan. He said, 'Rest assured we are here for you, Jenny. Don't be afraid.'

'It's Father, isn't it? Or Mother? Has something happened to one of the littl'uns?'

Her lashes sparkling with tears, Serenity nodded her head. 'Jenny, I'm so sorry, it's all of them. It happened through the night. Cholera. They were all taken.' Before the girl was overwhelmed with grief and horror, Serenity, forgetting she was in an upper-class place, scurried to her friend, kneeling at her feet and grabbing her hands. 'But they all knew the truth, everyone does, about you and Mr Hearne. Mrs Hearne told us outside the chapel. You're not under any shame. Your father died regretting the way he treated you, but feeling proud of you.'

Logan was touched by the scene. Mrs Brookson and Maudie were proud their protégée was reacting with dignity. Jenny, in fact, was too numb to be plunged into wailing or hysterics. 'Th—they didn't suffer?'

'Betsy and me were at the house first. We're sure it was over quick.'

Jenny nodded. 'They're all together.'

'It's better that way, Jenny,' Alice Brookson said. She was sorry for Jenny, but relieved that there were now no complications in the girl's life. She couldn't help feeling glad that now Jenny could remain her companion, saving her from a lonely old age. After Jenny had mourned, it would be easier to train her for her new life.

'Yes,' Jenny agreed. It was better her family were all at peace, her young brothers and sisters never to have to bear any more hard work and deprivation. 'Where are they now?'

'They've been laid out and are all at home.'

'They need shrouds. To be buried. How . . .?' She looked up at Logan. Not with pleading, Serenity noticed; Jenny trusted him. He was taking the role of guardian seriously and with generosity.

'I shall see to it that your family are buried with dignity, Jenny,' he said softly. 'I shall consult with my kinsmen who own the carpentry business about caskets this very night.' It was a good feeling to offer kindness to Jenny rather than to be selfish and quarrelsome all the time, but Logan would never change completely. The people of Meryen would know him as a hard man never to be mocked; some he had marked down for revenge. The village would know his presence keenly.

'Thank you, Mr Kivell,' Jenny said, pinched and pale, fighting to hold back her new misery.

'I expect you would like some time alone, dear,' Alice Brookson said soothingly. 'Maudie will take you upstairs and then bring you some hot milk. You may leave the funeral arrangements to Mr Kivell and me.'

'Thank you, Mrs Brookson,' Jenny said in a whisper, rising weakly. Maudie was preparing to usher her out. 'Thank you too, Mr Kivell. And thank you again, Serenity. I shall never forget the kindness of you all.'

Serenity was uncertain how to withdraw politely. Dipping her knee to Mrs Brookson, she said, 'I – um – will bid you goodnight, ma'am. I must go or my mother will start to worry.'

'We are very grateful for your thoughtful deed, Serenity,' Alice Brookson said, with a gracious nod of her lace-capped head. 'Good night to you.'

'I'll see you to the door, Serenity,' Logan said, already halfway across the room. Out in the hall he retrieved his hat. 'I'll see you safely on the way. Any manner of bad fellow might be abroad at this time of evening.'

Serenity thought back to the occasion when he had accosted her and her two friends in broad daylight. He was the most likely danger. If she was seen in his company alone her reputation would be lost, but she could think of no plausible excuse not to walk down George Road at his side.

'You are well, Serenity?' he said. 'Could there be any danger to you of contracting cholera?'

Was he concerned for her or worried there might be an epidemic? 'I think everything has been brought under control.'

'I'm pleased to hear it. I'll arrange the funeral service for next Sunday, at the chapel. I understand it's the preferred day among the mining workers, so all may attend. I'm sure the village will want to pay its respects in force to the Clymos. I shall then take Jenny straight home. Holding a wake can be a village affair.'

Serenity heard the element of scorn in the declaration. 'Indeed, all of Meryen will turn out. People will be relieved that Jenny is alive and well.'

'Jenny will have no more association with the villagers,' he said loftily.

'No one will expect her to,' she hit back. 'And no one will be jealous of her new position. All will wish her well.' Except for Blythe Knuckey, but she didn't matter any more. They had reached the end of the road. 'I'll go the rest of the way on my own.'

'As you please.'

She was relieved he did not insist on staying at her side.

'But I will see you again, Serenity,' he said in husky tones.

To Serenity he was hinting of wicked intentions. 'Only on my terms,' she hissed, and walked quickly away.

Logan smiled. 'Any terms will do,' he said under his breath.

Thirteen

Her head throbbing in muzzy pain, Feena Kivell lay in bed, wishing she had never been moved out of the more comfortable, happier surroundings of the farmhouse at Burnt Oak. If she had been offered a choice she would be giving birth to her baby, due any day now, within the old family community. Her father-in-law, Seth, had denied her forthcoming child its centuries-old birthright, and her the peaceful, safer environment of Burnt Oak in which to endure her confinement.

Last night she had tearfully told Adam that his father was a bully and that she hated it here at Trenbarvear. Moreover, she was sure she wouldn't be any happier in their own home, now just completed. Adam had confessed that he too wished they had not left Burnt Oak. He blamed himself for not thinking through the consequences of Seth's arrogant whim, and he blamed Seth for all the strain and misery in their present home.

Closing her eyes to ease her pain, Feena tried to picture her new baby, and imagine how it would feel in her arms. She smoothed gentle hands over her enormous bump and whispered passionately, 'I promise you, my darling, that I won't let you be unhappy. I'll beg your father to take us back to Burnt Oak. I don't think he'll take much persuading for us to be where we all belong. You and I won't ever set foot in that new house.'

Calmer, more optimistic, she prayed her labour pains would start soon, but not today. Adam was at the new house, moving in their belongings – many of the things crafted by the Kivells themselves. Verena and the others were helping him to get everything ready to receive her and the newborn baby. Only the two housemaids were left in the house with her. Someone from the family would be back soon to check on her and she would ask for a soothing cup of liquorice tea. She drifted off to sleep but moments later she awoke, urgently in need of the commode.

It was a struggle to sit up, with her head in pain and her body so cumbersome, and to wrestle the bedcovers back and drag her heavy legs over the side of the bed. The whole of her body felt like a lead weight. The baby moved and kicked inside her and she lovingly placed her arms around her huge belly. 'I love you, my little one.'

She gripped the bedside table for support while she heaved herself up, pushing down with her other hand on the bed as a lever. Gingerly, she slid down on to her feet, and carefully tested her weight on them. Her heart thundered crazily in her chest and it was difficult to breathe. This was harder than she had expected. She needed help. She flopped back down on to the bed but missed it and, with a strangled cry, thudded like a sack of coal to the floor. The beat of her heart went haywire and she felt as if it were about to explode inside her. Her back was pressed against the bed. Keeping her eyes shut, she could only grit her teeth and wait for her body to check itself. She had no strength left to bang on the floor and alert the maids. She would have to wait for someone to come and help her up.

To her relief, her heart suddenly behaved itself. She felt warm and relaxed, light and bright, as if she were floating on air; she was launched on a wave of euphoria. Everything was going to be all right. She and the baby were fine, and they and Adam had a wonderful future to look forward to; she could see every moment of it. Then her whole body heaved and she slumped in a heap.

'Do you like it, Clemmie?' Adam asked. They were in the nursery of his new house. 'Do you think it's right for little Jacob or Faith?'

Among the toys and baby linen were some that Clemency had stitched with Hattie at Poltraze. There was a new rocking cradle made jointly by Jowan and Thad. 'It's all lovely. It's a pity though that Feena can't be here to put things where she wants them to be.'

'She won't be all that bothered,' Adam said blandly, pulling on the ears of a small cotton rabbit.

'You don't seem particularly bothered either, Adam. Are you worried about Feena going through the birth?'

'Of course – more so than any other expectant father. Feena's been so low. She hates it here, Clemmie. When we moved here I thought – well, I don't know what I thought. All of us are so used to doing everything Father wants. Mother's miserable. She doesn't say so but it's easy to tell. Oh, well,' he worked up a grin, but it was unconvincing, 'perhaps things will get better when the baby's born and we've moved in. Our own place, we've never had that before.'

'You could leave here, like Logan,' Clemency said. She and Verena had visited Wingfield House and had come away impressed by Logan's return to his proud manner and his benevolence towards Mrs Brookson and the mine girl, Jenny. He had stood at the communal graveside of the tragic Clymo family supporting Jenny, who had been veiled in black – a touching, tragic figure of village folklore. Accompanying Logan and Jenny had been the highly respected widow Mrs Alice Brookson and a female servant from the household. Jowan and Thad, and Uncle Henry Cardell and Uncle Cary had also attended. The villagers had appreciated that. Logan was making strides into gaining the villagers' respect, breaking down the long-held barriers between Meryen and Burnt Oak. There had been a bit of an incident after the interment when Jeroboam Hearne and his wife had offered Jenny a home, to live with them in the same manner as she was now living at Wingfield House. Logan had told them bluntly not to interfere and never to suggest such a thing to her again. A stony-faced Mrs Brookson had led Jenny away. Still mortified by the accusation levelled against her and Mr Hearne, Jenny had not once met his eyes. After their rebuff Mrs Hearne had left the ceremony in tears. At least the malicious agitator Blythe Knuckey had not been there to listen in and gloat. She barely showed her face anywhere nowadays.

Logan had recently been staying with relatives in the Truro area, forming contacts in preparation for investing in the profitable business of mining and shipping. He seemed so far away. Clemency felt sure Adam would move out of here by and by. She hoped he would, for his and his family's sake. Her father was downstairs crowing about this house being the next step in his empire. It was pathetic that he couldn't see he had no such thing and never would have. One large farm wasn't of much account. And he was oblivious of the misery he was creating. Stupid, ignorant fool! She wanted to clatter down-stairs to him and shake him, but that wouldn't thrust sense into him or toss out his selfishness.

Adam was suddenly anxious. 'Someone should be with Feena.'

'I'll go. I'll stay with her until you come in for lunch.'

Clemency walked quickly over to the farmhouse, thinking about Feena, who was growing paler every day. This thought reminded her of the pale-skinned person she had acciden-tally met recently, Matthew Faraday. She had dreamt about him every night since, which was odd; she had only spoken to him for a few minutes. Her dreams were always the same: he was pulling Hattie into a book of poetry, which he slammed shut, never to let her out. Hattie was imprisoned for ever in his strange world, alone and desperate for any sort of company. In her dreams Clemency watched from afar, unable to go to Hattie's rescue. Clemency had enjoyed reading Matthew's poems; he had a brilliant imagination and each one was a story that stayed in her mind. There was nothing morbid or menacing in his words, but because of the dreams she had held on to the book for Hattie's sake, although that was illogical.

Clemency was vexed to find the farmhouse empty. Through the kitchen window she could see both maids hanging out washing. They had been ordered to stay within calling distance of Feena. She hastened upstairs and tapped on the bedroom door. 'Feena, it's Clemency. Is it all right to come in?'

There was no answer. Feena was probably dozing. She peeped inside to ensure that all was well and saw immediately that the bed was empty. Feena must have slipped along to the in-adequate bathroom. Then she caught a glimpse of fair hair just below the level of the bed. 'Feena!' It was obvious what had happened: Feena had taken a fall and was too weak to call for help. 'It's all right, I'm coming.'

Clemency knelt beside the mother-to-be. 'Feena?' With careful hands, she lifted up her sister-in-law's head. It was a heavy, lolling weight. 'Oh no, please God. Feena? Feena, wake up!' But she knew it was no good. She was too late. Feena was dead.

Gently releasing Feena's lifeless head, she sat back on her heels, the back of her hand up to her mouth. *No, this wasn't true.*

This terrible thing couldn't have happened to Feena and Adam. But
Feena wasn't moving or breathing. Clemency thought of the
baby. Was there still time to save the baby? Feena would have
wanted her baby to live. And Adam, too – surely he'd want to
try to save his child?

She scrabbled to her feet, pelted down the stairs and ran
shouting to the new house.

Logan returned home the next day satisfied with the new
investments he had made. He was now a shareholder, albeit
a minor one, in the Wheal Verity mine, he had bought a
local oyster dredging company and, to cap it all, he had won
two and a half hundred guineas at the card table in Truro's
Assembly Rooms. He had bedded a baronet's lonely wife,
and met a shy young heiress who might possibly make him
a bride, although there was no shortage of likely ladies who
would bring him in more money. He had yet to meet
someone who looked as if she would breed him fine, healthy
sons.

He presented Mrs Brookson and Jenny with an indulgent
amount of lace and confectionery. He gave Maudie boxed
handkerchiefs and brought home a square tin of ginger fair-
ings for the other servants. Let it be said that Logan Kivell
kept a good house. He retired to his study. He had recently
lined its walls with both classic and modern books, and his
favourites, accounts of contemporary explorers. One day soon
he would take a trip overseas; he had plenty of kin on several
continents.

He lounged back in his padded leather chair with his
boots up on the desk and eased his arm out of the sling.
The padding and splints could be discarded soon and then
the lasting damage to his arm determined. It would be
weaker, less agile, and give him sharp twinges throughout
the rest of his life but at least he would be spared the indignity of having one arm noticeably shorter than the other.
He lit a fat cigar, basking in his glory. It was he, not his
father, who would shine in the world. And the world would
be his. He would increase his wealth as he travelled it. Later
today he would go to Burnt Oak and down a barrel of ale
with his brothers and kinsmen.

There was a knock on the door and, in response to his

command, Maudie entered. 'Miss Clemency Kivell, sir,' she announced.

'Clemmie!' He sprang up. 'How good to see you. How are you? Let me tell you all about my . . .'

Then he saw that Clemency was wearing black and her eyes were red from weeping. 'What's happened?' He dropped the cigar in an ashtray. 'It's not Mother, is it?.'

'Thank God you're back, Logan. It's Feena. She died yesterday, suddenly. The doctor said it was her heart, that there must have been a malformation in it from birth. He said she didn't suffer.' Her eyes filled with tears. 'The baby perished too. Adam's inconsolable. He blames himself for taking Feena away from Burnt Oak. He blames Father too and says he wishes it could be him who was dead. He took Feena's body straight over to Burnt Oak. He's at the farmhouse with Tobias and he says he'll never leave there again.'

She ran to Logan and he gathered her in. 'What's happening to us? I've never been scared before but now it's as if we've been cursed.'

'It's Father who's cursed us,' he said, a sob rising in his throat. 'Poor Adam. Feena might have died anyway but we'll always wonder about that. I'll go straight away to see him. Clemmie, don't be afraid; you can come to live here with me – you and Mother. I'm afraid too, for all of you left at Trenbarvear.'

Fourteen

The church bells rang the one-note knell of death and mourning. From behind her net curtains Blythe watched the steady, slow trickle of horses and carriages, riders and pedestrians passing on the way to the church for the Kivell funeral. When the hearse had gone by, a carved black wood and glass vehicle, pulled by four, black-plumed, black ponies, and there was a lull, Blythe reckoned it was safe to sneak out and get some food. Her intention was to steal some from the back gardens of the villagers who had left their houses to stand outside the churchyard and gawp.

Blythe's dismissal disqualified her from applying for Poor Relief, and she was fiercely hungry, having long since consumed the contents of her larder and the few vegetables in her garden. She'd had two hens but they had stopped laying eggs and she'd killed them for the stew pot. She was also late with the rent. Shunned by all, abused by many, and her little home constantly under bombardment from stones, litter and even excrement, her only hope was to get out of Meryen and, in future, to keep a tight rein on her tongue. She had applied for a live-in housemaid's job in the next parish of Gwennap but had been turned away because she couldn't produce references. There was one possibility to avoid destitution. A middle-class, ageing spinster in Gwennap had advertised for a cook-general – actually, a dogsbody – in a less grand house near to the one where Blythe had failed at the interview. Apparently the lady was a hard, miserly termagant who couldn't keep staff long and therefore was not in a position to be too fussy about who worked for her. Blythe had an appointment there tomorrow.

She slunk off, stooped over with a shawl pulled about her head, along the back paths, making quite a detour until she reached Edge End. The Clymo house had been taken over by a young family related to the Treneers. She would not take anything from their garden for fear it might be contaminated, although there had been no more reports of cholera. Some people thought it strange that the Clymos had suddenly succumbed in the way they did. As weak as the parents had been, they and Jenny had kept everything as clean as possible. Blythe had been blamed for the deaths – if Jenny hadn't had cause to run away, the tragedy might never have happened. Blythe hoped the Clymos were rotting in hell. And she ill-wished Jenny every day, hoping she'd suffer a reversal of her good fortune. Living with the gentry and a Kivell indeed! Well, there was only one reason the lustful Logan Kivell would give her a home: he probably had a liking for childlike waifs. It burned in Blythe that she dared not start such a rumour.

She peered over the low dividing stone walls of the terraced cottages and through the back gates. All seem quiet and deserted. The Deverils had a goodly crop of greens, turnips, potatoes and onions. Blythe had a small sack hidden under her skirt.

She'd flit in and out, try not to make bare spaces among the vegetables too obvious, and pull out something for her next few meals.

She opened the gate, closed it slowly so that it wouldn't make a tell-tale click, and nipped up the ash path. She lifted her skirt, pulled out the sack and crouched down by the cabbages, her hand reaching out greedily for a fine specimen.

'What the hell do you think you're doing?' Abe shouted. In his chapel-going suit, he was running late to watch the funeral at the roadside. He wanted to demonstrate to Clemency his sorrow for her and his support. 'You've got a bloody cheek, Blythe Knuckey. Get away from here before I fetch the constable on you.'

Frightened by his sudden angry voice, and being caught out, Blythe fell back on her bottom. 'Now, now young Abe, you're a good boy. You wouldn't want to see me up before the magistrate just for trying to put a little food in my belly, would you? I'm starving, honest I am, haven't had a bite in three days. I'm getting weak as water. Don't turn me in, I beg you. I know everyone hates me and I don't blame 'em for it. What I did to Jenny was wicked and I'm sorry. Look, I'm getting a job and will be leaving the village soon. It's what everyone wants. Just let me go on my way, eh? I promise I won't try this again.'

Abe enjoyed watching her grovel. He had the power to have her thrown in prison, perhaps transported to the colonies. 'You've got no right to be stealing. You could have gone to the Kivells for charity. You got no right to steal from your hard-working, law-abiding neighbours who find life a hard struggle themselves. Your troubles are of your own making. You're responsible for the terrible end of the Clymos. Get out of here before I kick you all the way to the bleddy gate.'

It took an effort for Blythe to get up on her feet. She pointed a finger at Abe, her face creased in venom. 'Death, hell and damnation, and years of suffering to you and your family, boy. From now on may you never know a minute's peace!'

'You can take your curse and beat your own head with it. Now get out!' Abe made to charge at her and she shrieked and scuttled down the path. Abe followed, watching until she was out of sight; then, shaking his head over the sheer nerve of the woman, he strode towards the High Street and the church.

In a fury, but remaining furtive, Blythe's first thought was to look for gardens elsewhere for possible looting. Then she remembered that Dilly Trewin kept a good crop round the back of the Nankervis Arms, set back behind the inn stable block, backing on to a field. She'd reach it by way of the field. Blythe made off. She climbed over a style into the field then crept along the side of the hedge, as close as she was able to, as there were dead brambles, wet grasses and catkins and hawthorn hanging out from it. She was a few steps along then stopped. There were rustling noises behind her. Could it be a stray dog or a sheep? She turned her head slowly and her skin prickled in alarm.

'Who are you? What're you up to?' She was being followed by a scruffy, bearded stranger. He was leaning on a short staff and had the look of a tinker about him.

'I've been following you since you left home, Mrs Knuckey. Thought you might like a bit of company.' His voice was rough and he angled his hips at her lewdly.

'How do you know my name? I want you gone – I'm not that sort of woman. How dare you?'

'You may not be a whore,' he said, advancing on her rapidly, 'but you're a vindictive bitch.'

'What's that to you?' Blythe was getting edgy. 'What do you want?'

'Me? I only want money.'

'Well, I haven't got none. Get away or I'll scream.'

'There's no one to hear you and no one would rush to your side anyway. You're the most hated woman in the locality. You've upset too many people, one in partic'lar, and that person is paying me good money to take retribution for what you did.'

'Did? I never did nothing bad, not really bad.' Fear had Blythe in its icy grip. Someone had set this man on her with the intention of causing her grievous harm.

'You've taken away something precious that this person wanted more than anything, taken it away twice in fact, and you've got to pay the price for that.'

As the man raised the staff above his head, Blythe opened her mouth to scream but a crushing blow reached her face before she could utter a sound. Her jaw was smashed and she was hurtled down to the muddy ground. Unable to cry out, she put up her hands to defend herself. The next blow exploded into her stomach, the third cracked the bones in her thigh. The weapon was raised again and slammed down on her shoulder. Through her terror and agony Blythe knew this was the end; her attacker intended to murder her and he was enjoying doing so, slowly.

Finally the man wiped his staff clean of blood on the damp grass and pushed it out of sight up the sleeve of his coat. A short time afterwards, on the outskirts of the village, he kept an appointment with a lady who was sitting stiffly up on a trap.

'Is it done?' Mrs Jeroboam Hearne asked.

'It is, ma'am.' He touched his forelock and took a bag of coins from her.

'Did you do it well?'

'Oh, yes, ma'am, very well indeed, just like you said.'

Mrs Hearne smiled a malevolent, vengeful smile. 'Good man.'

'Anything else I can do for you, ma'am?'

Mrs Hearne had hired this rogue to poison Thomas Clymo for driving Jenny away with his cruelty, and denying her of her child's replacement. It was a pity about his wife and poor, ragged children but, in her eyes, they were expendable. On her orders, the tinker had also been behind most of the vandalism caused to Blythe Knuckey's home. The witch had had to pay for trying to sully Jeroboam's reputation with her evil lies. There wouldn't be much of a hue and cry for Blythe Knuckey. The village would think it had been done a favour. Mrs Hearne had cried with relief when she learned that Jenny was safe and well; the sweet girl had reminded her so much of her dear departed Lydia. And then, at the Clymos' funeral, Logan Kivell had offended and grieved her. She thought for a moment. Could this killer remove Kivell so that she could approach Jenny again? No, it would not be as easy as getting rid of the others and it would be too dangerous. She had planned murder in cold blood but she wasn't a fool. Better to let things lie and to try to see Jenny if the opportunity arose.

'No thank you, your work here is done. Goodbye to you, sir.'

Fifteen

The funeral service was over. Clemency left the church on Logan's arm and they joined the long procession that wound its way to the open grave. At its head were the vicar, carrying his prayer book, and the verger, carrying the gold cross. Next was Tobias, physically supporting a distraught Adam, and after them were Feena's parents and relatives from Redruth, where the couple had met. They were followed by Seth and Verena, and their sons and families and the rest of the Kivells. Mrs Brookson and Jenny were there to support Logan, and finally came the well-to-do, the local traders, shopkeepers and farmers, and the Trenbarvear workers. The church had been filled to overflowing and the graveyard was packed. All the while Adam had sobbed like an uncomprehending child.

A female figure in a heavy veil appeared and joined Clemency. It was Hattie. She linked her arm through her friend's. 'I had to come. I was so sorry to receive your letter about your dear sister-in-law. How very sad. All at Poltraze pass on their sympathies too. My brother thought it acceptable for me to be here if I leave immediately afterwards.'

'It's very good of you to come, Hattie, and thank you for sending a card,' Clemency said through her tears. 'People have been so kind but it doesn't really help. This is one of the saddest occasions there has ever been for the family.'

'I wish there was something more I could do.' Hattie glanced at Logan, who was standing behind Clemency. He cut a fine figure in his long coat and scarf. 'I'm sorry to meet you again under such circumstances, Mr Kivell.'

'I thank you for your kind thought, Miss Faraday.' Logan bowed his head to her. What a dainty, considerate little thing you are, he thought. Then his mind reverted back to his poor brother's sorrows.

It took a lot of shuffling for those closest to the deceased to form themselves around the graveside. The extra sadness of the death of an unborn baby affected many of the men as deeply as the women. Clemency felt Logan clinging to her as tightly as she to him, and she was glad to have Hattie there. The vicar solemnly intoned the readings and prayers, and to Clemency it went by in a blur until he said the words, 'Dust to dust, ashes to ashes.'

At this point Adam cried out in despair, 'They're not dust, they're not dust!' He fell to his knees and Tobias had to restrain his brother from flinging himself down on to the coffin. 'Feena, don't leave me! Let me go with you and the baby!'

Verena knelt beside her stricken son and Adam allowed her to take him in her arms.

'Get him up.' Seth moved round and hissed in Tobias's ear. 'He's making a fool of himself.'

Tobias shrugged him off fiercely. 'What does that matter? We're not interested in anything you have to say.'

Clemency stiffened. Never before had any of her brothers spoken to their father so aggressively. There was resentment in Tobias's hard expression, and the look Adam gave Seth was shot through with loathing. Affronted and furious, Seth stepped round the boys and grabbed Verena's arm. 'We're going. I'm not staying here while my own sons publicly disrespect me.'

'Go if you must, Seth, but I will not.' Verena was firm. 'Couldn't you for once in your life think about how one of your children is suffering? This isn't about your stupid pride.'

Clemency held her breath. This was the first time her mother had gone against her father. Would he explode in temper and cause more distress? Making an angry rumble in his throat, Seth pushed his way through the mourners and strode towards the lych-gate.

The rest of the burial went ahead, punctuated only by Adam's mournful wailing. He allowed Tobias and Verena to lead him away, his legs barely holding him up. Clemency had been to many funerals but this one was the most heart-rending. She leaned against Logan's shoulder, while holding tightly to Hattie's hand. Hattie too was moved to tears.

'We're going on to Burnt Oak for the wake,' Clemency told Hattie. 'You're welcome to join us, but of course . . .'

'I had better get back. Do come to Poltraze as soon as you feel able to, Clemency.' Then Hattie addressed Logan. 'Perhaps we will meet again, Mr Kivell.'

'My door will always be open to welcome you, Miss Faraday. I'm sure Mrs Brookson and my ward, Miss Clymo, would be pleased to meet you,' Logan replied gallantly. He turned away from her, wanting only to get himself and his family out of the public glare and to reach the comfort and solidity of Burnt Oak. He therefore missed the expression of delight that came over Hattie's face at his words.

At the lych-gate, up above the steps leading down into High Street, Verena asked Cary Kivell to substitute for her at Adam's side. Seth, not caring about the spectacle he was making for the villagers to stare at, was waiting for her, his bearded face never before so dark and brooding. Glaring at his wife, he stuck out his arm, and she threaded hers through his with dignity and a determined glint in her eyes. He kept her there until all the family had filed past.

Clemency and Logan, with a young lady everyone had guessed was Miss Hattie Faraday, brought up the rear. The vicar had engaged Hattie in a few moments' conversation. He had been pleased to learn that she was sure her parents would welcome a visit from him to take the sacrament of communion. Hattie had decided that it would be good for her parents to see the churchman. He was compelled to keep his counsel where his parishioners were concerned, so there would be no gossip. Hattie hoped this would lead to a little more contact for herself with the village.

Logan escorted the girls down the steps, and after the two friends had exchanged an embrace, he saw Hattie into her carriage.

Abe was across the street from the church, standing next to Serenity and Betsy.

'So the Kivells are friendly with them up in the big house.' Serenity made a face.

'Stuck up mare,' Betsy muttered. 'It's said they're a funny lot up there.'

'Miss Hattie's nice,' Abe said.

'How would you know?' the girls echoed each other.

'I've met her and spoken to her,' he said teasingly.

'When?' Serenity sparked with sudden jealousy. Abe wasn't

in Miss Faraday's league but she didn't like him being on friendly terms with any other girl. 'Oh, poaching, I bet.'

Then Logan Kivell looked their way – or, rather, straight at Serenity. He held her gaze for a second and she was sure she saw interest and warmth in his dark eyes. As she finally looked away, she was amazed to see Miss Faraday, on noticing Abe in the crowd, lift a hand in greeting to him. He waved back. Clemency Kivell stepped back from the carriage and it set off, and she too nodded to Abe and said, 'Good afternoon, Abe.'

'Good afternoon, Miss Clemency,' Abe replied confidently, as if he was particularly familiar with her. 'Please accept my sympathy for your loss. I speak for the whole of Meryen.'

While the gathering issued many an 'Aye' in agreement, Serenity traded stunned looks with Betsy. 'He's well in with those two.'

'Mmm,' Betsy tossed her head. 'P'raps they don't mind him sowing his wild oats in their direction.'

'Can't see that,' Serenity said loftily. She decided she was no longer interested in Abe Deveril. He in no way compared to Logan Kivell. Now he was a real man, tough, rich and powerful, and far better looking than Abe.

Seth had homed in on Clemency at the exact moment when she spoke to the young miner. Why the hell was she so familiar with him? He wouldn't tolerate this. Clemency was a young lady, every bit as fine as the Faraday girl. He wouldn't have her passing the time of day with mining dross, especially the one who'd humiliated her brother.

'Home,' he commanded Verena.

'The wake is at Burnt Oak,' she reminded him.

'I'm not going. If sons of mine can treat me with contempt then I don't want to be near them. We'll fetch Clemmie and go.'

Verena held back as he started down a step. 'Adam is my son and he needs me. How can you be so heartless? I'm going to Burnt Oak with Logan, and Clemency is coming with us. If you want to go back to that wretched farm then go, but you will go alone.'

'You dare to defy me?' Seth roared, shaken by Verena's determination and by her evident dislike of Trenbarvear.

'Take it as you please.' She pulled free of him and went down the steps. 'I'm just being a loving mother.'

Seth was left standing alone, a big man cut down to size by a woman. He made tight fists as he trembled with rage. All eyes were on him, mocking eyes in the mob. Not one member of his family showed him understanding or concern. He stayed put. He would not run away from ridicule and hostility. His own wife and children had turned against him; something he had never believed would happen. He'd win them back; he'd make sure of it. And after that none would ever dare disobey him again.

Sixteen

'Mrs Secombe said you wanted to see me, Matthew.' Hattie had gone straight to the east wing after changing out of her mourning clothes. He was rummaging through a large chest set down on his dining table, pulling out Christmas decorations. Despite his limited sight he enjoyed the sparkle of them in the firelight and candlelight, and was able to decorate his rooms on his own. He had written poems about every aspect of Christmas, some breathtakingly magical, some bleak and dark. He didn't respond immediately and this meant that somehow Hattie had displeased him. She went up close to him. 'Matthew?'

He carried on taking brightly painted tree ornaments out of the box, and shimmering sugar plum boxes, little toy drums and jewelled silk lanterns. 'Where did you go in the carriage, Hattie?'

'Nowhere in particular.' She picked up a stuffed fake robin and fluffed up its feathers. 'I fancied a drive.'

'Barker saw you leave. He said you were dressed as if for a funeral. Well? I want the whole truth.' He was stern, his posture straight and commanding, as if he were addressing a guilty soldier in the ranks.

Hattie was unconcerned by his anger, as she was by the fact that she had lied to Clemency when she said she had his permission to go to the funeral. She had returned home burning to say something to him. 'I went to a funeral in the village, of a sister-in-law to Clemency, actually. She died suddenly before she could give birth so it was a double tragedy. I didn't want to intrude so I didn't go inside the church. I only spoke to Clemency, her brother and the vicar.'

Matthew turned his extraordinary, luminous eyes upon her. 'It was agreed that we would keep our distance from Meryen.'

'That was yours and Kingsley's decision. You pushed Papa and Mama into agreeing with you. Well, I think it's a mistake for them to live in such seclusion. They enjoy being with people, they like to mix. It's a crime to deprive them of all company.'

'It was the right decision and done to protect them.' With his hands clasped behind his back he walked a few steps then strode back to her, hard and unyielding. 'Hattie, don't be naïve. Papa in particular is vague and vulnerable. Miners tend to be hard and uncouth. The Kivells, even your precious Miss Clemency, are not an easy breed. I won't have Papa and Mama exposed to people they might find hard to cope with. I won't have them laughed at.'

'I am not as naïve as you would have me be,' Hattie railed. 'Papa and Mama are not senile. They are charming still. Their friends in London were always eager to seek their society. You are using this argument as an excuse to keep your own anonymity. You're running away from life, both you and Jane. It's wrong!'

'Still your tongue, Harriet Faraday.' He shook at her emphatic attack. 'You say too much.'

'I have only just started.' She would tell him exactly what had been running through her mind of late.

'You will keep it to yourself,' he thundered before she got out another word. 'I have a notion you get these outrageous ideas from your Miss Clemency.'

'She has said nothing about you. Why do you disparage her? The men in her family face life squarely and all their problems and weaknesses. ' It should have been a quiet statement, a bid to make Matthew see life from a different perspective, but her anger had made it sound like an insult. 'Matthew, I'm sorry, I didn't mean to be ungracious.'

'Insolent and cruel would be a better description, Hattie.

I shall write to Kingsley forthwith. He would do well to leave his friend and resume his duty to you. In London you will have the opportunity to remember that you are a young lady who should always be civil of manner. When you are in the best of company, I pray God you will think through issues before venturing to make a remark or give an opinion. Do you really think Kingsley and I are so hard that we would deliberately keep our parents prisoners? If you had not always had your head up high in the clouds perhaps you would have noticed that they were finding life increasingly difficult to cope with. They forgot to pay the bills, they inadvertently ran up debts and they were defrauded out of their savings. They were very frightened. They wanted to move away and live where the world couldn't get at them. Kingsley and I have done our best to protect them and will continue to do so. They know they can consult me at any moment of the day. Are they lonely or unhappy? No. They have never been more content. The way Jane and I choose to live is irrelevant to their situation. Well, young lady, what do you have to say now?'

Throughout his reprimand Hattie had felt herself shrinking. She was silly and naïve. She had tried to be mature and forthright like Clemency and had failed miserably. She curtsied to her brother. 'I can only apologize to you sincerely. Forgive me, Matthew. Please don't take Kingsley early from his friend's side. I promise to be careful in all I do from now on. I would like time to consider all you have said, and to spend more time with Mama and Papa. I won't go to the village again. If you'll excuse me I'll run along.' She scurried for the door, not wanting to cry with shame in his presence.

'Hattie,' he said, softening, 'I understand that it's unexciting for you here. I shall endeavour to entertain you more. Come back after supper and play chess with me.'

'I would like that very much, thank you, Matthew.'

She shut the door quietly, and he listened to her slow dragging steps retreating. He pictured her with her head sagging, her eyes wet with tears, her arms hanging limply over her dress. Hattie was a sweet, innocent soul, never destined to be a feisty independent individual like Clemency Kivell. It was true he had disparaged the Kivell girl; she was an unlikely friend for Hattie to have anywhere away from Meryen. Why did he dislike Clemency? He knew the answer to that question.

At their single meeting she had compared him unfavourably with the Kivell men. Clemency was braver than Hattie, able to fight like with like, and no man would ever be able to extinguish the light in her. She would not be held down. Hattie was different; she could easily be dominated. He and Kingsley must ensure that she married a kind man who adored her, who would not trample over her goodness and ruin her life. But how could he protect her, or indeed their parents, while they were here at Poltraze, if it was not apparent to all that someone strong and capable was in charge? Hattie had not accused him of being selfish; she had not recognized that fault in him, concluding instead that he was weak. She was right; by hiding himself away he was weak, and he was also selfish. He was plagued with terrible memories and nightmares, and he had a dreadful secret, but he could not obliterate them by shunning the world and not fully living his life.

He had made a deliberate decision to end Hugh Hartley's life, to prevent him from hurting and humiliating Jane. Kingsley had confronted Hugh over his numerous sordid affairs and habitual drunkenness. Hugh had then started a fight and, in the presence of the regiment's fellow officers, mayhem had resulted. Tables were overturned and a candle flame had come into contact with spilled alcohol, starting a raging fire. Hugh had tried to run his sword through Kingsley. Matthew had saved his brother, pushed him out of the dining room and then gone back in and led four officers who were trapped in the conflagration to safety. Hugh had still been in the room, sprawled on the floor, and Matthew had gone back in again to drag him out.

Blackened by soot and coughing and retching, he had got Hugh nearly to the door when Hugh had flung an arm round his neck. 'The last laugh will be on you, Faraday. I'm going to tell your irritating, frigid sister about every time I went with a whore. How I had to get in my cups to bed her, to touch her clammy skin. It was like servicing a corpse. Then I'll leave her and tell the world what she's like.'

In a split second Matthew had hauled up his gloating brother-in-law, and with the flames raging around them and hiding them from anxious eyes, he had thrown Hugh into a heap of falling burning timber. Flames had seared the whole length of Hugh's body and he'd held out imploring arms, his mouth in a silent scream of terror and agony, and then his handsome face had melted away. Matthew would never forget the hideous sight and he had since accepted this recurring vision, that came to him by day and at night in his dreams, as his rightful punishment. Kingsley's voice had reached his ears through the cracking and crashing timber and exploding glass. He had stumbled for the door and hot pain had struck his face. With his eyes closed he'd somehow reached the doorway and waiting hands had pulled him out of death's clutches. He had been left scarred and almost totally blinded – again, a just reward for the murder he had committed.

He and Hugh had brought dishonour to the regiment, but Hugh's attempt on Kingsley's life had not been seen, and only he and Kingsley knew about it. Matthew would have confessed and gone to the gallows for Hugh's murder if it had not been for the disgrace and hurt this would have caused his family, particularly Jane. He had been given a medal and an honourable medical discharge. Harbouring his private shame, and with his parents' and Jane's problems to contend with, he had retreated from the world like a hermit and brought them all to this lonely, socially insignificant house. He had come to realize that Jane actually relished her widowhood, for he had overheard her tell Adela Miniver that now she would never again have to suffer the advances of a man.

He put his face in his hands. What a terrible example to Hattie he was. It was all credit to her that she had flourished and kept her verve and goodness despite the gloom he had allowed to descend on his family.

He went to the window, felt for the blinds and lifted them to peep out. The light hurt his partially sighted eye but he closed it for just a moment. He could only make out blurred shapes but out there were trees and flowers, grass and sky, and so much more. And he could still see something of these wonders if he went outside, closer to them.

He rang for Barker.

'You are ready for the fir tree to be brought up, sir?'

'No, not yet, Barker. Put out my outdoor things and fetch my dark glasses to protect my eyes. I'm going to Miss Hattie. I'm sure she would be delighted to take a stroll with me in the gardens.'

Seventeen

The Christmas dinner table seemed sadly empty to Clemency with only one of her brothers at home. Jonas and his family had moved into Adam's house, but he and his wife Elizabeth said the house 'didn't feel right' and they doubted if they would ever feel at home in it. Under Verena's direction, Clemency and Elizabeth helped to make the day special for the sake of the four-year-old twins. Clemency put together a centrepiece of candles, holly and ivy for the table. Verena brought out her best silver and china and served pheasant, beef and plum pudding. Elizabeth had stitched festive table linen.

Seth ate solemnly, maintaining the sombre mood he had been in since Feena's funeral. After her return from the funeral wake, he'd spoken to Clemency, seriously but civilly. 'I hope you've not taken up with a miner. I saw you speak to one today.'

'Abe Deveril is just an acquaintance,' she'd replied warily.

Seth had seemed to accept the explanation. He was no longer argumentative but strangely subdued. Nevertheless, those seated round the table today were on edge, waiting for him to rage again about the rest of the family, or afraid of incurring his angry disapproval.

He drank wine, white and red freely, topping up his glass without offering the bottles round. Verena smiled often, but Clemency could see how bleak her mother felt at having so many empty chairs.

When food was over and the servants had cleared away, the diminished family drifted off to the sitting room. Decorations had been put on a small fir tree that stood in front of the window, and holly had been placed over the pictures. There were presents under the tree to be opened. While Jonas junior and Julia ripped off the wrappings excitedly, delighted with their gifts, the adults offered polite thanks for theirs. Seth gave Verena pearls and pushed out his lips for the kiss he always got in return for his customary generosity. His usual affection was missing and Verena placed the kiss on his cheek. Clemency received a hope chest from him, a hint that he intended to have her married in the near future. She accepted it with indifference, as her father did with all his own gifts.

Clemency missed the joyous communal celebration that would be in full swing at Burnt Oak at this time. She missed the noise and constant traffic of people around her. She missed falling over the men's outstretched legs and their raucous laughter at bawdy jokes, and the trying on of new jewellery and dresses with the women, and playing with the mass of excited children. Most of all she missed her other brothers, especially Logan. After dining with Mrs Brookson and Jenny, then handing out extravagant gifts to his household, he was to ride with Jowan and many of the village Kivells to Burnt Oak, to make merry. At the end of the day, Logan, Jowan and many of the men would likely pass out, inebriated, and sleep where they sat or had fallen. Clemency used to tut as she clambered over slumped, heaving bodies in the morning but she had always been amused by their antics. This Christmas wasn't really worth celebrating. She aimed a resentful glare at the man responsible, her hard-hearted father.

While his children played with a spinning-top, a doll and mechanical toys, Jonas shared Verena and Clemency's misery and exchanged sorry looks with them. He usually ended up saturated in drink at the end of Christmas Day, but today he was slow to imbibe, despite his father's exhortations to down another rum, and another. Elizabeth, usually a cheerful chatterer, offered only an occasional comment. Sitting beside Jonas, she began working on a gift of embroidery linen and silks she had received. No one mentioned the two brothers who had decided not to move into Trenbarvear or the two who had deserted it.

Clemency knew her mother shared her anxious thoughts about Adam. How would he cope with this day, when the need to be with loved ones was at its deepest? Would his wish to be dead and to be with Feena and their baby intensify?

It was terrible to witness his unbearable grief, to hear him blaming himself: 'I should never have left her to go to that damned house. She never wanted to live in it. If I'd been there I could have done something to save her. I could have stopped her leaving me. She shouldn't have died alone. I shouldn't have left her.' His grief was never-ending. 'I shouldn't have taken her away from Burnt Oak. She hated the upheaval, all the bad feeling. I let her down. I let my beloved Feena and our baby down. I can't go on, I don't want to. I want to be with them – I just want to be with them.' Poor Adam. Today he and Feena should have been celebrating their child's first Christmas.

Seth suddenly rubbed his big hairy hands together. 'Right then, time for a party game.'

'There aren't enough of us,' Verena said grimly. 'And it's not appropriate.'

'Eh? Why not?'

'Because we're in mourning, remember?'

Seth eyed Verena, noting her undisguised irritation with him. She had rarely been in a bright mood since their two sons had stormed out of Trenbarvear, refusing to see it, as he did, as a betrayal. She should think herself bleddy lucky he hadn't reckoned with her over her disloyalty in the graveyard! He took in the gloomy expressions of Jonas and Clemency. It used to be unusual for his family to go a day without rafts of laughter and fun, now it was the reverse. He'd brought his family here to start an important new branch of the Kivells, yet no one shared his dream. They had all turned against him.

Hell and thunder! It now dawned on him that they all blamed him for the problems and misery. He had brought up a brood of vipers! And Verena, his once loyal, adoring wife, had turned against him. He flew to his feet, ready to chastise them over their rebellion, but then Logan walked in with an armful of presents. 'What the hell are you doing here?' Seth roared. 'You're not welcome in my house.'

Young Jonas and Julia ran to greet their uncle but at Seth's enormous bellow they veered off to their parents, climbing up on to their laps.

Logan squared up to Seth calmly and coolly. 'I've come to wish Mother and the family a happy Christmas, and to see if they are well.'

'They are, but it's none of your business while they're here under this roof, where they belong. Get out before I throw you out the bleddy door by the scruff of the neck.'

'You will do no such thing, and mind your language,' Verena said sternly, rising. 'It's Christmas, and I am very pleased to see Logan. I hope you had an enjoyable dinner, Logan, dear. We have presents for you.'

'He can take them and go to the devil!' Seth growled, shaken to the core by Verena's flagrant rebellion.

'Clemency, dear,' Verena said, ignoring her puffing bull of a husband, 'pass round the sweets. Logan, what would you like to drink, dear?'

'I won't stay in the same room as him, this stranger,' Seth snarled in disgust. How dare Verena go against him and belittle him. He would put her right about that. He caught what looked like a smirk on Clemency's face. He would deal with her later as well.

The moment Seth stomped out of the room it felt as if a crushing weight had been lifted from the others. They broke into animated talk as the next round of presents was opened. At last they started to enjoy themselves. Verena allowed a game of hunt the thimble and was pleased when it evoked much giggling from the children. Clemency was pleased that Christmas wasn't completely spoiled. She joined Verena in the kitchen to fetch hot mince pies and cream, and to invite the cook, the two housemaids and the boot boy to join them. Verena smiled with genuine pleasure while she handed out the servants' presents. They each had something that was useful and something that was a treat.

At five o'clock Logan kissed everyone goodbye. 'Mama, you know that you and Clemency can come to me,' he whispered, holding her tightly. 'I fear for you both.'

'Your father would never hurt us,' Verena said, as sure of this as she was that she loved her family.

When Logan took his leave, a shiver spiked all the way down Clemency's back. Somehow she knew this was the first and last Christmas any of her immediate family would spend at Trenbarvear.

As Logan made to mount Spartacus he was pulled round roughly. Seth, drunk and breathing heavily, spat hard into his face. 'If you ever come here again, I swear I'll kill you.'

At Burnt Oak, inside Morn O' May, where the whole community was gathered, Logan told his brothers, except for Adam, who was helplessly drunk in a corner, about his father's threat. 'He meant every word of it.' Logan shook his head, troubled by the event. 'There was hatred in his face. His big plans have fallen down around him and he's not man enough to accept it.'

'Jonas will watch out for Mother and Clemency,' Tobias said. 'If any of us go there it will only anger Father. He readily accepts Jowan. Now that a sort of understanding had been made between him and Clemency, he's the best one to keep an eye on things.'

'We'll ask him to pay regular visits, starting tomorrow. If he gets worried about anything, we'll all gather together and get Mother and Clemency out of there,' Logan vowed.

Seth kept out of the house until Clemency and Verena were preparing to go up to bed.

'Clemency,' he said loudly.

'Yes, Father?' She groaned inwardly. What now?

'I've got good news for you.'

'Really?'

'I've decided it's time you and Jowan made your engagement official. We'll throw a party, and,' he stressed, plastering on a grin, 'we'll invite all our kin, and I mean all of them. It's not right to be estranged from your own flesh and blood, even if they did go against me. I've been thinking about them two innocent little mites here today. They're little angels and shouldn't have a care in the world. It isn't right they should have worries thrust upon them. So we'll throw a big party, announce your engagement and everyone will be happy again. Good, eh?'

No it isn't, Clemency wanted to yell at him. He was daring her to object to his plan. He was looking for another opportunity to rant and rave, to blame someone else for the rift he had caused, to wallow in self-pity. She didn't believe he really wanted a reconciliation. 'I'm not sure Jowan is ready for that yet. He hasn't really shown a particular fondness for me. It's Christmas Day and he hasn't come to see me, or given me a special present or anything. And I'm not ready for that commitment yet.'

'I agree with what Clemmie's said, Seth.' Verena spoke quietly. 'Let's wait and see if a romance actually happens.'

'You want to see this family back together again, don't you?' Seth glared at them blearily.

'That's not my responsibility,' Clemency retorted. She would not be used as a pawn in whatever game he was playing.

Seth's eyes narrowed to mean slits. Then he smiled. Clemency discerned the cunning behind the smile. 'Actually, Jowan does want you. He told me so. You'll get engaged before next year is out and that's an end to it.' He strode out of the house.

'He means it.' Clemency sighed crossly. 'If Jowan and I don't go along with his plans then he'll wreak more trouble.'

'Don't worry,' Verena murmured wearily. 'I won't allow you or Jowan to be used. Your father must take responsibility for his own actions. We must be very careful not to antagonize him. He's like a cannonball waiting to be fired.'

'Stupid man.' Clemency closed her eyes in frustration. 'He seems to be hell-bent on destroying us all.'

In the early hours Seth stumbled into the dark house by the back kitchen. His head thumped from a hangover and his throat was sore and parched. Putting his head under the tap above the stone sink he slaked his thirst and splashed water over his face and neck, relishing the stinging, ice-cold wetness.

He heard a noise and spun round to the stable door. Someone was coming in. Thrusting out his arms he dragged the intruder inside. There came a girl's high shriek of panic. 'That you, Clemency? You been sneaking out, damn you?'

'N–no sir, it's D–Daisy Prouse, the kitchen maid.'

Seth pushed his bushy beard into her face. Daisy Prouse was a year older than Clemency, without charm or good looks. 'What've you been up to?'

'I needed a breath of fresh air, Mr Kivell. I haven't been up to no good, honest.'

Seth pulled off her shawl and felt about her body in the darkness. She was of a comely build and fully clothed, although wearing no stays and her bodice was loose. 'Why're you not in your nightdress? My guess is you've been meeting a man, a sweetheart. Who is it? And don't dare lie to me or I'll throw you out without a reference and it'll be on the streets for you.'

'I–I've been with one of the farmhands. Wilf.'

Seth guffawed. 'That boy? Give him a good time, did you? A Yuletide present?' He wrapped his paw round her chin, pressing her head against the door. 'No lies or I'll 'ave you out the bleddy door.'

'Yes, sir,' she croaked beneath the painful pressure on her throat.

Easing his hold, Seth twiddled with her hair. 'He your sweetheart?'

'Don't think of him as that.' Daisy was too frightened to lie.

'Like that sort of thing, do you, Daisy?'

'It's all right,' she whispered.

Seth ran a thick finger down her neck. 'Don't reckon you could have got much enjoyment out of the boy. He's too wet behind the ears. How would you like to be with a real man, Daisy? And earn two shillings to keep it between ourselves?' He had never been unfaithful to Verena and had never thought he would be, but his loins were burning with need, and at this moment his wife didn't matter. Verena had let him down, as good as betrayed him, by going against him so many times in matters concerning their children. He was slavering and breathing heavily. He pulled Daisy's bodice down and made free with his hands on her shapely breasts.

'Two shillings?' Daisy automatically arched her back, her thighs trembled and she splayed out her legs. It was more money than she earned in a week, and the encounter with Wilf had been fumbling and unsatisfying. This was heaven. She enjoyed sex and craved it every day. She put her own hands to work. 'You're my master, Mr Kivell, and I'll do anything for you, sir. I don't leave nothing out.'

Growling with lust, Seth threw himself into his second festive feast.

Eighteen

Serenity was down at the bottom of the garden, tipping vegetable peelings on to the compost heap. It was another Saturday afternoon and, as so often lately, her thoughts turned to Logan – not to the time when he had offended her and shamed himself, but to subsequent occasions when their paths had crossed. Thanks to him, she'd had the best Christmas ever. On Christmas Eve, a delivery man had arrived at the Treneers' house with a large wicker hamper packed with meats, fruits, pies, preserves, lemonade and ginger beer. The accompanying note had stated, 'To Miss Serenity Treneer and family, the season's greetings. In gratitude from Miss Jenny Clymo, Mrs A. Brookson and Mr L. Kivell'. No doubt Logan had instigated and paid for the gift, which had been a source of great joy and wonder to the Treneers.

'Well, that's a fine sentiment, but only one you deserve, maid,' Mrs Treneer had said, pink with excitement, as she took charge of the hamper. 'We wouldn't normally accept charity but this is a just reward for you saving poor young Jenny from more distress.' She was obviously prepared to overlook the fact that Logan Kivell had once insulted her daughter. The Angove family had received a similar consideration for Betsy's support of Jenny. As thoughtful Methodists, both families had shared the bounty with their most needy neighbours.

Serenity had since come across Logan twice in the village. He had lifted his tall hat and addressed her as Miss Treneer and had inquired about her health. Both times she had been pleased to see him, and had curtsied and asked about Jenny, each time to be told Jenny was very well. She tried not to admit that she looked out for the rogue turned gentleman and businessman. But what was the use of it, she asked herself now, shivering by the compost heap. She should rekindle her hopes for Abe Deveril, before another girl snapped him up. Betsy was walking out with a young miner and looking forward to becoming a married woman and housewife.

Abe, however, seemed happy to stay single and free. Sighing, Serenity told herself to accept her lot; it was the only way to be content. Several young men had asked her to become their sweetheart. One or two of them she quite liked. She decided that the next time one of them asked her to, she would agree to go for a walk, the usual first meeting alone. Well, perhaps she would.

Beyond the gate, on the rough track, a tiny black and white mongrel appeared. The family dog had the habit of dragging home sticks as big as itself, as well as all sorts of rubbish. This time it was tugging a long piece of cloth.

'Tink! What on earth have you got now?' She laughed, opening the gate and hurrying towards the little dog.

Pleased with herself, Tink shook the cloth, making Serenity leap back to avoid being hit. Then Tink dropped the cloth and wagged her tail, barking as if inviting Serenity to congratulate her. Serenity peered cautiously down at the cloth. Tink had been known to bring back stuff that had been dragged through a dirty stream or a cowpat; once she had brought home something that had the entrails of a dead animal stuck to it. Tink's trophy this time was a shawl. Serenity frowned; it looked familiar. Then she gasped, knowing to whom the shawl belonged – Blythe Knuckey. The vindictive old gossip had run off weeks ago, owing rent. Her few things had been confiscated in lieu of the money by her landlord, Cary Kivell. The village had collectively said, 'Good riddance.' New tenants, an elderly couple, had moved into the cottage.

Why had the hag left her shawl behind, and where had Tink found it? Gingerly, Serenity picked up the shawl between a finger and thumb, looking at it closely. She turned it over and was shot through with horror to see blood and hair on it. With a shrill scream she dropped the shawl and jumped back from it. Tink scurried up to reclaim it. 'No, Tink! Leave it!' she shrieked, snatching the tiny dog up in her arms. She must run and tell her parents what she had found.

Abe was leaving by the back door for the newly built, Kivell-funded Miner's Institute. 'Serenity! Wait there.' He leapt over fences to reach her quickly. 'I heard you scream. Is it Tink? Is she hurt?'

Pointing to the shawl, Serenity explained. 'Tink usually explores the back fields. Could Blythe have gone there – perhaps to hide or something? She might have died and foxes disturbed her body.'

'One thing's for sure,' Abe said, unease settling inside him, 'a search will have to be mounted.'

Ten minutes later Abe, with half a dozen men and older boys, set off with Tink to the fields that arced around the south edge of the village, in the hope that the little dog would take them to the spot where she had found the cloth. As if knowing their minds, Tink led them back along the way she had come.

Serenity and Mrs Treneer put on their bonnets and hastened up Edge End and then High Street, picking up interested parties on the way. They turned off at the former Nankervis Arms, to reach the fields by the easiest, cleanest route. Logan Kivell had bought the inn, allowing Dilly Trewin to enjoy a comfortable retirement in a cottage. The dirty building had been demolished and was to be replaced by a hotel, which would include a room for business meetings. The new establishment would be called the New Oak. Serenity felt her heart lurch at the sight of the powerful, handsome Logan, dressed as fine as a town dignitary, looking over the building work of his new undertaking.

As he handed the plans to the foreman, Logan was bemused to see a gathering of villagers hurrying along with Serenity at its head. Softly pink, her chest rising in some sort of excitement, she was as gorgeous and desirable as a woman could possibly be. How could he have left her alone? He had no answer to that, except that he respected Serenity and would do nothing to hurt her. He stood in the path of the villagers, his commanding authority bringing them to a halt. 'Miss Treneer, what ails?'

'We're looking for a body,' a leather-skinned old man croaked, eager to get on, hating to miss anything.

'A body?' Logan raised one brow, partly in amusement, keeping his eyes on Serenity. Apart from her, and a woman who he guessed from their resemblance to one another must be her mother, the crowd was like a gaggle of children intent on a prank. 'And who is presumed to be dead?'

'Blythe Knuckey,' Serenity said, bobbing a polite curtsy,

pleased to be singled out by Logan. 'Just now my little dog came home with her shawl.'

'And it was covered with blood, and if she's dead 'tis a good job too,' a female voice shouted from the rear. 'She's b'lieved t'be in the fields. That's where we'em goin', if we can get on, that is.'

'I agree with your sentiment, and I'll go along with you,' Logan said. Go along with Serenity, he meant. He offered his arm to her mother. 'Shall we go, Mrs Treneer?'

'Oh, yes, Mr Kivell.' Mrs Treneer blushed to the brim of her bonnet. For weeks afterwards she was to speak of the honour of actually walking on the arm of a gentleman.

Before the troop reached the hedge on the other side of Dilly Trewin's former vegetable patch, they heard a commotion. 'What is it?' the old miner yelled. 'Have you found her?'

A second later Abe appeared, grim-faced, on top of the stile. 'Tink took us right to her. Her body's sunk down in the ditch,' he said. ''Tis no doubt it's Blythe Knuckey. She's been there for some time, and was badly beaten about the head and body.' He stared in surprise to see Mrs Treneer with Logan Kivell.

'She must have been murdered the day she disappeared.' Serenity shuddered.

Logan placed a hand on her back for a moment. Serenity felt as if she had been touched by warmth and strength and her skin tingled with the most wonderful sensation. He said, 'I'll get the authorities on to it. Well done, Deveril. I'll take the ladies away. It's no place for them.'

'I'll bring Tink home,' Abe said to Serenity, directing a stony gaze at the man standing very close to her. Logan Kivell might have been generous to the Treneers but there was no need for him to be so familiar with them. His glances at Serenity were too often and too friendly.

All the women, except Serenity and her mother, were for clambering over the stile to take a look at the corpse. To Logan's pleasure he backtracked with a Treneer woman on each arm, and no others in tow. Because it had been she who had penned the letter of thanks for the hamper to this young gentleman, Mrs Treneer didn't feel overly shy in saying, 'It's a sorry day for Meryen when we have suffered a murder in our midst. What say you, Mr Kivell?'

'A sorry day indeed, Mrs Treneer,' he agreed. 'But I think,

without doubt, this is a crime of personal revenge and no one else need fear similar violence. I trust you ladies are both well?'

'We are, thank you,' Mrs Treneer answered importantly. 'And if I may ask, how is young Jenny? Or, as I should say now, Miss Jenny?'

'She does very well. Mrs Brookson has taken her to stay at Truro for a few days. The house is very lonely without them.'

Serenity felt Logan's eyes on her. She looked ahead, not wanting to risk her mother noticing the connection between her and Logan; for it was there and it was very strong. Before she knew it she had squeezed on his arm. For a second she felt an answering pressure from his arm against hers. A rush of euphoria mixed with fear and daring flooded her from her head to her toes, making her feel strangely energized. It was too late to retract her action, she had shown Logan she was interested in him on a deep level and he had replied in kind. The course was set and she had no desire to back out of it. What happened next was up to him. She was too shy and inexperienced to know what to do.

More villagers were heading their way, having heard the shocking news. Grandly, Mrs Treneer informed them of the gruesome find. She was enjoying her privileged position, knowing that the sight of her and her daughter being escorted by Mr Logan Kivell would provide nearly as much talk in Meryen as the murder. The newcomers dashed off to view the grisly scene.

Back at the building work, Logan relinquished the women from his charge, holding on to Serenity for a fraction longer. 'What do you think of my new enterprise, Mrs Treneer?'

The older woman clasped her hands in pride at being asked. Shopkeepers and trades people clamoured to be on good terms with the Kivells, who were ever growing in importance, and here she was being asked by one of them for her opinion. She was rarely asked about anything outside the domestic sphere. 'I'm very pleased that rough old place is gone for good. A grand hotel will attract finer people and be better for the village.'

Serenity thought it sad and ironic that this new place her mother approved of would never welcome her through its exalted doors. Although, with Logan as its owner, that might not necessarily be the case. Don't, she cautioned herself. Don't get silly ideas. You'll only end up coming down to earth with a humiliating bump.

Mrs Treneer went closer to the hotel to see how it would look on completion.

'You've made my mother very content today,' Serenity said.

On the pretext of rearranging his high collar, Logan leaned his head towards her and whispered, 'I've also bought the old mill from my Uncle Henry. Will you meet me there in an hour, Serenity, just for a while? I swear I mean you no harm.'

'If I can get away, I'll be there,' she whispered back, her heart thundering so fast she thought it would knock out all her breath.

With his toecap Logan prodded rubbish strewn on the stout wooden flooring in the derelict meeting place, which verged on to the fields that sheltered the back gardens of Edge End. Serenity did not have to go very far to reach him. Henry Cardell had bought the old empty mill years ago but had never decided what to do with it. Nor had Logan yet, he was merely set on accumulating property. The giant cogwheels and millstone had been removed to the new mill, in a more scenic spot outside the village, on the Gwennap road.

He had met women here before, for the sole reason of having sex with them – for the most part in acts of seduction. He had insisted on paying them all after each encounter, so that if they thought to complain or bother him when he tired of them he could keep the edge by accusing them of prostitution. There were women in the village who hated his guts over that. Two had said they were expecting his child but in each case no baby had materialized. He had not cared about them at the time but now he was ashamed. Part of him hoped that Serenity wouldn't come to him. He didn't want to sully her reputation. Although he wanted to make love to her, he wasn't planning to ease her down on the floor and take his pleasure with her. What's the matter with me? he wondered. I'm losing some of my Kivell hardness. Or is it because Serenity is sweet and innocent, like Jenny, or because I respect and like her deeply?

The door creaked on its bent hinges and was heaved aside, letting in a crack of daylight. 'Hello?' Serenity called softly.

'I'm here, Serenity,' he called back. He closed the door after her and they stood just beyond it, gazing at each other in the limited light. Flour dust, which would never be totally eradicated, floated all around them. If lovers who used this place were not careful at brushing themselves off, it caused a snigger in the village that they had 'been dusting their knees or back with white, you know where'.

'I can't stay long.' Serenity was breathless with nerves. 'I told my mother I was going to see my friend Betsy.'

'Let's not waste a minute then.' Heaven help him, he was blushing. That had not happened even when he'd lost his virginity at the age of fourteen.

Serenity swallowed the lump that was gathering in her throat and about to choke her. Did he mean they were to do *that*, right this moment? Was that what he expected? Had he thought she had agreed to sex by agreeing to meet him alone? She should flee but his gorgeous dark brown eyes rooted her to the floor, and she didn't want to leave him. The uncertainty, the fear, the longing in her, made a painful combination. She was so completely drawn to him, wanted so badly to claim something of him for herself, she knew she would actually go through with the frightening, wicked act of allowing him inside her body. He had made her shameless, a lost cause. The terrible consequences of becoming pregnant and shunned by society she merely pushed aside.

'This is the wrong place to meet you. I'm sorry about that.' Logan smiled at her. She was nervous, a little scared. He didn't want her to feel discomfited, rather he wanted to reassure her that he held only good feelings towards her; not long ago he would have scoffed at such a notion. He would like Serenity to meet Clemency, he was sure they would get along. 'Did your little dog return home safely?'

'Tink was tired out by all the fuss. She's fast asleep beside the hearth right now.' Serenity was glad at this small talk, and that for some reason Logan seemed to be feeling shy too.

'I think I'll get Jenny a little lapdog. It will be good company for her.'

'She would love that. Jenny was always soft about animals. She hated rabbits being killed for the pot.'

Instinctively Logan held out his hands to her. Serenity lifted her hands towards him. His big warm ones encapsulated hers. It was a joy and an intense pleasure for them both, but Logan was saddened to feel how rough Serenity's hands were from her many years of hard labour, begun when she was just a young girl. He couldn't bear the thought of her enduring another day of trudging to the mine in all weathers, bashing ore like a peasant, and trudging back home at the end of each arduous day. He must do something for her. He searched his mind, came up with the ideal solution and smiled into her eyes.

Serenity returned the smile and glanced down shyly. Quickly her eyes roamed back to his eyes and then settled on his lips. He was lingering over her lips and it sent tingles of wonder up and down her spine. Bending his head he grazed her mouth with tender lips. Serenity closed her eyes. His touch was gentle, blissful, and she prayed to God it would remain so and this wonderful encounter would not be turned into something sordid.

'You're the loveliest girl in the world, Serenity,' he murmured huskily, pulling her gently into his arms. Holding her firmly he kissed her fully. She tasted so sweet. She was divine, giving herself over to him a little at a time as her confidence grew. It was like kissing a woman for the first time.

Hugging his neck, Serenity felt her whole body becoming weightless as her lips gradually yielded to his string of soft, tentative kisses, and then to his more demanding, searching ones. She was aware of nothing but the wonderful pressure of his arms around her and his mouth giving her raptures.

He brought up his hands to cup her face and kissed her eyes and brows and cheeks. 'Darling Serenity, let's go from here.'

'Where? I can't go far. Suppose someone sees us?'

'Shush, my love, everything will be all right. I'm taking you home. I want to speak to your parents.'

'What about?' There was real panic in her voice. What did he intend to say to them? Her father would take his belt to her if he thought she had lowered herself into disgrace.

'Don't worry, Serenity, darling.' He eased her towards the door. 'Trust me. I'll tell you on the way.'

Nineteen

Clemency could tell Adam was in his darkened room only by the bump of his curled up body under the bedcovers. He was facing away from the door and she went round to him, carrying a tray of crusty bread and steaming hot leek and potato soup, his favourite. 'Adam, it's Clemmie. I've brought you something to eat.'

He didn't stir and she put the tray down. She shook his shoulder, but there was no response. She pulled the covers half off him and looked down with pity on his twisted face and painfully taut, wasted muscles. He had lost nearly half his body weight and seemed like an old man. He smelled of musky, stale sweat; beads of fresh sweat plastered his black hair to his scalp. He had not shaved for days. 'Adam, I know you're awake. Please open your eyes and sit up and try to eat a few spoonfuls. Tobias says you haven't eaten in days. You must try to make an effort. It's what Feena would want.'

He fluttered open his eyelids but otherwise did not move. 'What Feena wanted I didn't give her,' he rasped, his throat dry, his words bitter. 'I let her down. I didn't have the courage to stand up to our beastly, rotten father. It's he who should be in the grave, not my dear wife and our innocent little baby.'

Clemency blinked back tears of grief, for Adam had died inside the same day Feena had drawn her last breath. She knelt down to him and stroked his damp, greasy hair. 'I understand. But Feena wouldn't want to see you like this. Please, Adam, think of Mother. Her heart is broken every time she returns to the farm after seeing you. The rest of us love and need you. Please let that be enough to give you the strength to go on.'

'Clemmie, I'm sorry, so sorry.' A tear trickled silently down his cheek and soaked into the clammy pillow.

'You've got nothing to be sorry for.' She kissed his feverish cheek. 'Try to take a spoonful of soup, Adam. I'll help you sit up. Shall I get some hot water and help you wash and shave? You'll feel a lot better. When you feel stronger you could go to Feena and the baby's grave. It might help if you feel close to them. You could build a memorial to them; do something good in their memory. It might help if you had a new purpose.'

'Like Logan, you mean, taking in underprivileged mine girls? He's told me all about the new girl with the peaceful name. She's a companion of the other one, and the old lady delights in teaching those girls proper manners and to read and write properly. Logan says he has a particular fondness for this second girl. He's not bedding her yet though. I told him not to waste his life on someone else if he thinks she's the right one for him. What about you and Jowan? Has *he*' – Adam could never bring himself to say the word 'Father' now – 'made arrangements for an engagement?'

'No, and I'm praying he doesn't. Jowan and I know we can only be cousins to each other.'

'Never forget what I'm going to say now, Clemmie. Marry only for love. You'll only meet your soul mate once. I did, and now she's just a soul.'

'You'll meet Feena again one day and you'll never be parted again, Adam. Cling to that thought. She's watching over you. Why not do something to make her proud of you?'

His head spinning, for he'd heard all this before, he blew out sour breath. 'I'll think about it.'

'Good,' Clemency said brightly. 'Will you try a little soup?'

'Just to please you,' he murmured. Just to get rid of his dear little sister. He cared so much about her but just at this moment she was annoying him nearly beyond his reason.

With a heave and a struggle, Clemency propped him up. He was floppy and uncoordinated and she watched him anxiously. She filled the spoon and carefully aimed it at his mouth. Adam swallowed reluctantly and gagged and coughed, but he was surprised at how good the soup tasted on his dehydrated palate. He took three more spoonfuls to please Clemency and to ease his thirst then, feeling full, he pushed the next spoonful away.

Hopeful now, Clemency turned to a bottle of tonic and pulled out the cork. 'Uncle Henry mixed this up for you specially. He says it doesn't taste too awful. Take two spoonfuls and I promise I won't nag you again today.'

Adam gulped down the tonic then, weak and dizzy, he shifted down the bed and lay on his side. 'Hold my hand till I fall asleep, Clemmie.'

She did so, caressing his brow and stroking his hair. He was asleep in moments, breathing shallowly and jerking and moaning. Hoping he wasn't having a nightmare, Clemency kissed and hugged him. She covered him loosely in just the sheet. A hearty fire was kept burning and it wasn't healthy for him to be so hot. She left to tell Tobias she was cautiously hopeful that Adam had reached a place in his heart and mind where he might work towards his recovery.

The house was silent as a graveyard and felt as bleak as the downs on a harsh winter's day. Once she had enjoyed a houseful of children with their happy noise and clutter, and then little grandchildren running in and out. Trenbarvear had never been home to Verena and now it was empty and meaningless to her. And her marriage was fast heading the same way. She was standing in the middle of the clean, clinically neat sitting room gazing up at the painting above the carved overmantel. Jonas was a born farmer but also a fine artist in oils, and last year he had painted his father as the magnificent, godlike man Seth had been then. It seemed an age ago when he had been a loving husband and a proud father. Although autocratic and often severe, he had made a happy and secure home for his family. Now nearly all the children lived elsewhere and all of them hated their father. Jonas was bending beneath the strain of running the farm under Seth's belligerent management. It was only a matter of time before he too moved his family away from Trenbarvear. Verena didn't know how she would bear to live when Clemency married and set up her own home. It was too selfish to hope and pray that her daughter would marry and bring up a family here.

She stared into the commanding dark eyes above her. Did she still love Seth? It had been instant attraction for her, the daughter of a Camborne ironworks owner, when she had caught him gazing at her across the street in her home town. Seth had swept out a thick, muscular arm to halt a horse and cart so that he could immediately approach her. He had been more than rough round the edges, but full of laughter too. Her parents had been steadfastly set against him, but with Seth's son soon growing inside her they'd had no choice but to consent to their marriage. They had never called at Burnt Oak and had shown scant interest in her and her family ever since. Kivell men had little time for in-laws and tended to separate their brides from their kin.

Yes, Verena acknowledged, looking at the portrait, I still love you, Seth, and always will. But he had killed off her respect for him and she was afraid of what he would do next. For the most part he was still good to her, and a thoughtful and passionate lover, but he sensed he had lost a part of her and he often looked at her strangely and sometimes with hurt and resentment.

With Clemency out and the servants no company at all, especially the maid, Daisy, who had recently become rude and rather lazy, Verena wandered aimlessly into the next room. Tucked away in the corner of the house, it was a small room used as an office. She made to leave, but suddenly decided she would like to learn something about Trenbarvear and perhaps get some affinity with it. There were some ancient scratched file cupboards and she poked about in sections and cubbyholes. There was a lot about the farm's beginnings and the Nankervises but she couldn't stir an interest in any of it. Some rolled-up papers in one of the highest cubbyholes appeared to be new and she reached up and pulled them out. After untying the black ribbon round them she flattened out the papers on the desk.

Very soon she was seething with rage. She rolled up the papers and took them away with her. Then she put on her mantlet and bonnet and changed into boots, secured the papers on her person, out of sight, and went outside and round the house to the stable yard. Wilf was mucking out, and an older man was chopping mangolds. They stopped work and touched their forelocks.

'Mornin', ma'am,' said the elder. His weather-wizened features betrayed bemusement. The mistress had never shown herself here before. Lovely in appearance, and usually soft-natured, today she seemed as hard and uncompromising as any Kivell man.

'Good morning,' Verena replied, grim and peering about sharply. 'Has the master ridden out yet?'

★   ★   ★

Daisy Prouse met Seth in the shed at the end of the kitchen garden. She had asked him at breakfast to meet her here as soon as possible.

'Well, what's so urgent?' he demanded. 'Does someone know about us?'

'No, I've been careful, just like you said,' Daisy replied, head cocked and batting her thin lashes. ''Tisn't that, Mr Kivell.' He insisted she keep to his title. 'I've got some news for you. I think you're going to be pleased. I'm pregnant. I could be about to give you another son.'

Seth glared at her. He was to have a son with this lewd trollop? The way this girl dished out her favours the brat could be anybody's. Even if it was sired by his seed it wouldn't be the same as the children from his beautiful wife. 'I'll give Wilf a few pounds to marry you.'

'I don't want he! He don't know what he's got it for. I thought you could set me up in a nice cottage then you can come to me any time you like and even stay all night. Think of the things we could get up to with no need to keep quiet.' Daisy was so sure of him, for she saw to the basest of his needs, that she had no idea her thrust-forward hips, the finger she was running along her sparsely covered cleavage, were causing him only disgust.

'Then I'll give you some money to disappear!' he hissed into her face.

It was like being hit by an icy blast. 'What? But I thought . . .'

'You thought? Slut! Bitch! Why the hell would I want you as a mistress? You're the biggest whore ever to come out of Meryen. Take the money and get out today or I'll throw you out with nothing!'

His hands were reaching for her and Daisy jumped back, whimpering. 'B–but the baby. I thought you'd want it.'

'It could be anybody's. Think I'm stupid? Get in the house and pack your things. And mark my words, girl, bother me again or try to cause trouble and I'll kill you with my bare hands. In fact you can get out of Meryen for good. If I set eyes on you again you'll be a dead'un.'

Daisy was so horrified she couldn't move. Seth grabbed her by the back of the neck, clamped his hand over her mouth and dragged her out of the shed. He hauled her all the way to the kitchen and stormed in, frightening the cook, who dropped the eggs she was holding. He dumped Daisy on the floor.

'Cook, get this girl's things together now! She's got a brat in her belly. I won't have that sort of thing going on under my roof.'

Once the woman had scuttled out, Seth turned to the girl, now sobbing into the back of her hand. He threw all the coins he had in his pockets at her. 'Here! I'll get Wilf to take you on your way. That's the only charity you'll get out of me. You can work the streets from now on. You'll enjoy it.'

He went outside to order Wilf to make ready the trap and to take his passenger all the way to Camborne.

Clemency trotted into the stable yard to find her parents facing each other, both in a dark mood. If anything, her mother was the angrier of the two; in fact she was incensed. She jumped down off her pony. 'What's wrong?'

'There's a crisis in the house. I've thrown out that blasted kitchen maid,' Seth growled. 'I've just met up with your mother and for some damned reason she's glaring at me so aggrieved.'

'I'm glad Daisy has been sent on her way, but never mind her,' Verena said bitingly. 'Clemency has returned home at just the right moment. I want to speak to you both and I suggest we go into the house.'

'I'm busy. It can wait till evening.' Seth was angry that two of the labourers had overheard his wife's acid tone.

'Unless you want me to shout out what I've got to say so everyone can hear, Seth, go inside. Now.' Verena's voice was like steel clashing on steel and she was flushed with an unquiet heat. She took Clemency's arm.

'What's it all about, Mother?' Clemency matched her steps to Verena's quick ones while glancing back at her father. Her mother had left him with no option other than to follow them, but it was obvious that the instant they were indoors he would vent a volcano of fury.

'I've something to tell you,' Verena said, leading the way to the sitting room, ignoring Daisy's wailing, which was issuing from the kitchen. 'And you're not going to like it.'

'What on earth's going on?' Clemency wondered why the cook was lugging a carpet bag to the kitchen.

'It's nothing to do with the servants,' Verena muttered.

Seth shut the sitting room door with an angry click. Before he could vent his anger, Verena whirled round and whipped the papers out from under her mantlet and waved them at him. 'Before you turn your wrath on me, Seth Kivell, perhaps you'd like to explain to your daughter why you are trying to cheat her out of her rightful property!'

Clemency's jaw sagged. Her mother was so angry she was shaking.

'You've dared to go through my things, woman!' Seth roared, his face turning red and purple with rage.

'For goodness' sake,' Clemency pleaded. 'What is this all about?'

Her eyes blazing at Seth, Verena handed her the papers. 'Read this, Clemmie, and you will see.'

Clemency expected her father to rip the papers out of her hand but he stayed rigid, with his fists clenched at his sides. Quickly she gleaned the nature of the documents. She went towards her father and now it was she who was furious. 'You lied to me; you lied to all of us. Squire Nankervis did not sell *you* this farm. He gave it to me in gratitude for saving his son. From the date written here, it seems it was his intention to do it before the day you saw him. If I'd known this then things would have been very different. We might never have left Burnt Oak. Adam might not be in his present agony and all my other brothers upset and Mother in despair. How could you be so underhand and rotten?'

'What Nankervis actually did or did not do don't really matter,' Seth uttered in deadly tones. 'You're just a girl and under my complete control until you come of age.'

'Do you want to know something, Father?' Clemency thrust the papers into his hand. 'If this wretched place means so much to you then you're more than welcome to have it. I don't want it, not now or ever. I hate Trenbarvear. And so do Jonas and Elizabeth. We've only been staying here for Mother's sake.'

Shooting out his free hand, Seth caught her hard by the shoulder. 'Jonas can do what he damn well pleases, but you, girl, will stay under this roof until you're married, and that had better be sooner rather than later. I'll be seeing Jowan later today and I'll see about your engagement going ahead imme- diately. Now both you women get out of my sight. And you'd both better be very careful from now on. I won't tolerate any more disobedience, do you hear?' He pushed Clemency away with a profanity.

'Is that it?' Clemency stormed. 'You do something sly and terrible, and Mother and I are to take your condemnation? Not on your life. And I will not marry Jowan. It's not what either of us wants.'

'You'll do what I bleddy well say!' Charging his hand, he slapped her face, first one side then the other. 'One more word out of you and I'll take my belt to you.'

Verena put herself in front of Clemency. 'If you ever touch her again,' she screamed, 'I'll make you pay, Seth Kivell. I'll leave you and take Clemency with me, I swear.' Her voice dropped to become flat and deadly. 'I'm beginning to hate you.'

The next bellow died inside Seth. It was unthinkable that Verena should threaten to leave him. For her to mention hate hurt him worse than a death blow; it crushed his soul and forced him into seeing himself for what he had become: an embittered, self-centred, pathetic brute who had lost most of his family and was in grave danger of forfeiting the rest. His pride had made him a fool. Logan, the son he had prided the most, had seen the error of his ways and turned his life around. While Logan was accepted everywhere, he himself had turned his world into a steadily shrinking domain, where the few loved ones he had left craved to break free from him.

'Verena, I—'

An ear-splitting commotion broke out in the passage and was coming their way. Daisy and the cook were screaming at each other. 'You mustn't do it! Daisy, don't, the master will kill you.'

Ignoring Seth, Verena left Clemency and went to the door. 'What on earth is going on?' She blinked in shock when Daisy threw herself on her knees in front of her and grasped her legs.

'Help me, ma'am. Don't throw me out. It wasn't all my fault. I'm sorry it happened but I can't let an innocent little baby suffer. Please help me, ma'am. I'm terrified I'm going to die!'

So much had happened to stun and horrify Verena today that she was incapable of making a response.

Clemency saw the murderous look her father aimed at

the maid. This had something to do with him, she was sure. Easing past her mother, she yanked Daisy away from her and tossed her back. The maid ended up on her rear, leaning on her hands. Daisy's troll-like face was livid red and swollen from weeping. She seemed like a cornered rat, and as spiteful and treacherous as a hobgoblin. 'Well? Explain,' Clemency ordered. 'And make it quick and civil or I'll throw you out myself.'

Daisy glanced at Seth. Her lover didn't seem so outraged, blustering or dangerous now. It was strange he wasn't shouting the odds. She would take advantage of this. She put on a hard-done-by expression and hung her head. 'I'm sorry about this, ma'am, and miss. The thing is, I've done wrong. I'm having a baby and it's the master's. When I told him he threw me out, said I could become a prostitute. I'm sorry about all the ruckus. I panicked, see?'

Verena heaved a mighty sigh of defeat. She had believed Seth would always be faithful to her. And it wasn't even as if the maid were some lovely *femme fatale*. She was a plain-looking trollop who hung around the male staff.

'You *are* little more than a prostitute,' Clemency said coldly. 'You can't be sure that it's my father's child.'

'It is, honest it is,' Daisy pleaded. 'I was so thrilled the master took a liking to me that I was never unfaithful to him. You ask any of the men round here, they'll say I've not been with none of them since Christmas.'

The word 'unfaithful' cut Verena to the core. 'Are you saying the affair started at Christmas?'

'Yes, ma'am, on Christmas night,' Daisy whimpered, feigning shame.

Keeping her head high, with icy bearing, Verena turned to her husband as if she were addressing a peasant. 'Well, Seth, you have succeeded in pushing out your entire family but now you can start a new one with your whore. Clemency and I are leaving now, today. I'm confident Jonas will bring his family with us. The only way you can stop us is to kill me.' She moved out of the doorway. 'Clemmie, say goodbye to your father, if you wish to.'

Clemency couldn't have been more pleased to be leaving. She would leave the full import of today's revelations to implode on her later. 'Trenbarvear is yours,' she told Seth. 'Enjoy it, if you can.'

'Walk out of that door, the pair of you, and I'll never forgive you. I'll hate you to your graves,' Seth spat.

'I don't care,' Verena said. 'The man I fell in love with no longer exists.' She sailed out, taking Clemency with her, sweeping past Daisy who was scurrying to her feet.

Howling like a savage, wounded animal, Seth rolled up the papers in his hands. He would take them straight to his lawyers and have the necessary documents drawn up for Clemency to sign over the farm to him legally. He wouldn't give her the chance to change her mind in order to spite him.

Daisy grabbed her carpet bag and flew through the kitchen and towards the lane, in terror lest the master should try to carry out his threat to kill her. She was only too well aware of the rift her revelations had just caused and she knew he would be a hundred times more furious with her now.

She had covered only a little ground before Seth, on horse-back, caught up with her.

Twenty

Hattie went to Matthew in the summer-house where he was writing poetry. His favoured place nowadays was anywhere outside, accompanied by his new loyal friend, a young golden retriever, trained by Barker and himself to prevent Matthew from falling over obstacles or wandering over the side of the pool. He was lolling in an armchair on the veranda, his legs up on the balustrade, reading aloud as he scribbled, concentrated and content. The theme of his poetry this past week had been the fresh hope of spring. The season hadn't yet arrived, but his poetry reflected his newly acquired optimism, something Hattie did not share with him.

This morning a letter had arrived from Clemency. In it she explained that there were more problems in her family, and because of them she and her mother had moved back to Burnt Oak, together with her remaining brother at Trenbarvear.

Hattie had seen little of Clemency since Feena Kivell's funeral and now she might have even less time to spend with her. Hattie missed her friendship. Life at Poltraze was increasingly boring. Since learning of some old woman's violent murder in Meryen, Matthew had repeated his order that Hattie keep out of the village. Her parents had been pleased when she'd begun to spend more time with them, but only at first. They lived in a private bubble, preferring their own routines, and to fuss over and preen the spaniels. Hattie realized that her father and mother did not really see her or her siblings as their children, but rather as people they felt at ease with and relied on. Hattie had then gone to Jane, who had more or less ignored her. Hattie was soon grateful for that. A few minutes with the morbid, lifeless Jane and Miss Miniver had quickly brought her spirits down. Thank goodness Kingsley had now left his convalescent friend and returned to London. He was to travel down to Poltraze next week, having written to say he had some important news to impart.

Matthew took off his dark glasses and put his poetry aside. 'Hello, darling girl. There was a heavy tread to your feet. Are you lonely again?' Sandy, the retriever, ambled up to Hattie and she stooped to pat his broad, curly head.

'I'm positively bored out of my mind. There's nothing to do, entirely confined here in the house and grounds. How can you stand it, Matthew? It's unhealthy.'

'All of us have a different outlook on life. I'm pleased this will enable you to see life in London is right for you. Take cheer, you will soon be going up with Kingsley. You won't be bored for a moment from then on.'

'I shall make sure of that,' Hattie promised with feeling. She perched on the balustrade. It was an unladylike thing to do, but it didn't matter here, nothing did. She supposed that could be summed up as a sort of freedom. Those members of the family who chose to reside here in virtual seclusion were content in their preferred way of life, dwelling inside their safety nets, doing exactly what they wanted to do. But Matthew could place a guardian here for their parents and live a life that enriched him. Kingsley had said as much after Matthew had been blinded.

She regarded him with affection. 'Not long ago nothing would have enticed you outside the east wing, but now you enjoy the gardens. Now you consult with the gardeners and direct the placement of plants. You've ordered new chippings to be laid and that sort of thing.'

'I am the master here. It is my responsibility.'

'You could enjoy so much more, Matthew.'

'Such as? What are you trying to wheedle from me now?'

'It's time you rode again. You need the exercise. Your muscles are wasting away. There's a good-tempered mare in the stables that would be just right for you. Take a ride with me, just a short one. I'll make sure you come to no harm. Barker could come too. You keep that poor man too static. Think of him.'

'A ride?' Matthew mused. 'That might be a good idea. I'm afraid I have an appointment with the steward in about twenty minutes. Now there are troubles at Trenbarvear he wishes to recommend that we buy our meats and dairy products elsewhere.'

'You know that Clemency has left the farm?'

'I do and I'm very sorry for her. Her fortunes have taken a considerable turn for the worse since you first met her.'

Hattie relived that first meeting with Clemency and the friendly poacher. At the time she thought she had made two friends, although of differing backgrounds, to have adventures with. How naïve she had been. She, Clemency and Abe Deveril were fated to live with and probably to love members of their own ilk, but she and Clemency had formed a real friendship and because of that she owed Clemency her support.

'Well, I think I shall take a little ride and burn off some energy.' Hattie was on the verge of asking permission to go to Burnt Oak, pointing out that she had a duty to extend solace to her one and only friend hereabouts. But Matthew was bound to argue against her entering a community where complex and thorny characters abounded.

Hattie took a roundabout route to reach the lane that ran past Burnt Oak, after which she soon reached the sprawling property. The wide iron gate was thrown open. A grit track led down to the valley where the community nestled. Sparrows and thrushes twittered in the hedgerows, flew in and out of the thickets and pecked at the ground. It was a peaceful, ordinary scene. Surely nothing detrimental to her safety would be found inside the walled compound. She had heard that the Kivells were a more peaceful breed nowadays; surely they would not seek to harm a friend of Clemency's. Even so, she was as nervous about meeting them as if she were about to be presented before the Queen. She rode on down and a pack of rough-looking, barking lurchers came bounding up to her. Clemency had mentioned that everyone received this canine reception and that it was nothing to be feared. Nevertheless it was disconcerting. 'Hello there,' Hattie called in a cheerful way to the pack. She watched the dogs warily as they shepherded her down to the houses.

The compound gate was also open. Before Hattie passed through the gaping gateway two men and three women joined together to offer her a friendly welcome. There were no children about and Hattie presumed they were at home or in the schoolroom. Her first impression of the Kivells matched that of most people who encountered them: they were an attractive breed, strong and confident, with an air of independence. All were well dressed, even those in work clothes.

'Good morning to you. I'm guessing you are Miss Faraday,' said a man of middle years, well built and with lavish sideburns. His blackened hands and leather apron revealed him to be a blacksmith. 'I take it you've come to see Clemency.'

'That is correct, sir. Where may I find her?' Hattie felt herself blushing under the scrutiny of the greeters' keen gazes.

'She's at the farm. You'll need to ride past the houses and you'll see it immediately beyond,' the man said. 'It's not far.'

Reassured by his polite, welcoming manner, Hattie trotted on. She saw a lot more Burnt Oak inhabitants. Some raised a hand to her, all watched to see where she was heading. Leaving the main body of Burnt Oak behind she followed the slightly dipping track to the farm, which veered slightly off to the south. The farmstead was situated behind its own protective walls and a towering stand of oak trees. The farmhouse was old and homely, and of thick whitewashed stone. She trotted up to the front door, weaving between pecking hens and waddling ducks and more lurchers. A strapping youth appeared from round the far end of the house and offered a hand to help her dismount.

'Is it Clemency you've come to see?' he asked, after she was safely on the ground. 'She's inside.'

'No, I'm not, I'm here.' Clemency beckoned brightly from the porch. 'Hattie, this is a welcome surprise. Come in, come in.'

'I got your letter, Clemmie. I'm to leave Poltraze next week and I wanted to spend some time with you.'

'Logan is here. Come in and join us.'

Hattie was disappointed not to see Clemency alone, but the most rugged of her brothers was always worth a look. Her stomach flipped at the thought of seeing the awe-inspiring Logan again. 'I hope I'm not interrupting anything. I'm so sorry your life is in turmoil. Would you like to tell me what has happened? How is your brother, Adam?'

'We're all hoping Adam's beginning to come to terms with his grief. He's getting stronger and is presently doing light tasks about the farm.'

Clemency ushered Hattie into the sitting room. Hattie found its intricately carved furnishings intriguing. Most of them seemed as old as the house's staunch foundations. The fireplace took up almost one wall, with its massive, dark-varnished over-head lintel. The room had a comfortable, cosy ambience.

Logan got to his feet and bowed to Hattie. The pale, sorrowful-looking woman seated regally at the hearthside, middle-aged but still beautiful, was obviously his and Clemency's mother. Hattie was taken aback to see two girls of about her own and Clemency's age, also there. They did not possess a lady's sense of poise and elegance and were no doubt the two mine girls Logan had taken under his wing. One was shy with sweet eyes and pretty ginger hair. The other one glowed with dark loveliness and appeared to have the greater character. Knowing their place, they jumped up and bobbed to her.

'It's a pleasure to meet you again, Miss Faraday,' Logan said. 'And it's a pleasant surprise for Clemency. Allow me to intro-duce my mother, Mrs Verena Kivell, and Miss Jenny Clymo and Miss Serenity Treneer.'

Hattie felt unaccountably jealous of Serenity Treneer, for Logan had introduced her with something of an intimate manner. She curtsied to the older woman. This was not neces-sary since Hattie was of a higher station, but Mrs Kivell was a presence to whom respect should be shown. 'I'm pleased to meet you, Mrs Kivell. Clemency has told me much about you. Good morning, Miss Clymo, Miss Treneer.'

Verena said, 'It's good to meet Clemency's friend at last. I'm sure you would prefer to be alone with her, Miss Faraday. Do feel free to take her away from us.'

'I would like a while alone with Clemency, if it's not an imposition,' Hattie said, feeling something of an intruder. She had been remiss. She was a stranger to the family. She should have written first, requesting to see Clemency at a more opportune time.

Clemency threw on a shawl and suggested to Hattie they go outside in the garden. They stepped along neat paths between flower borders blooming with polyanthuses, narcissi and camellias, then on to the lawn where they stopped under an apple tree. Hattie sat on the swing that was swaying in the breeze from its strongest branch and apologized for intruding on the family. However, Clemency dismissed her concern. 'Everything that needs to be discussed privately among the family has been resolved. My mother and I will live here from now on; and Adam will live with us. Jonas and his family have moved into a cottage. Nothing will induce any of us to return to Trenbarvear. My father has served us all ill in so many ways.' Darkness and pain cast shadows over Clemency's face. She wrung her hands until they turned white. 'Among other things, it turns out he's been carrying on with a slut of a kitchen maid. She is expecting his child. He has moved her into her own cottage near Redruth and after the birth, which is to be at Trenbarvear, he plans to pay off the mother and rear the child himself with the help of a nursemaid. It's the greatest insult to my mother and to us all.'

'Oh, Clemmie, how terrible.' Hattie was at a loss what else to say. Her cheeks burned at the callousness of Seth Kivell and the shame thrust on her friend. 'I'm so sorry.'

'It's crushed us.' Clemency felt defeated just saying the words. Her initial fury had petered out and she was beginning to experience some of her mother's despair. Her father had chosen the cruellest way to publicly humiliate her mother who, despite everything, was prevailing with dignity. And at least here she could keep a watch over Adam. The whole extended family, here at Burnt Oak and in Meryen, had disowned Seth. Adam and Logan hated him; so did Clemency. He had thrown away all those years of marriage, turned against his children in favour of his illegitimate child. Well, that child would never inherit Trenbarvear. Clemency would rip out her own heart before she would sign the house over to her father. His lawyer had sent her some legal papers to sign and she had sent them back with a terse letter of repudiation. Looking at Hattie's sympathetic face now, she squared her stance and brought up her chin. 'But we have to accept it. The family has weathered dreadful things before and will again. Tell me, Hattie, are you looking forward to returning to London?'

'I am now. I've so enjoyed meeting you, Clemmie, but the excitement has gone out of my time at Poltraze,' Hattie admitted. 'Kingsley is travelling down to collect me, but he also has some important news for us. Papa and Mama are excited, they're sure he's going to announce his engagement.'

'Do you share that view?'

'No, he's always maintained marriage is not for him. I suppose he might have fallen in love. It does happen suddenly, I'm sure. I hope it happens to me,' Hattie ended dreamily, but hoping she would not meet a gentleman who disturbed her in the strange way Logan Kivell did.

'I hope you get all you want out of life,' Clemency replied warmly. 'Are your parents well?'

'They are, thank you.'

'Does Matthew still make forays out of doors?'

'I would never have imagined the change in him. He's out of the house more than he is inside it. However, I am afraid that will be the limit of his horizons. You must come over soon, Clemmie. You haven't seen Matthew's dog, he's a fine creature. Papa and Mama would so love to see you. Perhaps, now that I am soon to leave Poltraze, your mother will allow you an overnight stay.'

'I'd like that,' Clemency said. Time away from all this heartbreak would be good. 'Logan has invited me to stay at his house whenever I want.'

'Do you get on with his . . . charges?' Hattie asked a trifle tartly.

'Jenny and Serenity are nice girls.'

'Does he have a particular liking for the attractive one?'

'So you've noticed that. I think Serenity is special to him.'

'Does your mother mind?'

'She only wishes for each of us to be happy.'

'So she wouldn't mind if you married Abe Deveril, say?'

Clemency couldn't hold back a small laugh. 'Why on earth do you say that? There could never be anything between Abe and me, why did you mention him? Have you seen him recently?'

'No, but I shall never forget the kind, rough young man who came to my aid.'

'You're such a romantic, Hattie. You and I differ greatly, but I'm so glad to have you as my friend.'

A rider came up fast to the farm. Clemency peeped round the house to the stable block. 'It's Jowan. He always rides like the wind.'

'Oh, your cousin two or three times removed – the one your father wanted you to marry. I'd like to meet him.' Hattie grinned mischievously.

'Be careful not to fall instantly in love with Jowan,' Clemency returned in the same light vein. 'Jowan is very agreeable but he's a committed womanizer.'

Serenity had been to Burnt Oak with Logan half a dozen times, with and without Jenny. While Jenny preferred to stay with Mrs Brookson, Serenity felt at home here and accepted by the community. Mrs Kivell, who had reverted to her old matriarchal position on her return to the farm, was always kind and interested in her. Serenity was happy to be anywhere Logan was.

She was irretrievably in love with him. She adored him. So far his secret attentions to her had not gone beyond intense kisses and caresses. Although some verged on the intimate, he had not yet hinted at a more physical union. Serenity would willingly have given her whole self to him in a beat of her heart. He spoke lovingly to her and treated her as if she were precious and irreplaceable, but he had not spoken of love and an everlasting commitment. Although she dreamed of becoming his wife, her life now was wonderful beyond anything she could have imagined in her bal-maiden years; just to be near him, to see him almost every day was bliss. It was a crude sort of agony she underwent when he spent a day or two away at Redruth, Camborne or Truro on business. At first she had wondered if he bedded other women to feed his normal male desires or for pure pleasure. She told herself she would love him just as much if he did, and gradually she had come to doubt him less and less. There was never any sign, such as a lingering trace of perfume about him, to suggest that he was seeing anyone else, and he always sought her out first the instant he was home. He brought back additional secret presents for her that far surpassed the simple ones he gave to Jenny and Mrs Brookson.

Her biggest fear, something she could never bear to think of, was that Logan might one day marry a wealthy bride. This fear was offset by his generosity in moving her family into a house that was a cut above their old home, had four bedrooms and the luxury of plumbed-in water. Her parents were welcome to call at Wingfield House at any time and Logan had called twice at theirs with Serenity. He did not care what people thought about this. Serenity was on the receiving end of a certain amount of sarcastic, jealous comments from her former peers, with suggestions that she had 'sold her soul to the devil' by becoming Logan's mistress. Jenny fretted for her friend's reputation, denying the nasty rumours whenever she could, but Serenity didn't care.

Serenity smiled contentedly when Clemency and her guest reappeared, for Logan took no particular notice of Miss Hattie Faraday, who was the envy of all young women in her tailored riding habit and with her pretty hair carefully tended by a skilful maid. She had the proud bearing of the high-born, but Serenity remembered that Miss Faraday had not been too proud to acknowledge Abe after Feena Kivell's funeral. She thought that she would like Miss Faraday if she were given the chance to know her better. Serenity felt she had another reason to be contented; no one could take away the fact that she now mixed with real ladies.

Hattie looked eagerly at the door, awaiting Jowan Kivell's arrival. He breezed in, a darker-skinned version of Logan, with even more exciting rough edges. Although it seemed he was probably less uncouth than Logan had once been, there was an animal rawness about him. At the corners of his wide mouth were laughter lines. He was handsome, skilled and well off. Why did Clemency not see him as more than just a relative? Jowan looked straight into Hattie's eyes during the introductions and her tummy fluttered alarmingly. Here was a man who thought no one was better than he. He would be inclined to rebellion and stubbornness and would always seek his own way. He was perfect for Clemency. Hattie determined to point this out to her.

Jowan kissed his aunt, buffed Clemency's arm, shook

Logan's hand and smiled at those referred to in the family as 'Logan's girls'. 'It's a pleasure as always to see you again, Miss Serenity and Miss Jenny.' He smiled, his gaze lingering over Serenity.

Logan was aware of his admiration. It was not the first time Jowan had chanced to be familiar with Serenity. When Logan had taken Serenity into his home, Jowan had made a point of remarking that he'd noticed her in the village. Serenity had looked away after his salutation. Jowan grinned and angled his head thoughtfully. Logan glared at him. Was his cousin after a chase? His anger rose. Jowan could dally with any other woman in the world but not with Serenity. She was his exclusively. He had been playing out a quiet courtship with her. It was time to have a frank talk with her father.

Jowan was entirely unaware of the anger he had aroused in Logan. He glanced at Miss Faraday, who was looking at him from under her fair lashes. Simpering fragility wasn't for him. One tiny advance of his would scare her into multiple palpitations. He gave a long sigh. 'I'm afraid there's a to-do in the village. There's been an accident down the Wheal Verity.'

'Oh, no!' Jenny's hand flew to her mouth. She turned to Serenity. 'People we know, some of our old friends and neighbours, might be hurt – or dead.'

Serenity thanked God that Logan had seen to it that her younger brothers and sisters were taking full advantage of schooling and need never work down a mine or on a mine face. 'Logan, can we go to the village and see if there's any news?'

'Of course my dear,' he soothed, but his face was full of concern. He had financial interest in the mine and responsibility. 'Have you any details, Jowan?'

'It happened not long after the morning core went under grass. There have been fatalities and the surgeon has performed at least one amputation. Men are trapped, including the mine managers who went down early for their inspection.'

'Mr Hearne!' Jenny squeaked. 'I hope he's all right. He was kind to me.'

'Abe might be down there.' Clemency exchanged worried looks with Hattie.

Serenity reached for her bonnet, and snapped at Jowan, 'Why did you not tell us of this at first? This is terrible news to us. We want to help.'

Jowan bowed his head. 'You are right to chasten me, Miss Serenity. I am sorry. But rest assured, the Kivell Charity Fund have sent a wagon of supplies and medicines to the mine.'

While Jowan was speaking, Logan slid his arm around Serenity's waist, leaving none in the room in any doubt about his special closeness to her.

Hattie saw the love in his eyes. He would probably marry this village girl. Setting aside her usual disapproval of people marrying out of their class, she hoped fortune would be kind to Serenity. She changed her mind about urging Clemency to see her cousin as a good match for her. Love, it seemed, settled where it would. Clemency would make up her own mind anyway.

Twenty-One

He did not know what was worse: the weight of the rubble pressing down on his legs or the weight of the utter darkness. Dust and grit clogged his nose and were plastered across his lips. A deafening ringing was still reverberating inside his ears. The dark was thick and cloying, all-consuming and airless. Rock was all around him. Abe had tried in vain to feel a way out, or rather to find a way in for rescuers to reach him. How long would the air last? Minutes only, it seemed, judging by the way his lungs were fighting for oxygen. He tasted blood inside his mouth and swallowed it down. It was a hard task and it hurt. To ward off the fear of suffocation, the panic of knowing he was already in his tomb, he focused on the pain below his pelvis. He hadn't known pain could be this bad; unbearable, searing jabs and throbbing agony that felt worse than being roasted in a fire. His legs were twisted one under the other, the roof of the galley pinning him down inexorably. If his legs were crushed beyond repair he would welcome a quick death. His poaching days would be over; he'd not be up to outrunning the farmers and gamekeepers. Nor could he

endure the pity that would be directed at him as a cripple, or
the tormenting ridicule of cruel children.

He might as well make peace with God and try to wait
passively for death to take him; try not to think what might
have been. It wasn't as if he'd wanted a lot out of life. He
hadn't planned on marriage and a family. He'd been happy as
a free wheel. All he'd wanted was to be respected and to be
able to support his parents. His parents! They needed him. He
was their only child to have survived childhood. They would
mourn his death and struggle to survive and eventually give
up on life. His mind played him a clear picture of his little
mother, aged before her time, draped in her old black funeral
dress and shawl, her black bonnet swamping her grey hair,
weeping in the churchyard at this latest mining disaster, he in
the communal grave, a broken corpse in a shroud alongside
God knows how many other dead miners.

How long had he been down here? He tried to gauge how
much time had elapsed since the sudden roar of the murderous
blackness that had crashed down on him. One moment he
had been talking to Mr Hearne, the next he was being
bombarded, seemingly by Satan's hordes. He gulped. He
screamed for help. He found a fist-sized rock and pounded it
against the impenetrable wall at his side and then above his
head. He tried the other side. No luck. He was totally trapped.
He was being eaten up by terror, which had him in its relent-
less grip, plumbing him down into the abyss he had never
known existed inside him; the place where all his life his fears
and demons had been slumbering. 'No – no – *no!*' He banged
with the stone, producing foaming spittle. 'Please, God, don't
let me die a coward.'

He didn't want to die. He would be twenty years old next
month. There were a great many blue skies ahead of him, and
primroses in the hedges, and drinking and laughing and loving.
There were good meals and frugal meals to be eaten with his
parents. He should be there to see them into their graves. It
was his duty and his hope to ensure that they passed into the
next world with at least some dignity, avoiding the shame and
the destitution of the workhouse or the gutter.

He thought of Mr Hearne; he was also under the deadly
rubble. If he was still alive he might be languishing with
his own demons or praying out his last wishes for his wife.

'Mr Hearne,' Abe croaked, coughing and spitting up dust, 'can you hear me?'

No answer.

Where was his work partner? Wilf Treneer, Serenity's married brother, had been alongside him. Had he survived or was he mangled and dead? It would be more of a tragedy if Wilf died than if he did, since Wilf would leave behind a large brood of children. If the man engine that levered the men and boys up and down the shaft on a platform had been put out of action it could be hours or even days before he, or his body, was dug out. If dynamite were needed to clear the rocks that were trapping him, his remains would be blown to bits and there would be no body left to be sunk down into the grave.

He didn't want to end up in little pieces mixed with particles of rock and dust. Panic slashed at his guts and flooded through him. He couldn't run or flee so he flailed out with his arms, pushing on the rock with the little bit of might he had left. 'Let me out! God, if you're here, help me. For pity's sake, have mercy!'

Something moved, but where? In his crazed fit he wasn't sure.

Crying, screaming, he threw both arms to one side of him and pushed at anything he reached. No movement. Frantically, he swung his upper body to the other side. There was rock, thick in places, and rock and rubble with sharp edges. He could find no space big enough to take his hand. 'No use! No bloody use! I don't want to die here. Get me out, get me out, someone!'

His strength drained away suddenly, as if his last breath had escaped him. This was it. He was so tired. If he closed his eyes he would go to sleep, drift towards the gentle hands of death. It wasn't so bad; in fact – it was strange – he felt serene. It didn't matter how his body ended up; he, the essence of him, what he really was, would no longer be inside it. Without him his parents would soon die and they'd all be reunited in heaven. He'd see his dear old granny. She had smelled of mothballs, and white hair had bristled on her chin, but he had been fond of her. And Snowy, his boyhood cat, might be there; a grimy, white ball of fur with a single smudge of black on the tip of her long scruffy tail. His father used to joke that Snowy could be used to sweep the floors.

He was floating on soft waves of euphoria. Beautiful images filled his mind: a sunlit meadow; the sea – or what he imagined the sea and coast were like; girls, in gorgeous silvery dresses, bathed in an unworldly, shimmering golden light. The girls looked familiar; he knew them. They were Serenity and Jenny and Hattie Faraday and the most beautiful of all, Clemency. Her image lasted while the others faded away. Clemency was beckoning to him. Could she be dead, killed this very day and sent to take him to paradise? She exuded strength and determination.

Of a sudden she was gone and there was nothing but the overpowering leaching darkness and the certainty of grim death. 'No, come back!'

He wept tears of desolation. Why couldn't he have died while he was cocooned in that sublime peace? In desperation he yelled, 'Clemency!' and summoned up her image. She came back for an instant. Her strength and determination stood out above all else and he latched on to it. 'Damn it, I won't die like this. I won't!'

Reaching behind his head he pushed and pushed on the rock that met his struggling hands. He felt something give way, something really moved. But the treacherous dust and rock debris rained down on him again. He would not stay like this. He'd bring the whole bloody roof down and get death over with. Closing his eyes, gritting his teeth, he squeezed in his stomach, let out a terrific breath and pushed again, grunting and swearing until he could do no more. Matter fell down on him, gathering momentum. He was about to be buried alive but at least it would be a more merciful end than suffocating on the dirt he had worked in for the past six years.

Feeling about with a hand, his fingers touched something different from the unyielding rock. He grasped it. It was a hand; a hand that was cold. He didn't know if he'd found Mr Hearne or Wilf but, whoever it was, it must be too late. The dust was winning, sucking up the last of the air. Terror and panic were things of the past. In their place had come mercy, heralded by the return of that wonderful feeling of serenity. Serenity. Serenity Treneer; Hattie Faraday; Clemency; Jenny. Sweet young Jenny was the final image in his head. He actually smiled as he sank down into the endless sleep.

Twenty-Two

On one side of Jenny was her family's joint grave, with its simple headstone bearing their names, ages and date of death. On her other side stretched away the mound of the communal grave of those lost in the Wheal Verity tragedy. There were seven in all: five men, four of them married, and two boys aged fourteen and fifteen, down under the damp earth and the soggy, blackening wreaths. The mouldy scent of the saturated, dying wreaths was overpowering, emphasizing death in all its forms. A thin drizzle pattered down into the puddles tramped out by the great number of feet that had squeezed around the edge of the miners' grave for the interment. As was fitting, Mr Hearne had a grave to himself, at some distance from the communal one, where the better off were laid in their eternal rest. Mrs Hearne had left Meryen immediately after his separate funeral, muttering about just retribution against her, whatever that meant.

In heart-wrenching sorrow Jenny stooped to lay bunches of flowers, tied with black ribbon, on her family's grave. 'I hope you like these red and pink flowers, Mother and Father, my little brothers and sisters. They're called camellias and come from Mrs Brookson's garden. You'd have liked to have some in our little back garden, but I'm sure you all wander round gardens now where the flowers and trees are so much more beautiful.' At times Jenny felt acute loneliness at being separated from her family. She would curl up on her comfortable bed in her room that was larger than her parents' kitchen and front room put together, and ache for her former life. She longed to step back in time, with the knowledge she had now. She would know better than to accept the gift of Mrs Hearne's brooch; she would be there to protect her family from the disease that had wiped them out. She would happily forego all she had now, the privileges and security that would be hers for the rest of her life, if she could have her family back again. Mrs Brookson had told her she had made a will leaving her all her worldly possessions and Mr Logan had settled a generous sum of money on her in the event of his death.

When things got too much for Jenny, she remembered her loved ones were at peace and that they would wish her well. She was sure she felt them watching over her and that they were delighted she had a life so wonderful in comparison to what theirs had been. And she renewed a vow she had made on emerging from the worst of her grief and the depression that had gone with it: to work diligently in any way she could to help the wretched poor. When she was given money for herself she bought only token items for herself and secretly gave food, medicines and much-needed things to the worst off in Meryen, and to the occasional beggar passing through. She understood the unique sufferings of the underprivileged and how even the smallest scrap of relief could make a difference and lift some of their grinding worries. She and Serenity had given Betsy small household items for her future home and lace to sew on her bridal dress. Jenny's eyes filled with tears, for Betsy wouldn't get to wear her special dress now; her bridegroom had died under a mass of rock, along with Serenity's brother, Wilf.

Brushing away her tears, she smiled over her family's grave. She liked to give them a smile; she didn't want them worrying about her. Then she gazed up at the sky, believing they were all up there, very close to her, rather than under the crushing, cold earth. This exposed her to the chilly rain. 'Look, all of you, I've got an umbrella. Who'd have thought I'd own such a thing? I don't feel the rain at all when I'm under it. I'm happy, really happy most of the time. I'm sure you know that, but I miss you all so much. But one day we'll all be together again. It will be so wonderful.'

She popped back in under the umbrella and turned round to the horribly new mound, and whispered, 'You poor, poor people. I pray for you and for the ones grieving for you every day. Rest in peace.'

It was time to go. Visiting her family's grave was always going to be sadder from now on with the reminder of this other great tragedy so near to it. Lifting her skirts she wound her way through the other graves over the uneven, slippery grass to the path. There was a muddy slope to contend with before the return to a firm foothold on the path. At the place where the rich were buried there were steps down to the path, but Jenny was of humble birth and didn't dwell on that sort of unfair division. It had been a slippery climb up the slope and would be a tricky descent. Jenny chose a spot where a yew tree loomed nearby and was handy to grab, to aid her balance. She was behind the church, so there was little risk of anyone seeing her undignified scramble down to the path.

She reached the narrow path easily and experienced the sense of wonder that was with her so often nowadays. Someone, God she presumed, was intent on smoothing her way since she had lost her family. There was no one about, just the sexton's hut and the silent graves, and the trees and bushes disturbed by the sulky wind, so she lifted her skirts and wiped her ankle boots clean on the grass verge. She straightened her skirts demurely and lifted her chin, as Mrs Brookson kept reminding her to do. 'Always keep your chin up, my dear, so that if you see gentlefolk you are ready to curtsy and to wait for them to speak to you. Others are now beneath you in station and you must show them their place.'

She walked off but almost at once came to a stop. The tiny brown body of a sparrow lay crumpled and covered in grit where it had been kicked towards the verge. Another death, only a tiny, insignificant bird, but it seemed to symbolize the village's suffering and gloom, and illustrate how suddenly and unexpectedly the monstrous invisible force that was death could, and did, pounce on any form of life. She couldn't leave the little bird down there to rot, and end up a tiny skeleton to be crushed under some careless foot. If the sexton discovered it he'd merely throw the poor little thing in the hedge or burn it on a bonfire. To Jenny, to abandon the little body would be heartless and obscene. It was one of God's creatures and deserved a proper resting place.

She gathered up the bird – Mrs Brookson would be horrified at her contaminating her kid gloves – then spied a small sharp stick. Cradling the little feathered corpse in one hand Jenny went back to the yew tree but stayed down on the path. She leaned forward and used the stick first to dig away the soggy fallen leaves, then to gouge out the wet earth, which parted obligingly for her. She made a little bird-sized grave.

'What are you doing, Jenny?'

She straightened up, prepared to show the sparrow, then to have to justify finishing her task. When she saw who her companion was she was instantly her usual soft self.

The serious expression on Abe's battered face showed that he understood. He hobbled forward on his crutches. 'Let me help you.'

Jenny wrapped the tiny deceased thing in her handkerchief, while Abe, resting on one crutch, dug away a little more earth. Very carefully Jenny placed the shrouded body down in the little hollow. With a bare hand, scarred with cuts and bruises that were now healing, Abe filled in the grave and patted it down, then dressed it with leaves. No one except the pair of them would ever know that one tiny sparrow out of thousands was buried under the tree. They kept a minute's silence.

'Thank you, Abe,' Jenny said in the softest whisper. She wanted to convey to him that she had no intention of intruding on his time here. He had been too injured and weak to attend the joint funeral and this was the first occasion on which he had been able to pay his respects to the fallen, in particular to his partner, Wilf Treneer. 'And I'm so sorry.'

'Thanks for coming to the house, Jenny, and for the food you brought for my parents. Thank Serenity for me too.' He kept his head down, his gaze fixed on the secret grave, for his neck hurt and he did not want this gentle girl to see him wince in pain, or the tears beginning to well up.

'I'll leave you now, Abe. I'll call on you and your parents again, if that's all right.'

'Thank you,' he whispered, his voice just a rasp. With his chin still lowered he watched her dainty feet moving away. People called Jenny 'a dear little thing'. She was exactly that and more. She deserved her change of fortune. He shared something with her now; death in force – her family, his work-mates, and the secret burial place of a tiny bird. God knew every sparrow that ever was and ever would be. Up there in heaven He would approve of what Jenny had done. God knew exactly when that sparrow had dropped out of the sky, never to fly again, and He knew too that there was a natural weakness in the rock down the Wheal Verity, and when it would give way. He knew beforehand who among the miners would live and who would die.

It was a struggle but Abe managed the climb up the slope and reached the big spread of recently disturbed earth covered with the blackening wreaths. The terrible scene hit him like a thunderclap of reality: these seven men and boys he had known all his life really were dead, and Mr Hearne also. Abe was the only survivor among those who had been trapped. 'God wanted all of you gone but not me. He had a reason for letting you die but not me. I'm sorry you all had to die. Some of you had more responsibilities than me. It might make some sort of sense, so the minister says, at the end, on Judgement Day. They say we should give thanks for everything. God is working out His purposes.'

He stopped. If he went on his words would turn bitter over the tragic loss and the suffering of those left behind; at what the accident had done to him personally. He mustn't feel sorry for himself here and now. That could wait until he was lying in his bed tonight, with the candle burning because he was now terrified to be in the dark. Without light he was soon fighting for his breath, convinced he was suffocating.

Even if he could bring himself to go back down into the bowels of the earth again it was no use. He had a twisted leg that would never be fully right, and the other leg had lost a slice of mangled muscle and would never again be strong. His hearing was not so good and there was a constant ringing in his head. He had headaches that felt as if his temples were being pounded by hammers, and as if his brain were being crushed by a cruel hand. He hoped that in time his hearing loss and headaches would ease. Henry Cardell had treated his wounds for nothing. The apothecary's expert poultices, ointments and dressings would guard him well against infection. And he wasn't a cripple, after all; he could be thankful for that, at least.

After being dug out – the cold hand he had gripped had not belonged to the dead Jeroboam Hearne or to Wilf Treneer, but rather to a dogged rescuer – he had lain in his bed, sliding in and out of consciousness until yesterday morning. His parents told him that Jenny and Serenity had dropped in to see him. They'd visited all the bereaved too. He didn't have to worry about losing his wages for six weeks; the benevolent among the Kivells would see that he got a weekly sum of eight shillings, and as always during these times the whole mining community rallied round. His frail parents were being well supported.

Yesterday, Clemency had called, finding him shaky and his eyes red, swollen and crusty. His hair was still matted, the dust that had nearly choked him refusing to be washed out. She had said all the usual things and he had thanked her. Then he had suddenly blurted out, 'You were down there with me,' as he fought to keep breathlessness at bay. If he gave way to it he knew he would be clenched by panic.

'Was I?' She waited patiently for his explanation.

'I saw you in my mind, you and Jenny and Serenity and Miss Hattie; she sent me her good wishes in a letter, by the way. Then you all faded away, but when I thought I was about to die you alone came back. Somehow, seeing how strong you are made me fight for my life. I was rescued in the nick of time, thanks to you. Then I saw all of you again. It was such a comfort.'

'I'm pleased about that, thank God for it.' She pondered. 'I don't feel particularly strong but I suppose I'm not afraid to stand my ground. Abe, what will you do now?'

'For work, you mean? I'll try to get by on odd jobbing.' His inner ear started itching wildly. He rubbed a finger along in the crevices and dug out thick horrid dust. 'Sorry.' He was embarrassed and ashamed at not waiting to be alone to do it. 'Stuff's got everywhere.' He coughed up more of the wretched dust and blew more out through his nose. 'Sorry, I can't help it.'

'Don't worry, I understand. I'm sure you'll do very well in the future, Abe. Just be sure to rest and get well. I don't want to patronize you, but if I can do anything for you, please do say. I'll go now. Good luck.'

Clemency had had the sensitivity to go because she could see he was filling up with tears from deep inside him. He was often tearful these days, but just at that moment he'd needed a damned good cry, in private, to sob out the feelings of hopelessness and fear he'd undergone in the deep, deep darkness and which still clung to him. He'd cried too for the things he'd never again be able to do.

He wept now. He would never again wrestle with Thomas Steadman, one of the men who lay in the earth beneath his feet. Thomas had been a thirty-four-year-old father of four children, a stocky man with a wide girth, whiskers that stuck out like a cat's, and feet like slabs of granite; he'd been a

devout Methodist and a teller of hilariously silly jokes. He'd
been a good man, a kind man and a willing mate. Thomas
Steadman hadn't deserved to be crushed to death. None of
his six-feet-under neighbours deserved to die that day. But
it was a fact that in the midst of life was death, and death
lurked everywhere, and not just in Meryen. Abe had heard
that life in the big towns and cities wasn't as close and caring
as in small communities. He had a lot to be grateful for. He
was alive and would soon be able to look for work. He could
turn his hand to most things, fixing and mending, gardening,
ditching, cleaning windows. He'd always earned extra each
summer in the harvest fields. He would do anything to keep
his parents in food and clothing and to pay the rent. Best of
all he had friends, not only among the men he had worked
and drunk with, but in three pleasant young women and a
dear young girl.

Jenny hung about his mind. Dear, sweet young Jenny, who
had reverently buried an unimportant little bird out of the
gentleness of her heart. Sharing that poignant occasion with
her would stay in his mind for ever.

Twenty-Three

The money was rolling in and she was making it by doing
the thing she loved to do best. Daisy indulged herself by having
sex in every way and with any number of partners, of both
genders. Her budding pregnancy was an added attraction to
some of her lovers. Luck had been on Daisy's side the day the
Kivell marriage was rent apart. As soon as Seth Kivell, who
these days had nothing to do with her except for sending his
manager to check regularly on her, had paid for his safely
delivered brat, her fortunes would change dramatically again.
She would leave this cosy detached cottage on the fringes of
Redruth, where the locals ostracized her for her immorality
and sometimes threw mud and stones at her, and she would

set up a high-class brothel far away from the town. Trenbarvear's manager, lusty Jimmy Ellery, was looking for another temporary home for her until she returned to Trenbarvear for the birth. Jimmy, a single and easy-going man, had enjoyed many a furtive tumble with Daisy at the farm, and was now taking full advantage of her skills and perversions.

Following a rip-roaring drunken party the night before, Daisy had slept in late. She emerged from a drugged sleep in a muddle of bedcovers, with a fuzzy head and parched throat. She was alone – her clients, three respected businessmen of Redruth, and a lady, had left in the small hours. Daisy had been careful to lock up after them. Naked except for white stockings – ripped in the fun – and scarlet garters, she relived last night's debaucheries, giggling, and staying excited for as long as it pleased her.

She staggered off the bed, avoiding the many abandoned gin and wine bottles, and went down on all fours to reach behind the washstand, where a thick drape hung, and felt for the reticule where she kept her nest egg. It was there, and she heaved a sigh of relief, always anxious lest it should be stolen. By the weight in her hand the monies she had earned last night were tucked up tightly inside the drawstring leather. Getting up, none too easily, she groped all over her bulbous stomach, nodded and sneered as she felt answering flutters of movement from the baby inside her. There were indentations of teeth marks on her bulge and many other parts of her sallow flesh. She giggled. It had been a rough night. She would have to stop all that when she got to eight months. Seth Kivell's midwife would tell him about the results of her pleasures and he wouldn't be pleased. She had better cut out the gin and opium. She didn't want to risk getting addicted to either, and if she gave birth to a damaged baby Seth Kivell would refuse to pay her off.

After sitting on the chamber pot, she pulled on a nightgown and shawl and slippers and went carefully down the steep bare stairs to the kitchen. She changed into old shoes, slipped outside to empty the chamber pot, then washed it out and left it to soak in diluted rose water until tonight's appointment with a different batch of clients. Inside the kitchen again, she returned to the slippers, washed her hands, and gulped water from the pitcher – it was tepid and had bits floating in it, but nevertheless she welcomed the stream that passed down her sore gullet.

Thank God, the black iron slab had red embers in the grate. She built up the fire and heated a kettle of water and vigorously applied a much-needed washcloth to clean her whole body thoroughly. Back upstairs she cleared up last night's chaos, singing chirpily all the while. She might be a trollop but she had once been a diligent cleaning maid. The whiter-than-white Mrs Kivell and her cow of a daughter could not have faulted her work at Trenbarvear. They might hate what she was, but how would they like to skivvy for a living, with no prospects other than to marry some ignorant oaf, live in a miserable tied cottage and turn out a brood of squalling brats, with never a new dress on their backs? Daisy sprayed lashings of perfume into the air and opened the window. Then she dressed, applied some rouge and lip paint, and dabbed perfume liberally over her neck, arms and cleavage.

Then it was back downstairs, where she used the curling tongs on her dull brown hair to produce tight ringlets. The allowance she received from Seth Kivell, coupled with her earnings, enabled her to dress well and pamper herself. The final result was quite elegant, if a little common; the look she liked best, and an invitation to new clients. She smirked. More than one man who had reviled her publicly had knocked surreptitiously on her back door at the dead of night, begging her services for payment.

There was porridge left over in the pot. She threw in some sugar, cinnamon and a few raisins and ate a large bowlful, following it with a chunk of cottage loaf thickly spread with butter and plum jam, all the while sipping sweetened tea. Mmm, she thought delicious. This is the life. May it long continue and in even better circumstances. Pleasantly sleepy, she went up to the second bedroom, the smaller one, which she kept to relax in, to doze and dream, or to look at the pretty pictures in ladies' magazines. In her former life she had never had the chance to be alone and to please herself. She anticipated this luxury as much as she did feeding her base appetites. Nibbling from a box of sugared almonds, she browsed through the fashion pages of a periodical and then noted a recipe for squab pie. She drifted off into a restful slumber.

She dreamt of her new home, a splendid mansion in which

there was everything she could ever want. She was not a madam
in a whorehouse; rather, she was married to a handsome, virile
young man, surprisingly a Kivell, only not one she knew of,
and they had a good-looking, strapping son and a beautiful
little daughter – wonderful, happy children. She was respected
everywhere she went and was the most sought after hostess in
the county. She knew that one day soon her loving, passionate
husband would be knighted and they would both be commanded
to attend the royal court. '*Ahh*,' she moaned in bliss. She didn't
have to become a whoremonger, very likely doomed to die of
some nasty disease, but a married woman held in the highest
esteem.

She was lying in filmy silks and on rose petals on a giant-
sized four-poster bed, dozing in sublime happiness. There was
no other furniture in the room and, all around, gold gleamed
and diamonds sparkled, and rose-framed mirrors reflected all
the glory. A soft breeze fingered the lace curtains at the crystal-
paned windows. Someone slipped into the room. It was a man,
tall and dark, with muscles that rippled in perfection, and so
handsome that it made her heart ache for him. He sat on the
bed, leaned over her and shook her shoulder gently. It was her
husband. He had come to wake her and make love to her.
Oh, bliss. Soon he would call her name, ever so tenderly. '*Daisy,
Daisy, my love.*' She reached out a hand to him.

He pushed her hand away. That wasn't right. He had never
rejected her before.

Daisy opened her eyes and sat up straight, frowning. A man
was sitting on the end of the bed. People came here without
invitation quite often but this stranger had broken in and she
was furious. 'Who the hell are you? How did you get in?'
Then she saw that his overcoat and the tall hat and muffler
that concealed his face were of fine quality. She had given one
of her businessmen clients, who paid more than her two-guinea
price, a spare key. 'Did Mr Kendle lend you his key?' she
simpered, keen now not to offend a potential new gentleman
customer. The sensuous conclusion of her wonderful dream
had left her in need.

'No, I don't find locked doors a difficulty. Don't you recog-
nize me, Daisy?'

The man's voice was deep and low and slightly rasping, but
it was familiar to her. As she stared, he removed the hat and

muffler. She knew him. His face was thin and gaunt, his eyes hollow and as if haunted; quite a contrast to his appearance the last time she had seen him. He had allowed a beard to take over his jutting chin. 'Mr Adam! You're a surprise. Have you come here for—?'

'Certainly not.' Adam Kivell curled his upper lip in disgust.

'Sorry,' Daisy blurted out. 'I didn't mean to cause offence. Of course you didn't. Mrs Feena was the only one for you. I really liked her. She was always nice to me. I never got the chance to say how sorry I was for what happened. I'm not surprised you left the damned farm right after. But I don't understand why you're here. Would you like to go down to the kitchen? I could make you a nice cup of tea. I've got the best in – real China tea.'

'I want to stay here. I've got something to say to you.'

Adam Kivell looked so hard and grave that it gave Daisy the creeps. 'You're angry about me and – and your father, is that it?'

'I don't blame you for that, Daisy. You're an uneducated girl following your instincts. You were a willing participant, but if you had not been you wouldn't have been able to stop my father from having his way with you. He got you pregnant and when you told him he threw you out. It's understandable that you'd lose your senses and scream it all out. But I can't let things go on.'

'What do you mean?' Daisy edged up towards the headboard. Grief had stripped Adam Kivell of all emotion, likely his reason too. He seemed as cold as winter, and a little crazed. 'Look, I'm sorry about all the upset I caused your mother. I shouldn't have done it. Mrs Kivell didn't deserve it. She's a fine lady and was a good mistress. I'm sorry, Mr Adam, I really am.'

'I won't let that child in your belly grow up at Trenbarvear as a direct insult to my mother. I lost my baby as a result of my evil father's will, and I won't let his bastard draw breath in this world.' Adam's voice was hard and cold. He was passionate about this one subject but, otherwise, except for his undying love for Feena and their child, he felt nothing.

Curling herself up protectively, Daisy put her hands to her throat. 'Well, that's easy.' Her voice wobbled. 'I'll get rid of it. I don't love it or anything. I can't wait to have it out of me

and carry on with my own life. Perhaps you can arrange a
surgeon to do it, Mr Adam. I don't know any.'

'I wouldn't dream of getting someone else involved.' Adam's
tone was as if from the dead.

'What then? God, no – oh, please,' Daisy wailed. 'You don't
mean to cut it out yourself?'

'Of course not; I wouldn't be so cruel.' Adam turned lifeless eyes on her.

His words did little to soothe Daisy. 'What then, for God's
sake?'

'This won't hurt at all, Daisy. You have my word, and the
word of a Kivell is watertight.' From a pocket of his overcoat
he produced a small vial. 'I got this from my uncle, the apothecary. He made it up especially for this purpose. All you have
to do is drink it down and lie still and it will soon be over.'

Daisy eyed the vial warily but she was a little less scared.
'Oh, to bring on a miscarriage, that's what you mean. All right,
fair enough.' This would spoil the best of her plans. Without
the baby she'd have to leave here, but she had nearly twenty
guineas in the next room, and her regular clients to provide
her with a good living. 'But how's it not going to hurt? It'll
bring on labour pains and I'll be in agony.'

'You'll feel nothing, Daisy. Trust me. My uncle is an expert
with his potions.' Adam held the vial towards her lips, ready
to pull out the cork.

'Labour, all done quickly and without pains? Your uncle
should sell the stuff,' Daisy cackled nervously. 'He'd make a
bleddy fortune.'

'Go ahead. He's assured me it won't taste too bad.'

Daisy looked at him above the vial. 'Will you stay and take
the baby away after? I don't fancy getting rid of it somewhere
meself.'

'You've got nothing to worry about. I've thought of
everything.'

'So I'll feel nothing and all I'll have to do is push it out, is
that right?'

'Drink it,' Adam whispered. 'Everything will be fine.'

Doubting she would give birth without pain, Daisy knew
that, nevertheless, she had no choice. She wouldn't have to
leave here until she had recovered, so things wouldn't be too
bad. She drank from the vial. The liquid was thick and strangely

sweet with a dry aftertaste. There was something familiar about it, she thought, while settling down on the bed. She wasn't wearing pantaloons and she drew up her knees and opened her legs. 'Oh, my good bedding – I need to get some towels and something to wrap the baby in afterwards. It won't live long, will it?'

Adam stood up and looked down on her from the foot of the bed. 'You don't need anything, Daisy. Just close your eyes and go to sleep and it will all be over soon.'

'Sleep?' she murmured, feeling a strange but not unpleasant floating sensation. 'How can I push a baby out, even a tiny baby, if I'm sleeping?' Next moment she was hallucinating. She was in the wonderful bedroom in her dream and she was walking towards a window. When she reached it the glass and wall had gone and she was high up on a mountain top bathed in a rainbow glow. Hundreds of feet below was a crystal sea, and she knew she could fly and soar over it. Holding out her arms she leapt off the mountain. Instead of flying she was falling, feet first, plunging down at rapid speed, the wind whipping at her ringlets until they were straightened out. She wasn't afraid. Nothing was going to harm her. The sea had disappeared and a lush green valley was rushing up fast to meet her. At the very last instant her descent slowed and she floated to touch down on the velvety green. In front of her was a mysterious pinpoint of light that she knew would grow larger if she reached out towards it. She started to walk – then she knew the walk would never end.

Adam waited. A cold stillness settled in the room. He lifted Daisy's limp wrist and pressed on it. There was no pulse. He put her legs together and straightened them on the bed. He went to the door and looked back at her. 'My baby died in his mother's womb. It's better that this child dies in yours. It would have had a terrible life reared by my cruel father, and as an outcast from the Kivells. And it's better that you should die this way, Daisy, than go on to a dissolute existence, probably ending up in the gutter. Your death won't be too closely looked into, not a girl like you. It will be believed you died from an accidental overdose of opium. You won't bring any more disgrace to the Kivell name and my mother won't suffer a daily living insult.'

Later in the day Adam was at Wingfield House.

'Is it done?' Logan asked.

'It is.' Adam shrugged off his brother's worried embrace.

'You should have let me come with you.'

'Two of us were more likely to be seen, and it was something I had to do alone. I was well wrapped up. I wouldn't have been recognized. The clothes and boots were new and I've burnt them. As Uncle Henry promised, she didn't suffer.'

Logan searched Adam's waxen, bony face, hoping to see even the tiniest flicker of light in his lifeless eyes. 'Do you feel any ease?'

'You know that will never be. I'm glad for Mother's sake, for Clemmie's. It would have been impossible for them otherwise.' Adam raised his head and now there was a new fierce passion in him. 'I wish with all my heart Father was dead. Don't you?'

'Every day, but Adam, take heed of this: his death must not come about by your hand. Do you understand me?'

Adam nodded grimly. 'I must return home or Mother will start to worry about me.'

Alone, Logan set his expression hard. He and Serenity were engaged, and in view of Adam's mourning, a quiet wedding was planned after Easter. Seth Kivell might take it into his rotten head to cause upset to his bride. Logan would not take that risk. The old bully was a stain on the family's character; a disgrace to all the Kivells. Future generations must and would be spared that shame.

Twenty-Four

The dawn sun was gently bathing Poltraze's sweeping parkland as Clemency pulled back the guest bedroom curtains, after the first night of her stay. There was no mist or murkiness. It would be a warm, fresh day. A young gardener, in rolled-up sleeves and apron, was digging in one of the formal tiered herbaceous beds, and Clemency watched in pleasure as a fearless robin, probably well known to him, followed on, picking out a breakfast of tasty earthworms. The mass of azaleas was in bloom, the rhododendrons in bud and the camellias dying off. The lawns were meticulously mown. Beyond them beech, birch and oak trees planted by long-ago Nankervises reached up to the sky. Clemency had never thought Poltraze could be naturally peaceful and beautiful, but of course the tranquillity was all outside.

Always an early riser, and knowing that Hattie would not surface until the eighth hour, Clemency put on her riding clothes – black, as were most of her clothes while she was still in mourning. Shunning a hat, she crept past the servants, who were scurrying hither and thither to prepare the old house for the day. She told Mrs Secombe of her intention to explore the grounds for an hour.

'I'm sure you already know every inch of them, Miss Kivell,' Mrs Secombe said knowingly. She cast a disapproving glance over Clemency's tumbling tresses, but added kindly, 'Do be careful. I'll have the bathroom prepared for your return. I trust you slept well last night.'

'Very well indeed, thank you.' Clemency had been surprised to awaken in the strange bed, after a deep, undisturbed sleep. Since her return to Burnt Oak Farm, every night had been marked by turmoil and anxious dreams. Perhaps the total change of scene, coupled with the late night of breathless entertainment that Clarry and Phee Faraday had put on in her honour, had brought the welcome respite. Jane Hartley and Adela Miniver had not attended, and although much of Matthew Faraday's poetry had been read out, with gusto or great drama, as each piece demanded, he had not been there either, to dampen the delightful occasion. Chairs had been positioned in a semicircle in the music room. Mrs Secombe and the steward and his wife were invited to take a seat in the middle row. The servants, according to their rank in the house, took up the back row or lined the walls. There had been a hush of expectation. Applause had broken out loudly as the master and mistress, decked out like actors on stage, took to the dais.

Clemency had been astonished at Clarry and Phee's energy and talent. During several changes of costume, they had acted short plays, recited the poetry with and without music, played duets, sung and even danced. The spaniels had charmed the audience by performing tricks. The old couple was not unlike a pair of adorable children and it was no surprise that the family and the loyal staff sought so diligently to protect them. Clarry and Phee were soul mates, and Clemency thought they might not have coped with the rigours of everyday life if they had not met. They would enjoy the raucous partying that went on at Burnt Oak. It was a pity they couldn't take part in it at some time. There had been no such activity there of late. Her brother Adam's tragedy was particularly grim, and her father's betrayal of his kin, and his subsequent despicable behaviour, had unsettled the family as nothing else had before.

'I'm gratified to witness that you're enjoying your time with us, my dear Miss Clemency. This is an important time for us at Poltraze.' Clarry had beamed at Clemency at the buffet table in the next room, during a break in the show. He was still revved up with adrenalin and was bobbing up and down on the balls of his feet. He was wearing Eastern clothes, complete with a jewelled and feathered turban, and some of the dogs were about his feet, begging for titbits of food. 'We have the delight of you spending a few days with us, and Kingsley, don't you know, is to arrive here soon after luncheon on the morrow. We shall have so much more fun.'

'And Kingley's bringing company with him,' Phee had piped up in a shivery sort of excitement. Her exaggerated smile exposed the gaps between her small grey teeth. The heavy rouge on her cheeks and the red grease on her lips were starting to run. 'He's been very mysterious about it. Hattie thinks it might be one of her friends, travelling down to help pass the tedious journey with her on the way up. If so, it will be some young lady who has her eye on Kingsley, no doubt.' Phee winked and giggled. 'He's always been very much sought after. Poor Mrs Secombe has been quite thrown by the arrangement of the rooms she's been asked to make ready, but she'll rise to the challenge. She's a treasure.'

Hattie had linked her arm through Clemency's and pulled her a couple of steps away. 'Now, Papa and Mama, don't monopolize Clemmie. I've got little time left to be with her.'

Clemency was very fond of Hattie but on occasions she found her friend's insistence on claiming every second of her time too demanding. So it was good to be able to take a ride alone this morning and clear her mind, to prepare herself for the excitement that would inevitably break out on the arrival of Kingsley Faraday and his companion.

In the cobbled stable yard she found a thoroughbred, new to Poltraze, already prepared for riding. There was no one about and she ran her hands over the horse's well-formed shoulders and neck. 'You're a fine beauty, aren't you?'

'I'm pleased you think so.' Matthew was approaching in riding gear, with a large hat pulled down to obscure his features. Watching for his master's steps, Sandy the retriever was striding at his side.

Her abiding impression of Matthew Faraday was as a stuffy weakling for wanting to hide himself away. He had recently been seen riding and walking, although not at close quarters, by delivery men to the house, and speculation was rife in the village as to who the newcomer at Poltraze was. Although some thought he might be a Faraday, none guessed he was the owner of the big house

Clemency stepped back from the horse. 'I'm about to ask for my pony to be saddled. I won't be interfering with your ride, Mr Faraday.'

'As you please, Miss Kivell,' he said blandly, reaching her. He took off his dark glasses. 'I would have invited you to accompany me.'

It was an insincere invitation and Clemency knew it. He had no more liking for her than she had for him. 'I'll leave you to get on.'

He nodded. As he lifted his head, she noticed the fresh air and exercise had added colour and strength to his face. His cheeks had filled out and he looked altogether much healthier. His body was more muscular and his carriage had reverted to its former military bearing. To her surprise she discovered that he was rather attractive, and his strangely exquisite eyes were even more mesmerizing. She had the notion to engage him in more talk. 'You will miss Hattie when she leaves here.'

'I shall be more relieved when she has safely and contentedly returned to London. The quietness of the country does not suit her and', he went on darkly, 'there is nowhere for her to go socially hereabouts.'

Clemency eyed him stonily. She understood his meaning: he didn't approve of Hattie associating with her. This was understandable, she supposed. She was part of a family that

had a dubious pedigree and that was presently in the midst of
a scandal. While Clemency was too proud to be hurt by his
opinion, it stung her into despising him for a pompous prig.
Apart from the act of bravery that had partially blinded him,
Matthew Faraday had little to be proud of. 'Huh.' She marched
off to locate the stable boy.

'Huh to you too, little Miss Rabble,' Matthew muttered
under his breath, and then swung up on to the saddle.

Was it the dead of night or was he actually dead? I can't be
dead, Seth reasoned after several painful moments in a foggy
haze, not with this thumping great headache. Over the past few
days and nights he had guzzled down enormous quantities of
ale and spirits. His binge had been provoked by concentrated
brooding; he was being shunned in the village by his kin. Deadly
whispers were circulating about him in farming circles. He had
been publicly called a fool for his decision to buy Trenbarvear,
and sniped at for losing his lovely wife and all of his family.
He had been jeered at as the instigator of his own downfall.
Even the whores in a brothel he'd stumbled into had been
reluctant to be chosen to service him.

The latest thing to plunge him into furious self-pity was
the withdrawal of the farm produce order from Poltraze. 'Don't
tell me something like that, Ellery!' he had yelled at the farm
manager, the high notes resounding off the walls in the house.
'Tell me something good, for Old Nick's sake! Why? Why
don't the Faradays want my choice meats and the best dairy
stuffs any more? Has someone been making trouble for me?'

'Not that I know of sir,' Jimmy Ellery had replied quietly,
marking off the Poltraze order in an account book. Confidence
was packed into his short, stocky frame. He was well thought
of in the farming community and could easily get himself
another good job, with a tied cottage, elsewhere. And it amused
Ellery that he was bedding the master's pregnant trollop when
he made a fortnightly check on her. Without a doubt Seth
Kivell would kill him if he found out, but his black moods
and drunkenness were blunting his perception.

'Did you talk things through with the Poltraze steward? Did
you offer him a better deal?' Seth bellowed. He had begun to
cough and splutter and was forced to wipe away the resulting
spittle on his sleeve.

Ellery looked away in disgust. The mistress would have been ashamed to see that. It was a good job she'd had the sense and courage to leave the pathetic old bugger. 'I tried everything to convince him otherwise, sir, but he was adamant, I'm afraid.'

'What reason did he give? Who's supplying the big house now?' Seth dug a paperknife into his palm, leaving deep indentations, all the while imagining that he was aiming the knife at the Poltraze steward's throat, terrifying him.

'All he would say was that Poltraze had its reasons. He wouldn't be drawn, as you'd expect, about who had been asked to fill the breach.' Ellery had closed the books and pushed back his chair. 'Is that all, sir?'

'All? You'd better fill the breach left in my books! It's your job,' Seth had thundered at the man. He had wanted to kill him, blaming Ellery as the latest one to let him down. Then he saw that Ellery wasn't afraid of him. Seth had been about to threaten him with dismissal without a reference, but he saw that the farm manager wouldn't care. Ellery no longer respected him. No one did. Seth was almost felled by the damning fact. 'Get out, curse you!'

Seth lost the struggle to get up off the bed and fell back with his face falling into Verena's pillows. He had not allowed the bed linen to be changed, desperate to hang on to the wonderful feminine smell of her and the rose and sandalwood perfume she wore. He might as well push his face deeper into the pillows and suffocate himself to death. Verena would never come back to him. His autocratic decisions, his belligerent conduct and, above all, his affair with the kitchen maid had seen to that. But Verena was his wife and she should have stood by him, even over his concealing the fact that Trenbarvear was actually Clemency's. It still was; the little bitch had refused to hand it over or to sell it to him. He was living under his daughter's roof; it was no wonder he was a laughing-stock. He might as well be dead. A great number of people must wish him dead, including some in his own family. He had started out wanting the big house and ended up with this blasted farm. All his grandiose ideas had been cut down to size; everything had been an utter failure. No Kivell before him had had such a downfall.

But to kill himself? No, it wasn't his way. There was still hope. All he had to do was to pull himself up. A man who did that diligently and with great success would regain respect. Clemency had no legal right to the farm until she came of age. She had just had her seventeenth birthday. He had four years to get her to change her mind and let him have Trenbarvear. He would have to use guile. He'd make it known to her that he had been wrong in lying to her and for trying to push her into marrying Jowan.

First he must clean himself up, behave as a respectable businessman, and return to patronizing Kivell businesses. In time he would apologize to his children, except Logan and Adam; he'd hate to do it, but he must be clever. If all else failed he would even pray to God to win Verena back. He was excruciatingly lonely without her. As for his child with Daisy, he'd find it a foster home. He should never have planned to bring up the child himself. That had been his biggest folly. The child would never step inside this house, not unless . . . unless his family refused to forgive him and Verena continued in her desertion. At least then he would have one child and would not have to face his greatest fear, of growing old alone.

First he would go over to Poltraze himself, ask to see Mr Clarence Faraday, and plead with him to return his custom to the farm. Clemency was welcome under Poltraze's roof and that meant he should be too. If he could get on good terms with the Faradays that would help his cause no end.

Struggling to his feet, ignoring his pounding head, he went to the bedroom door and called down to the cook to prepare him a hearty late breakfast.

His meal of fried gammon, eggs and potatoes was interrupted by the arrival of Jimmy Ellery. 'What's the matter with you?' Seth barked, sprinkling a mist of salt and pepper over his food. 'You got a face as long as a fiddler's bow.'

'I'm sorry to disturb you while you're eating, Mr Kivell.' Ellery shifted on his feet and twiddled his cap in shaky hands. 'I'm afraid I've come with bad news.'

'What news?' Seth let his knife and fork clatter down on to the platter. He was afraid for Verena. Ellery's face was too pale and twitchy for him only to be worried about farm matters.

'I'm afraid there's no easy way of saying this, sir. I went over to check on Daisy and found her dead.'

'Dead?' Seth stared at him. 'That means the child's dead too. Did she go into early labour?'

'Nothing like that, sir. I'm afraid she'd been dead two or three days at least.' Ellery had visited Daisy, hoping for sex. He was still overcome by mild shudders at the memory of her corpse, an empty vial next to her hand. From the numerous footprints visible, as well as a rug that was wrinkled and pushed to one side, it seemed others had come and gone in haste, failing to raise the alarm. As Ellery had recoiled, his hand over his nose, one of Daisy's customers had shown up, a magistrate from Redruth. Nervous and embarrassed, he had practically begged Ellery to agree to let the magistrate pass on the news discreetly to the coroner. 'By the look of her,' he told Seth now, 'death was from an overdose of opium and too much gin. Of course, it was too early for the child to be born; it would have died even if Daisy had been found in time to cut it out of her.'

'The bitch!' Seth hissed, puce in the face, shoving away his late breakfast, his appetite completely gone. 'I set her up well but she killed my child.' If he didn't succeed in winning Verena back, and that wouldn't happen unless he first convinced his children he was a changed man, he would have no one and nothing to work for.

'A magistrate turned up there, Mr Kivell,' Ellery said in an officious manner, and then he tapped his nose. 'I think he must have been seeing Daisy, if you get my meaning. She was making good money by the look of the grand things she'd got hold of. Anyway, I got him to agree to clear the cottage and get all legal matters over with quickly. Your name won't be mentioned, sir.'

'You did well, Ellery. I'll reward you if you make sure this is never mentioned again. I'm going over to Poltraze later to see if I can personally persuade Mr Faraday to reconsider the cancellation of the farm produce order. This farm is going to thrive, I swear it will.'

Clemency put on a dark grey day dress with a patterned shawl over her shoulders for Kingsley's arrival, in compliance with a vibrant Phee's request that everyone should 'dress up to greet our dear boy and his guest in style'. She added a diamond pendant necklace and bracelet, which had once been her paternal great-grandmother's, bounty from a shipwreck. She shunned the expensive jewels her father had given her.

Perhaps she would never wear them again. He had ignored her recent birthday and while part of her had been pleased, a bigger part of her was hurt and sad. Her hair obeyed her nimble fingers as she pinned it up, then she tweaked natural ringlets about her forehead and neck. She was pushing her feet into embroidered, heeled shoes when Hattie's maid Bridie popped her nose round the door. 'Would you please hasten, Miss Kivell. Miss Hattie has sent me to inform you that Mr Kingsley's carriage is about to pull up, so would you kindly go down to the hall.'

'Straight away,' Clemency said, smiling. She sprayed on a little light, musky eau-de-Cologne and glanced out of a window. The coach and four was weighted down with luggage. Kingsley Faraday's guest must indeed be a lady, and one of fashion. She was interested to see Kingsley again. She had a reason to be pleased to be saying goodbye to Hattie in a few days' time. She could see that Hattie was beginning to wilt in this house. There was little to give her joy and nothing to challenge her. If she stayed much longer she was likely to become terribly unhappy. Clemency's red lips instinctively compressed at the thought of Matthew Faraday being among the welcoming party.

After a deal of pitter-pattering and clomping and clattering down corridors and stairs, Clemency, the Faradays, the west wing mourners, the spaniels and the servants were all assembled in the hall. Clarry, Phee, Matthew and Hattie went outside through the open doors.

The hearty greetings from the parents were halted by their cries of surprise.

'Well, upon my soul!'

'Well, I never!'

'Children, little children come to stay with us, how wonderful. What a delight. They shall have great fun playing with our dear doggies.'

Children? Clemency glanced at Mrs Secombe, who shook her head; the housekeeper had not been warned to expect children.

Those outside began to fill the hall. There was a little shuffling and Clemency found Matthew at her side. He was well turned out yet managed to appear informal and even a little careless. His expression was grim. There were more guests than

Kingsley had intimated and Matthew was not pleased to have so many people in the house. The servants bowed and curtsied to the guests. Furtively they eyed the strangers – a tall, handsome, red-haired lady with an open, expansive demeanour, and a small boy and girl and their nursemaid. There was an expectant hush and all eyes settled on Kingsley, who had walked in proudly with the lady on his arm.

Smiling, with his chin up, Kingsley began. 'Papa, Mama, Matthew, Jane, Hattie, Miss Kivell, I have great pleasure in introducing to you my wife, Mrs Kingsley Faraday – Fearne, the former widowed Mrs Lewis, and her two children, Master Timothy and Miss Constance. The children will share the same room, and their nursemaid will take the adjoining dressing room. As you can see, Master Timothy has been unwell and Mrs Faraday does not desire him to be shut away up in the nursery.'

Matthew let out a sharp breath and Clemency looked at him. He knew who his new sister-in-law was and he did not like her. She seemed acceptable as a wife for Kingsley, Clemency thought. Hattie moved away from Kingsley and suddenly gripped Clemency's arm. Her perfect pale complexion was burning with hot colour. It seemed the lady wasn't to find approval from at least two of her new family. Then Clemency saw why. The children greatly resembled Kingsley; they were obviously his, and Fearne Faraday had either conducted an adulterous affair with him or she had been his mistress. From Jane's habitual dour bearing it seemed she had no previous knowledge of Fearne. Miss Miniver seemed only half-interested; she was, Clemency was sure, concerned only with her position here.

Stuck between the stiff-backed brother and the mortified sister, Clemency wished she were not here to witness what might happen next; embarrassment and recriminations? She was glad when Clarry and Phee, after ordering the spaniels to lie down, went forward to embrace Kingsley's wife.

'We are so very delighted to meet you, dear Fearne.' Bubbling like an excitable child, Phee gave and then accepted a kiss from Fearne Faraday. 'Kingsley married! He's brought us a daughter-in-law, indeed. Oh, what marvellous news. You must tell us all about your nuptials, my dear. You must call us Mama and Papa. Clarry, my old croak, did you hear? We're grandparents! There couldn't be anything better, eh?'

'No indeed, my old treacle.' His face split by the most enormous grin, Clarry bent over Fearne's hand and kissed it once, twice, and again. 'And such a beautiful bride you have, Kingsley, lucky, lucky fellow. And Master Timothy, you're a fine little fellow, eh? You look as if you need your bed, and no wonder after such a long journey. Hated every mile of the way down here, myself, by train and then carriage from Plymouth. And little Miss Constance – my, my, you have your mother's beauty. You're a fairy princess, I declare, and no mistake.'

The children were tired, the boy pasty-faced with huge dark shadows under his eyes, but they were a most attractive pair. They bowed and curtsied to their new relatives again and again, as Kingsley introduced them to their Uncle Matthew and Aunt Jane and Aunt Harriet. Clemency read Matthew's face. His mouth was set grimly, the rest of him like granite. Under the steady hardness of his glowering eyes the children clutched at their mother's skirts. Fearne Faraday swallowed uneasily and blanched. Clemency felt sorry for them.

'Say something,' she whispered to Matthew. 'Give them a welcome.'

Next instant she had to hide her shock and anger when Matthew prodded her in the back. How dare he? She would not allow him to get away with his spite and she had in no way deserved a reprimand.

'It's a long time since last we met, Mrs Lew—, Mrs Faraday.' Matthew practically hissed the words between his teeth. At the same time Hattie made much of gazing down at her feet.

Kingsley cleared his throat, darting stony glances at the pair. He was also displeased to note that Jane was high-nosed and indifferent to his new family. 'Mrs Secombe, would you please dismiss the servants and take the children and Miss Dance upstairs. Miss Dance will inform you of the children's requirements. Papa, Mama, shall we go along to the morning room?' He added coldly, 'Do join us, everyone, if you'd care to.'

'I'm sure Mrs Faraday doesn't want to be overwhelmed in the first moments of her arrival,' Jane said dully. 'If we may be excused, Miss Miniver and I will leave the pleasure of getting to know her until this evening over dinner.'

Just before she and her mousy shadow turned heel and headed for the stairs, Matthew stalked off down the corridor that led to the east wing. Kingsley scowled at their rudeness, and Clemency shot him and his bride a look of sympathy. Some people in this suffocating old house were unbelievably obnoxious. Thankfully, Clarry and Phee, in their innocence, were oblivious of the bad feeling.

'Hattie, will you come with us? And you, Miss Kivell?' Kingsley appealed, taking up Fearne's hand.

'I'd be delighted to,' Clemency said with meaning, receiving two grateful looks in return.

'If you don't mind, Clemency,' Hattie said, cool and seeming to have lost all her sparkle, 'this is family business. Would you mind finding something to occupy yourself with for a while?'

'As you please.' Clemency said. 'I know just the thing.'

She went after Matthew and was on him in a moment. 'Stop. I want a word with you, Matthew Faraday.'

'I do not wish for your company, Miss Kivell. I suggest you go elsewhere.' Matthew kept up his dogged pace.

'Stop you will.' Clemency stepped in front of him. He nearly collided with her. They were in the light of some French windows that led out to the front terrace. Matthew angled his head and adjusted his sight to make her out. Clemency was still furious but she found his strangely mesmerizing eyes somehow enchanting.

Matthew saw her fiery irritation, her eyes blazing with unswerving determination to state her case. This young woman, who was afraid of no one, was beautiful in the extreme. He found her insufferable but he knew he would have to write at least a dozen poems about her. No, it would take a lot more than that for there were so many fascinating aspects to her.

'What is it you want with me? Be quick.'

His arrogance made her lock her fists for she was sorely tempted to slap his face. 'First I demand to know what gives you the right to think you may touch me.'

'You angered me by telling me what to do in my own house and for pushing your nose into my business.'

'Don't be so pompous. I could see for myself how things are between Kingsley and his wife. Your brother has done a good and honourable thing by marrying the mother of his children, to give them his full protection and security.'

'You would say that, coming as you do from a ragtag breed that does not adhere to high standards of morality, not to mention that your family contains a strong criminal element.

Kivell men think nothing of displaying their turn-of-the-blankets to the world.'

'You despicable boor, have you no feelings? Can't you be happy for Kingsley? It is easy to tell that he greatly favours his wife and children, who, you should remember, are your niece and nephew. How dare you pass judgement on them when you choose to hide away from life in a cowardly manner? I should think your regiment is ashamed of you. It's hard to believe you come from such good and gentle people as your parents are.'

'I don't!'

'What?' Clemency was bewildered.

'They are not my true parents, none of us are their true children and none of us are true brothers and sisters.' Suddenly he caught her by the arm. 'I don't know why I am telling you all this. I came by the knowledge by chance while going through the family papers just before I expected to serve overseas. I don't think my parents could have children. I believe it's more than likely they're man and wife in name only. They adopted me and Kingsley and Jane and Hattie – we are all orphans. All of us come from impoverished gentlefolk. I destroyed those papers. My God, what have I done, telling you?' He shook her. He was trembling. 'Swear to me you won't tell another soul. It would particularly crush Hattie.'

'I swear. I swear on my mother's life. I – I don't know what else to say.' She truly did not. Matthew's secret must be a burden to him. All she could do was to stare back into his amazing, glittering eyes.

As if coming to his senses he let her go. 'I'm sorry. Forgive the liberty.' His voice was soft, his eyes kept steady contact with hers.

'You can trust me, Matthew.' She cared that his brother and sisters should never be hurt by the secret, but she didn't know why she was being kind and understanding towards him.

'Yes, I'm sure I can. That gives me peace.'

Neither of them moved, not wanting these intriguing, charged moments to end.

'I've never met anyone like you before, Clemency,' he murmured, gazing even deeper into her eyes. 'Men have said those words to women down the ages for a variety of reasons, but I mean them with all sincerity. You are an extraordinary woman. And you are so very lovely, a dream to men. I could go on and on.' His ruined sight had never seemed so clear; he was drinking her in. He wanted to consume her. Then he was stabbed through with desire for her.

Clemency felt drawn to him more and more, as if a part of her were melting and being absorbed by him. It was outlandish, as if they were creating some unknown force together. All else in the world was forgotten. She knew if she didn't step away he would kiss her. He leaned in, his arms reaching towards her, and she mirrored his movements. Their bodies drew together as one, they clung to each other, closed their eyes and their lips met.

Clemency had never kissed a man before but instinct and need guided her and it was an exquisite experience. The kiss went on and on, their lips moving keenly; searching, giving and taking relentlessly. At last they drew apart, but only a fraction. Their eyes met in the same passionate togetherness. They kissed again, neither wanting to stop.

The sound of a horse's hooves broke through to their senses. Disappointed beyond measure, Clemency looked through the French windows, and recoiled. 'It's my father. I can't think why he's here but it's sure to mean trouble.'

Twenty-Five

'I'll deal with this, Clemency,' Matthew said, never so reluctant to let anyone go.

'You don't want to stay out of sight?' Clemency knew the question was unnecessary. She had recognized in his voice the authority of the army officer he had once been and she was in no doubt Matthew could be hard and fearless.

'Not if you or my family could be under threat.' For the first time he smiled at her and it was a smile full of intimate warmth. He caressed her cheek. 'There are times when something suddenly happens and it changes your perceptions, don't you think, Clemency?'

'Things can change very quickly, Matthew. Perhaps that was how it was for Kingsley.'

'You've left me with no choice but to agree with you. I must rethink some of my opinions. Do you want to stay here and wait for me while I deal with your father?'

'Certainly not.'

Side by side they passed through the French windows. Clemency guided Matthew down the wide curving steps. Seth trotted up the last stretch of gravel and halted in front of them.

Hiding his disgust at seeing his daughter linked so cosily with this swank – the mystery swank – Seth hopped down on to the gravel and favoured them with a toothy smile. 'Clemency, my dear girl, it's good to see you. Are you visiting Miss Faraday?'

'Hello, Father,' Clemency replied in a level tone. 'Why are you here?'

'I've come to see Mr Clarence Faraday,' Seth said, offended by her cool reception. He looked over her companion. 'On business.'

'You'll need to speak to me.' Matthew fixed Seth with a hard, penetrating stare. 'I'm Matthew Faraday, the owner of Poltraze. Would you care to join me in the office, Mr Kivell?'

Not comprehending that the other man was partially sighted, Seth took his peculiar stare for condescending disapproval. His intention to rein in his prickly nature evaporated. 'I'd like to say that's very civil of you, sir, but I find your manner distinctly hostile. What're you doing alone with my daughter?'

Seth didn't wait for an answer. He was as welcome here as smallpox. His own daughter had seen fit to belittle him in the presence of this supercilious Faraday, who for some reason had chosen to conceal the real ownership of this property. His fury erupted like a storm. 'Clemency! Is he why you've been so eager to keep coming here? Speak up, girl. You're still under my authority and control until you come of age. What's been going on? And why has everyone been led to believe that Mr Kingsley Faraday owns this place and his father heads the household when he's away?'

'You have forfeited the right to be the head of my family,' Clemency said coldly, checking her own anger. How could her father believe he deserved respect while he behaved like a brute? 'You seem to be hung over. I suggest you leave.'

'Leave? I'll not leave till I'm good and ready to! You dare

to speak to your own father with such contempt?' Marching up to her Seth swung back his arm to give her a backhand across the face.

'Don't you dare touch me!'

At the same moment Matthew pushed her up the step behind him and raised a forearm to fend off Seth. Their arms clashed like crossed swords. 'Don't you ever think to hurt her! You're a bully and a failure, Seth Kivell. Why else do you think my steward and I decided to stop doing business with you? I would have been prepared to discuss the matter with you. But after this, get off my property.'

Seth was close enough now to see the truth about the other's sight. 'Yah, if you weren't a blind man I'd beat you to a pulp for that.' Thrusting his weight against Matthew he tried to push him off balance but Matthew stood firm. Seth stepped back and spat on the ground at Matthew's feet. 'You're not worth doing business with. This strange place is damned. You Faradays are a peculiar, secretive people. A curse on this place and all of you in it! And you, girl!' He pointed at Clemency, spittle lathering his beard. 'You're no daughter of mine.' He called her obscene names, then ended like a lunatic, 'Tell your wretched mother she's got twenty-four hours to return to Trenbarvear in her rightful place as my wife, or all of you, both Kivells and Faradays, will be sorry.'

'Oh, dear life,' came a horrified voice. Hattie had come looking for Clemency. She was up on the top step leading to the house, her trembling hands up to her face. She fled indoors.

Seth turned on his heel and whipped his horse away at a gallop. Clemency felt the breath had been knocked out of her. 'I must go home straight away and warn my mother and brothers. Will you go to Hattie?' She took Matthew up the steps and inside.

'I'll tell Hattie not to worry, but your father meant every word he said. He's dangerous.' Matthew sighed. 'I'll have men posted round the property and order an armed groom to escort you home. Clemency, as soon as we're able to, can we talk?'

Her father's threats were uppermost in her mind. 'What happened between us happened so suddenly, Matthew.'

'I understand but we do need to talk,' he said. 'Take good care and God go with you.'

Clemency dashed up to her room and changed into her

riding habit. Hattie entered. Her eyes were red from weeping, her ringlets dangling in disarray. Clemency had seen her pull at her hair before when she was vexed but this time she was distraught. 'You're leaving? I thought you'd come to me.'

'I'm sorry, Hattie, I need to go home.'

'Some friend you are!' Hattie stamped her foot. 'My life is in ruins and you are deserting me. My brother has married his mistress and turned us all into social outcasts. My marriage prospects, my future, my whole life are ruined beyond repair and you don't care.'

'I do care, Hattie, but I really do have to go now. Matthew will explain. Don't be angry with Kingsley. He's done the right thing by his children.'

'You would say that, Clemency Kivell.' Hattie put her hands on her hips and twisted her mouth in an unbecoming pout. 'Your brother is soon to marry a mine girl. Your family doesn't need to care about a good place in society. No gentleman will look at me now; I've got nothing to recommend me as a bride. I might as well marry Abe Deveril!'

Clemency viewed Hattie as she would a spoiled child. 'Well, I'm quite sure Abe wouldn't consider marrying you. His injuries took away his means of livelihood but he doesn't complain; he's supporting himself and his parents in a different way. Grow up, Hattie. Why be so obsessed with marriage? There are other honourable estates one can enter into.'

'Like becoming a nun? Is that an option you think I should consider?'

'Stop being so selfish, Hattie. Kingsley could teach you something about that. It's not the end of the world for you. Now, excuse me, I've got real troubles to attend to. I'm sorry if this puts an end to our friendship. I'll have you know that I've found some of your remarks downright insulting. Please pass on my apologies for my sudden departure to your parents and Kingsley and his wife. Goodbye, Hattie. I wish you good fortune in all that you do.'

Matthew found Hattie in her room, sitting rigidly with her hands clasped together, and gazing into space. 'Hello, Hattie, what are you thinking about?' Although feeling sorry for his sister, he was unable to keep his thoughts from drifting to

Clemency and the wonderful, deep kisses and passionate warmth they had shared, as well as his worries for her.

'I'm picturing myself at a reception, a ball or a supper party. Titled men and ladies and the eligible men and debutantes are ignoring me. Ladies are whispering about me behind their fans and the men are smirking. I am a wallflower and soon I won't be able to bear to go out any more. I'll be an old maid, spending the rest of my life doing good deeds.' Big hot tears streamed down her cheeks. 'Thanks to Kingsley I shall never gain a husband, have children or my own home. It's all I've ever wanted, Matthew. How could he do this to me? He should have waited to marry Fearne Lewis until after I had settled down. It would have made no difference to their arrangement, but his thoughtlessness has spoiled my whole life.'

Perching on the arm of the chair, Matthew wrapped her in his arms and she sobbed against him with her heart in pieces. 'I take in all you're saying, beloved, but if any man can shun you over such a thing then he's utterly worthless and un-deserving. Of course you'll find someone who will love you and give you all you've ever desired. Not everyone will look down on us Faradays.'

'But you reacted in just that way when Kingsley introduced his wife here – and Poltraze takes no part in society,' Hattie pointed out, gulping between her tears.

'I know and I had no right to be so high-minded. Clemency pointed out to me that honour should come before social standing, and that the two children are our kin. If Papa and Mama are happy to take Fearne into the family then I should be too. My aloofness must have hurt them as much as it did Kingsley and Fearne. Besides, Kingsley is wealthy and that is all that matters in most quarters.'

Hattie stopped crying and pulled away to look at him. 'You're right. And Clemency was right, and I was so beastly to her. I must beg for her forgiveness.'

'I'm sure she'll give it eagerly. Now why don't you freshen up, and go downstairs with me and we'll meet Fearne properly.'

'Do you think Clemency and her family are really in danger from that horrid man?' Hattie asked, making repairs to her appearance.

'That is my fear,' Matthew said. 'God help him if he harms Clemency in the slightest way.'

Twenty-Six

Two days passed. Clemency stayed at home to be part of the human shield surrounding her mother. Verena had sent a hand-delivered letter to Seth stating her displeasure at his hostility towards Clemency, and her own intention to remain for good at Burnt Oak. 'Our marriage is over,' she had written, 'ended by your unreasonable behaviour, especially over your intention to place your coming child in Trenbarvear. You must accept it. Please, I beg you, Seth, to get on with your life and leave the rest of us to ours.'

Clemency's brothers were taking turns to spy on Seth's movements. Tobias arrived home, having been relieved by Logan. 'He's just come round from the heavy drinking he turned to after he left Poltraze,' Tobias reported. 'Now it seems he's packing up for a long journey.'

'If only he'd leave and never come back,' Verena said, with a heavy heart. 'We could all relax and start a new phase in life.'

'There is nothing for him in this area any more,' Tobias said.

'Except his and Daisy's child,' Clemency reminded him.

'She's dead; they're both dead.' Adam issued the words from the dark corner of the sitting room. He was so quiet it was easy to forget he was present anywhere.

'How do you know that?' Verena asked, concerned. Adam rarely left Burnt Oak land. It had been taken for granted that the long hours he went off on his own he spent lingering in the places where he and Feena had done their courting. He occasionally visited the graveyard but he called on only Logan in the village and confessed he spoke to no one else.

'I have it on good authority from someone who saw Daisy's body a few days ago.' Adam's voice was flat and distant. 'Stone cold dead she was, with the child still in her body. She was using the cottage she was living in to trade as a prostitute. She drank too much and took too much opium. It was what killed her. Father must know. Perhaps that's why he's going away. God damn his evil soul.' It was eerie and disturbing, the manner in which Adam's tone stayed cold and detached. 'So there's nothing left in that regard to upset you, Mother. It's best the child died. It would have had a wretched existence.' Adam then executed what had become a habit of his, of curling up his body with his head out of sight.

No one spoke for a full minute. Frowning glances passed between Clemency, Verena and Tobias. The dreadful suspicion was forming in all their minds that if Adam's account was true, he himself might have been involved in Daisy's death.

Verena looked up at the ceiling despairingly. 'I wish this was all over. Completely over.'

'Will it ever be,' Tobias asked, 'while Father has breath in his body?'

'I suppose not,' Clemency said, going to Verena.

Logan was flat on his stomach under holly bushes watching Trenbarvear stables through spyglasses. This was just one vantage point he and his brothers had used from Poltraze woods. Spartacus was hitched several hundred yards distant, and Logan had brought food and water for them both for the long haul. Way down below him workers went about their tasks, scrubbing down the yards, mucking out, tilling the kitchen garden, and tending to the beasts. The new housemaid scurried in and out of the back door, tossing crumbs to the tumultuous greedy hens, geese and ducks, or shaking out her duster. She fought to throw a square of carpet over the washing line and gave it a good thrashing with the carpet beater. Logan thought she must be angry with someone or something. It was hardly surprising, working inside that house. The dogs, three traditional Kivell lurchers, sniffed in nooks and corners, worried tussocks of grass, marked territory, clashed with the barn cats, snoozed, or ran about. None wandered off; they had obviously been ordered to stay close to the house. Wood smoke, nutty and fragrant on the wind, meandered from the kitchen chimney. Life down there, apart from the vexed maid, seemed just as it should be, ambling along in scenic rural tranquillity.

Yet Logan knew that Trenbarvear was steeped in a chilling atmosphere.

After Daisy Prouse's killing, Logan had intimated to Adam that he would one day kill their father. It was terrible even thinking about it, deliberately snuffing out the life of the man he had once so venerated, but if it proved necessary he'd go through with it without too much torment to his conscience. Shifting to ease his stiff limbs, Logan longed for a smoke but couldn't risk giving away his presence.

'Hello, son.'

His every sense in shocked alert, Logan rolled over. 'Father!'

Seth trained a rifle on Logan's heart. His wayward hair and shaggy beard were wet from bathing; his casual work clothes were in good order, but he was rough and wild. 'Why the surprise? Wasn't it me who taught you to stalk and hunt – you and your brothers? You've been spying on me and I've been aware of it every moment. Grog don't mar my instincts totally. I haven't sunk to that. On your feet.'

Dropping the spyglasses Logan wriggled out from under the holly bushes. 'What are you going to do?'

'This.' Wielding the rifle Seth cracked it against Logan's skull, sending him plummeting back down to the woodland floor.

Hattie was wandering listlessly in Poltraze's grounds. Eventually she came to the pool, a place sheltered by trees and bushes and never used by the family. The boathouse, rebuilt just over a decade ago, was in good repair, its windows glinting in the occasional ray of sun. A rowing boat lay over-turned, newly painted in blue with a red upper band. Hattie could see no reason for its embellishment, unless the servants used it. Perhaps Kingsley would take his children on the water. Wild ducks glided on the surface or dipped for food; there would be ducklings soon. Matthew had talked about reintroducing swans after many years' absence. A wooden bench, losing its varnish, was set on the bank. Hattie sank down on to it. Within seconds she was near to tears. There was no peace to be found here.

Kingsley and Fearne had forgiven her, reassuring her that they understood her worries. 'I'm selling up in London,' Kingsley had said, enthusiastic about the future. 'We're going to settle in Devon. You will come with us, won't you? We will fit into local society. And we'll only be across the county border, not very far from the family. And that, as I realized when I feared I was about to lose my children, is all that really matters. Hattie, darling, every family has secrets, and many have a lot worse than mine. You'll meet the man of your dreams, never fear. It will be my first priority when we've all settled in.'

Hattie found the children a pleasing distraction but she knew she would never feel content until she had healed her rift with Clemency. She had written an emotional apology to her and was waiting on tenterhooks for a reply. Matthew had forbidden her to go to Burnt Oak. 'It's too dangerous,' he had stressed. 'Until the situation with her father is resolved you must promise me to stay in the grounds.'

'You and I could go together,' she had suggested. 'But I suppose you wouldn't countenance that.'

'Actually I would,' he'd said, 'but the Kivells must be allowed to solve their own problems. They're a proud people and would resent outside interference from me, someone who has previously shunned all contact with them. I have also written to Clemency, offering my support if her family so wishes it. All we can do is await the outcome.'

The waiting was dreadful. Matthew had told her to concentrate on her new future but she couldn't give it a thought until she had reclaimed her friend.

A chill went through her, yet the wind had not gathered strength nor the air turned cold. She shuddered. She had the uneasy feeling that something bad was close to her. She turned her head and her eyes widened in fear but she had no time to scream before Seth Kivell clamped a rough hand over her mouth.

'Is Hattie here with you?' Kingsley entered his brother's rooms.

'No, I haven't seen her this morning.' Matthew pushed aside the poem he was working on; another to add to the many he had already penned in praise of Clemency. 'Why? Do you have reason to be concerned about her?'

'Yes, I am rather. Bridie said she went out for a walk immediately after breakfast. It will soon be time for luncheon. I've been up to Jane and she hasn't seen her. Apparently, Hattie hasn't returned to the house at all. I've ordered the servants to search the grounds and every room, even the attics.'

'Sandy, come.' Matthew was striding to the door. 'We'll go to the stables and see if she's taken her pony. I have a bad feeling about this.'

Up in her room, Clemency had finished writing a reply to Hattie's letter in which she expressed her forgiveness and understanding. It was easy to forgive Hattie her insults, born of childish desperation; but Clemency, perhaps unlike Hattie, knew that their friendship could only continue if there was mutual respect between them. Matthew's letter to her was a different matter; it had amounted to a love letter. This had staggered her, although perhaps it should not have – they had exchanged passionate, unrestrained kisses. His slightly scrawling hand had begun with a formal offer of support of any kind from Poltraze and then had changed completely in tone. She had the impression that he had laid open some of his deepest feelings to her; something he had not done for years.

> *My very dear Clemency,*
> *Do forgive my words if they are not of the kind you desire to read. Our moments together alone meant everything to me and now I find I cannot get you out of my mind. I am so looking forward to seeing you again. There are many things I wish we might do together – ride, play music to each other. I would so like to read some of my poetry to you. I shall pray that your family predicament will soon be over and without added distress for you all.*

He had gone on with much romantic prose. Clemency had only read the first line. Such yearning embarrassed her. And, yes, it even annoyed her to be on the receiving end of such dedicated hopes from a man – one who had qualities she disapproved of – after just one intimate encounter. She had Kivell blood flowing through her veins. Her hopes and dreams for the future didn't conform to the traditional ones of love, marriage and children, which were those of girls like Hattie and Serenity. She wanted first to taste adventure; to kiss more men before meeting the strong-minded, dynamic one who would be her match and her soul mate – if there were such a man. What Matthew wanted from her she could not give. Love and all that went with it was for her decidedly in the distant future. Now she had to think hard how to find the words to answer Matthew.

Sighing, she rested her elbows on the little writing desk and cupped her face with her palms, racking her brains to compose a gentle let-down.

'Clemency, will you come down at once,' her mother called up to her, her tone urgent. 'Mr Faraday is here on a most pressing matter.'

Kingsley had come to see her? What pressing matter could it possibly be? Was Hattie in distress and in need of her?

It wasn't Kingsley she found gazing up at her from the hall carpet. She didn't need Matthew's drawn expression to tell her something was terribly wrong. His unprecedented leave-taking from Poltraze declared it in force. Barker was with him. Both men carried firearms.

'Clemency, forgive the intrusion.' Matthew's hurried speech betrayed his acute anxiety. 'Hattie has disappeared from Poltraze without a trace. She had gone for a stroll and now there is no sign of her anywhere. Sandy trailed her scent to the pool and there is evidence of someone else being there. I fear this has something to do with your father. He vowed revenge and he may be seeking it through Hattie. Kingsley is heading a wider search, and I've put my parents under guard. If Hattie has merely wandered off, would you have any idea where? Please think of the places where you both went.'

'I'll do more than that. I'll take you to them,' Clemency said without hesitation.

'Clemency, no.' Verena too was anxious. 'If your father is involved in this it could spell danger for you too. Let one of your brothers go with Mr Faraday.'

'Don't worry, Mother,' Clemency said, 'I'll be safe.' She had no doubt of that. Matthew's sight was impaired but the very stamp of him at this moment showed that he would be an adversary both calculating and dangerous.

Twenty-Seven

Adam slipped into Trenbarvear and stole up to the bedroom he had shared with Feena and where she had died. His mother had sent over all his and Feena's possessions to Burnt Oak and he still treasured everything that had belonged to his beloved wife. This room, with the same bedcovers, rugs and curtains, was horribly empty and bare, but it was where Feena had spent her last moments and he wanted to try to form a link with the essence of her.

He had come to see his father to give him something and then to do this afterwards, but his father was out. No matter; Adam had patience. The old man would return eventually and he was content to wait.

Lying on what had been his side of the bed he took hold of Feena's top pillow and cuddled it to his body. The linen had been laundered and there was no scent of her, but out of his pocket he took a lace-edged handkerchief. It still had a faint smell of Feena on it and it was this that kept him sane. Gently placing the handkerchief between the pillow and his face he closed his eyes and whispered her name. 'Feena. Feena, I love you.'

The sun broke through the clouds and radiated through the windows, covering him with warm light, and it was like a small blessing to him.

Serenity and Jenny were in the wooden summer-house of Wingfield House, talking excitedly about Serenity's wedding plans. Their surroundings were pleasant; the summer-house had recently been repainted on the outside with fresh dark green paint by Abe in his new role as a handyman. They were sitting on cushioned garden chairs, drinking fruit and mint cordial and nibbling Maudie's shortbread biscuits, rehearsing aloud the walk up the aisle of the church. It had to be the church rather than the chapel, at Mrs Brookson's insistence. 'People of standing attend church. It's how things are done,' she had said. And that was the end of the matter.

'I hope I don't trip over my skirts,' Serenity said, suddenly anxious.

'I'm sure you won't put a foot wrong,' Jenny said. 'Your father will be really proud when he takes you on his arm. You'll look so beautiful, Serenity. Mr Logan's eyes will be full of love for you.'

Serenity laughed; her young friend had never come out with anything like that before. 'And you'll look lovely as my senior bridesmaid, with my two little sisters trotting along behind.' She would have teased Jenny about catching many an eye – Abe's, for sure. Serenity had noticed how well they got along. Abe had smiled warmly at Jenny when he'd passed them earlier on his way to clearing out the gutters – launders, to the Cornish. But Jenny didn't particularly yearn for romance as most young girls did, and Mrs Brookson certainly wouldn't approve of her name being mentioned, even in fun, in connection with a labouring man. Jenny's birth wasn't likely to lead her into a marriage to someone of Mrs Brookson's class, and Jenny wouldn't desire it, but like Serenity, she might one day make a match with a Kivell. On second thoughts, Serenity decided that Jenny was too shy and sweet ever to consider a Kivell as a husband.

'Hello, ladies.'

Serenity's whole being rocked with alarm. She grabbed Jenny's hand. 'Wh–what do you want?' Her future father-in-law strode into the summer-house and shut the door after him. He trained a small firearm on the girls. 'Where's Logan?'

'Aw, he's having a little sleep right now,' Seth hissed maliciously, enjoying the girls' fear.

'What have you done to him?' Serenity blazed. 'If you've hurt him . . .'

'Hurt him? Why shouldn't I hurt him, you stupid young bitch, he don't care about what he did to me. He deserted me like the rest of my traitorous family. Double-crossing bastards, all of them. Get up, get in the corner.' He motioned with the gun.

'What are you going to do to us?' Serenity recoiled at

his venom. Hatred burned in Seth Kivell's eyes. But she had to know about Logan. 'Is Logan alive? Tell me!'

'Do as I told you!' Seth sprayed the girls with spittle, aiming the gun at Jenny's temple. 'Or I'll shoot this little bitch on the spot.'

'No!' Serenity snatched Jenny away and pushed her into a corner of the building where they huddled together.

Trembling, Jenny whispered, 'Please don't hurt us.'

'Shut up! Don't scream or I'll break both your necks in a flash.' Over his shoulder Seth had flung a bale of rope. He put the gun in his jacket pocket, yanked the girls back to back and bound them together tightly, trapping their arms and hands. Despite their peril neither made a whimper. It would be useless, and both knew not to feed this brute's lust for cruelty and power with pleas and tears. Seth whipped out two kerchiefs. He roughly knotted a gag around Jenny's mouth. He stared at her. She had her eyes closed, denying him a last jeer.

Moving round he leered into Serenity's eyes. They were full of loathing and contempt for him. 'You'll burn in hell for your sins.' The words grated from her throat.

'Aye, me and Logan together, but he'll get there long before me.'

'So he's alive?'

'For a while longer.' Seth stroked her face and she turned away. He yanked on her hair. 'You're a pretty wench. I can see why my son's taken with you. If I had a little more time . . .'

While he cruelly put the gag on her, Serenity prayed for Jenny and Logan, and thanked God she had been spared the ultimate violation from this monster.

Watched by Serenity, her eyes widening in horror, Seth picked up a flagon of rum that he had put down by the door. He took a long swig then started to splash the spirit over the door and the planked floor. He lit up a smoke and drew in, deeply filling his lungs. 'Bye-bye, girls, you'll never get out of here. This place will burn down in minutes and turn you to cinders. Now, excuse me, I've got an old lady to see and a nice big house to burn down.'

Struggling futilely against the bonds, Serenity's mind and body surged with panic and the inbred instinct for survival. She wanted to live and find Logan and save him. She wanted Jenny to live and have a future. She wanted to save Mrs Brookson and the house. Damn this evil beast! She wasn't going to die without a fight. She watched him open the summer-house door, throw down the glowing cigarette, and slam the door shut on the leaping flames.

Using her feet, Serenity dragged Jenny towards the window that made up nearly half of the wall at the opposite end of the summer-house. She planned to thrust her head through the glass and try to hurl Jenny over the top of her body and land them both outside. She'd probably kill herself but this way Jenny might live and, God willing, raise the alarm. It was Jenny's only chance. Abe was on the other side of the house. He would hear the splintering glass and come running.

'Dear Lord, save Logan and take my soul.' She made to surge forward.

Suddenly the glass was broken and she was showered in splinters. Instinctively she closed her eyes, feeling tiny stabs of pain all over her face. 'Get back, Serenity!' Abe shouted.

Serenity shuffled her feet, and Jenny, aware of what was happening, went with her. They stumbled and crashed to the floor but they were mostly out of the way of flying glass and breaking timber. The flames had reached the low ceiling and were licking across it. The girls felt thick, hot smoke filling their nostrils.

Then they were being lifted up as one. Abe had climbed in and was hauling them over the crunching glass. They felt the fresh air and could breathe more easily. Abe bundled them over the crushed glass and splintered wood of the window frame. Their flesh and their clothes were being torn but it was the only way if they were going to survive. They crashed down, ending up on a flower bed. Jenny's gag had been ripped down and she screamed shrilly to rouse more help and to warn the house.

Serenity knew they had to get away from the burning building; she felt the heat coming after them. She prayed that Abe would get out of the furnace in time. Something warm was running down her neck; she was bleeding badly. There was a madness of movement and pain and then she was sinking into darkness.

Twenty-Eight

Where am I? The thought changed instantly from confusion to sheer terror for Hattie. Coming round from a faint, she had no idea where she had been taken to and dumped by the brute Seth Kivell. She had been blindfolded, gagged, and bound round her middle, and then bundled over the back of a horse. She thought she had been taken through trees and under-growth, as sharp projections had snagged at her clothes and hair and painfully scratched her skin. After being pulled off the horse, she'd been dragged along by a thick arm around the front of her body. There had been a creaking sound and the next thing she knew was that she was being tossed down on to cold, dirty ground, her back slumped against something hard. There had been a loud bang. She could only think she had been imprisoned in a shed of some sort. Then she had heard grinding, clinking noises, probably of a padlock and chain being clamped and locking her in. There was a rank, musty smell.

God in heaven, why was Seth Kivell doing this to her? He bore hate-filled grudges against every member of his family but why did he want to hurt her? To get back at Clemency in some twisted way? He had of course clashed with Matthew. Was he holding her to ransom? How far had he taken her from Poltraze? How much time had passed? It was hard to work out anything with her stomach eaten by worms of fear. The fear whooshed into fully-fledged panic. Wave after wave of terror reduced her to someone without proper reason. Her situation was made a thousand times worse because she could neither scream nor flee. She couldn't breathe. She was going to die! She struggled against her bonds, thrashed her whole body about. Her head banged against something hard. She threw her head back again and again, wanting the ever-growing painful contact to prove she still had her senses, desperate to bring herself out of this vile black tunnel of chilling unreality.

Hattie passed out – or knocked herself out. She came round, her head feeling as if it had received a hundred hammer blows. Moments of suffocating dark stillness elapsed. Now she was breathing like a locomotive, her chest was heaving, her heart racing madly. Searing hot tears wetted the cloth blinding her eyes. Think, think, *think*, for heaven's sake, think! She broke through the panic by screaming inside her head. She was alive. If there was a way out of this she could only reach it by controlling her mind. Matthew and Kingsley would know by now she was missing and they would be making a thorough search for her. If it were a ransom Seth Kivell wanted, her brothers would pay it. And the searchers might find her at any moment.

Clemency came into Hattie's mind; strong, accomplished and clever Clemency. She had found the former squire's abducted baby. Clemency thought past the obvious and summed up the unusual. Between them, Matthew, Kingsley and Clemency would tear the area apart until they found her.

Think like Clemency, Hattie urged herself, to keep the stabs of despair at bay. What would she do if she were here like this now? Clemency wouldn't just cower; she'd fight to get free. Hattie knew she could not get out of the ropes binding her so tightly, but she might gain some advantage if she could see and cry for help. At least she might be able to work out exactly what kind of prison she was in. She needed something to rub against in the hope of dragging off the blindfold and gag. Gingerly she shifted her head about, hoping to find a protruding object to do the job.

There was nothing but hardness behind her, seemingly a planked wooden wall. She leaned to the side and almost at once her cheek struck the end corner of something immovable. Pain plumed out from her cheekbone. Ignoring the pain she angled her face in the hope of working off the blindfold. She managed to hook a part of the blindfold over the hard point of the object. One fast downward movement and the blindfold rose up to her forehead then fell down on to the bridge of her nose. Hooking the blindfold over the object again, she lowered her head and twisted it back and forth, her

neck searing with the strain, and bit by bit, she got the blindfold up and over the top of her head.

She was panting within the gag; the wet, chafing monstrosity
that was pulled in cruelly between her teeth. She took a few
moments to allow her eyes to adjust to the dim light. It was
still day, unless she had languished here unconscious throughout
a whole night. She wasn't in any ordinary shed. Light dotted
in through chinks in the drawn, moth-eaten curtains. There
was a small square table and a pair of chairs, laden with dust
and cobwebs, but otherwise fit to grace a parlour. She saw that
the object which she had successfully employed to drag off
the blindfold was the corner of a long bench seat, topped by
a full-length cushion. It struck her that she was in a place that
had been used for assignations by a long-ago well-to-do
personage. It had been abandoned for so long she feared she
would never be found.

Don't think like that. She had to keep trying to get free. One
step at a time; it had been the chant of her old governess.
'One step at a time; that is all we need to take in life, Miss
Hattie. The next will surely follow.' It was good advice. Pray
God it would work in her present predicament. Now she had
to concentrate on the gag – an easier task now that she could
see what she was doing. She put the top edge of the gag to
the seat corner. One, two, three! She brought her face down
rapidly, hoping the gag would be pushed down around her
neck. The gag shifted; she had freed herself from it. She was
elated, but next moment she was screaming in agony and felt
blood dripping down her cheek. In her desperate haste she
had been careless and the seat corner had gashed her face.

She moaned in pain and despair. If she survived this, her
face would have to be stitched and she would be scarred for
life. She thrashed with her feet, sobbing and struggling against
the vice-like grip of the ropes. Why had she ever come to this
wretched county, to the God-forsaken Poltraze? The place was
cursed. Now it had cursed her life. As a scarred young lady
she had no future at all. She wished she were dead.

There was a scuffle. Hattie stiffened. A mouse? A large creepy-
crawly insect? Something moved on the ground on the other
side of the table. Next came a strange noise, a sort of stran-
gulated groan. Her fear magnified this possible new danger
into some unknown monster.

In panic she shouted out, 'H–hello?' Another eerie groan, a scuffle on the ground. Dear God, what on earth was it?

There was another stronger movement. In a merciful moment of clarity Hattie saw that it was the sole of a boot – a man's boot. Someone else was here, someone who was hurt and in the same predicament as herself. Shuffling on her bottom she edged around the table, bumping into a chair, her skirts dragging and tightening about her and cutting into her armpits. She was forced to get down on her front and wriggle until she was flat and her clothes no longer restricting her. She wrestled to get up on her knees and, feeling it wise to attain the advantageous position, she somehow staggered up on to her feet, grunting with the mighty effort.

Her eyes travelled up from the boot to the slumped figure of a well-built man. She took a huge gulp. His head was down on his chest and there was blood on it. His black hair was soaked in dark red, caked blood. He was another of her abductor's victims, and the violence meted out to him chilled her to her bones. He wasn't tied up. There was no need for that. Both his arms had been broken. He couldn't get up on his legs, one had been broken and bone was sticking out through his trousers below the knee.

Hattie eased down on her knees. 'Hello. I'm Hattie Faraday. Can you wake up properly? Please wake up.' She was sure he was a Kivell but which one?

Leaning forward for a closer look her face touched against his, mingling their blood. The man lifted his head, barely conscious. It was Logan Kivell.

'Logan! Wake up. It's me, Hattie.' Using her teeth she worked his blindfold away and then his gag.

'Logan. We need to get out of here. Speak! Say something, please! Tell me what I can do.'

Logan licked his dry lips. 'M–my father.'

'I know he did this to us. What do you think he'll do next?'

'R–revenge. Coming back . . . tonight . . . burn place down.'

'Oh, my God! We've got to get out. But how?'

'No g–good . . . sorry.'

Hattie watched dismayed as Logan sank into unawareness again. If she didn't do something to get them out of here and safely far away, in a few hours' time Seth Kivell was going to burn them to death.

Up again she stumbled to the door, pushing against it and kicking it while shouting for help. There were two windows but even if she broke the glass they were too small to climb out of. There was nothing here she could try to cut her bonds with, no sharp edges, no bottles she could break. She went on shouting until her throat was painfully sore and her voice was completely gone.

Her strength left her and then her hope. Settling down next to Logan she rested her face on his chest. His breathing was shallow. He was gravely hurt. If he didn't receive urgent attention he might lose a limb or limbs or even his life. He was going to die anyway, they both were. She prayed they would both die from the smoke before the first flames reached them.

Twenty-Nine

'Are you absolutely sure there was nowhere else, Clemency?' Matthew was too late to help Clemency dismount from her pony. She slid down on to the cobbles of Poltraze stable yard before he'd got down off his own mount.

'I've taken you everywhere in the grounds and beyond where Hattie and I had ever gone together. She couldn't have gone any further on foot.' Clemency chewed her bottom lip in worry. 'Your gun dogs located her scent by the pool but they soon lost it. I hate even to think it but it seems she may have been taken away by an expert tracker. If so, then everything points to the possibility of my father being involved. Let's hurry inside and see, pray God, if Hattie is safely home.'

'Water the horses,' Matthew ordered the groom. 'Keep them saddled. We may need to go out again straight away.'

Kingsley came striding across the yard. One glance at his sorry demeanour told them that Hattie was still missing.

The silence was broken by the sound of riders pounding up fast to the stables. Clemency caught her breath. Matthew instinctively reached for her hand and she allowed him to grip it in their shared anxiety. It was Tobias and Jowan and there was no doubt they were bringing bad news. They pulled their horses up hard.

'I've been to the ridge where we've been spying on Father,' Tobias blurted out. 'Logan's gone. It seems he was dragged away. There was blood on the ground. Spartacus was either taken or set free. I rode down to the farm. Father has been out all day. He must have taken Logan. I went back to the ridge and searched about but Father's too expert at covering his movements. He could have taken Logan anywhere. The farm is now heavily staked out from all quarters in the event Father returns there.'

Clemency gasped and stiffened in fear for Logan and Hattie, and of what her father would do next. She stifled an exclamation of horror and looked at Matthew. He squeezed her hand and gazed directly into her eyes.

Jowan saw this and was rocked by a sudden burst of jealousy and anger. How dared this soft, strange man, this recluse he had so recently heard about, make free with Clemency? He wasn't the least bit right for her. Clemency had been pledged to him. He had taken little notice of his despicable uncle's wish that he and Clemency marry one day, but witnessing another man's interest in her stung him. Matthew Faraday wasn't good enough for Clemency. He couldn't have her, neither he nor any other man. Jowan plunged in with his news. 'There was nearly a tragedy at Wingfield House today. If not for Abe Deveril, Serenity and Jenny would have been burnt to death in the summer-house. It was Seth. He's gone mad. He threatened revenge and now he's carrying it out. He won't get to Aunt Verena, she's safely guarded at Burnt Oak.'

'Father's been in three different places going about his wicked deeds today.' Tobias looked from his cousin to his sister then to the Faradays. 'That means he couldn't have taken Logan and Miss Hattie very far away.'

'But a search for my sister has proved fruitless,' Kingsley said angrily. 'I should never have left Hattie in this place.'

Matthew stared at his brother. Kingsley's statement sounded like an accusation. 'I have been capable of looking after Hattie.'

'Really? Then why is she in this terrible peril? You'd better plead with the Almighty that she's found safe and sound. Then I shall take her away from this accursed place tomorrow.'

'None of this is Matthew's fault,' Clemency declared.

'No, Miss Kivell, it's not entirely. I share the blame.' Kingsley went on darkly, 'I should have ordered you out that first day I discovered you trespassing in the house. Then Hattie would never have got involved with you and your family.'

'And we should not have allowed Clemency anywhere near your peculiar and ridiculous kin,' Tobias retorted, seething.

'Clemency, come with us,' Jowan said. 'These people aren't capable of finding an acorn under an oak tree. Come now, we must hurry. If Logan and the girl are to have any chance we must hurry in a new search.'

Clemency pulled her hand away from Matthew. Her family had been insulted, and at any moment now there could be punches thrown, and she couldn't do with witnessing any more animosity between the Faraday brothers. She pushed past the groom and swung up on to her pony and rode off, her amber hair flowing out from her shoulders. Tobias and Jowan caught her up.

'Clemency, wait!' Matthew was running after her. She did not halt or look round. He turned on Kingsley. 'Damn you to hell! You have just put a rift between the Faradays and Clemency's impossible family. You may have denied me for ever the woman I love.'

Clemency headed towards the rear of Poltraze to reach the woods, where Logan had last been seen. Tobias and Jowan were on either side of her, as protectors. Jowan kept glancing at her and she got the impression he was trying to read her. She didn't care about that, or Kingsley Faraday's accusation. All that mattered was finding Logan and Hattie, and please, please let them both be still alive. If her vindictive father was crazed enough to try to burn two young women alive, God knows what other atrocities he may have carried out.

It made sense for Seth to have left Logan and Hattie somewhere that was close to the scenes of both their abductions. 'I think I have it!' she cried. 'I've an idea where Father might have taken them.'

Thirty

In the dark heart of night Seth stole into his study, the furnishings silhouetted by the silvery tint of the moon. He went to the drinks tray on the sideboard, poured a large splash of his favourite tipple, a hundred-year-old Scotch, and tossed it down. He needed that. He poured another and that went the same way. God, that was better.

He was in an agony of tension. His once rugged face was drawn and haggard with the strain of having to stay cunning for so many hours, and with the perversity of his situation. He'd failed to roast Logan's two sluts alive. How could he have missed that village oaf jobbing in the grounds? If not for Abe Deveril, it would have been believed at first that the pyre had been accidental and he'd have got clear away, but those wretched girls had been rescued and had screamed his name. After skulking away to retrieve his horse, left in a quiet thicket outside the village, he'd ridden off across the downs. With the demoniacal clanks and blasts of the Wheal Verity in the distance, his horse had been terrified into a quagmire. He'd jumped down, shot it dead and left its body to sink. Then, raging at himself for so carelessly ruining his plans, he'd left the scrubland and hidden out near his home until darkness fell.

He would have to abandon his plan to torch his once favourite son and the mealy-mouthed Faraday girl. What a sweet little handful she would have been. He should have made a feast of her, enjoyed every delicious second of her pain and horror. His worst mistake was not stashing money away from the house, including Clemency's rightful dues, for he had sold Trenbarvear and its holdings, via a land agent, and the new owner was to move in after two weeks. One agreement of the sale was that the buyer would not set foot on the property until then. By this time Seth would have left Bristol on a ship bound for the West Indies.

To get into the farmhouse he'd flitted as smoothly as a ghost past some of his treacherous, stupid sons and other male kin keeping watch. He crept to the bookshelf. Behind a false set of books was hidden the safe. He stretched up his arms to ease a sudden heaviness in his neck and shoulders. His arms wouldn't reach far, they were suddenly full of weight. A cloying weariness came upon him and his eyes felt strangely fatigued.

'Hello, Father.' Adam stepped out from behind the curtains where he had been concealed, patiently so, for some time.

'What the hell . . . ?' Seth staggered and nearly fell over his own feet. He stared at the tall thin profile. His sight was blurred. He shouldn't have drunk the Scotch so fast. 'Adam? Are you real?'

'I am, but I'd be dead if you'd had your way.' Adam's voice was as cold as the tomb. 'As dead as Feena and our baby because since I lost them due to your cruel, selfish ways it's all I've wanted. I'd kill myself this minute, die with you, but I couldn't do that to Mother and Clemmie. You've already put them through enough heartbreak. The only way they can really put all this misery behind them is when you're out of the way, which you soon will be, Father. Dead. And in hell.'

Seth felt strangely leaden but he let forth a hideous mocking laugh. 'You're going to kill me are you, you pathetic weakling? All you had to do was get yourself another woman and knock out some more brats. What've you got with you? A gun, a knife? You're a milksop, Adam, a mother's boy. Think you've really got the guts to actually kill me?' Seth went to shove his hand inside his coat pocket for the small gun he had there. He had other weapons about him too. No one was capable of taking him by surprise. Yet he was surprised, and puzzled. His hand refused to obey his intention to slip it into the pocket.

'You are a rotten evil bastard,' Adam said with slow, precise enunciation, closing in on Seth. Seth frowned for he had no strength to step back. 'But how could you know what real love is? If you did you wouldn't have sent all your family away. We all hate you, Father. Take that with you to the grave. You see, I don't need to do anything to kill you, Father. I've already done so.'

'Wh–what are you t–talking about, f–fool?' Seth couldn't fathom why he was slurring his words.

'I checked the safe. I knew you'd come back for the money. I knew what you'd do the instant you walked into this room. So I put a little concoction of Uncle Henry's in your Scotch. Something that would paralyse you; make you die suddenly and appear to have had a heart attack. No mess, little fuss.'

'Y–you . . .' Seth felt a thickening of fear and tried to put his hands to his chest to thump up some breath, only his hands refused to move.

Adam put out a finger and pushed Seth. 'I say this with pleasure. Drop dead, Father.'

For the first time in years Seth obeyed an order and did just that.

Thirty-One

Matthew took a letter to Hattie. She was in her room, in bed, which she had not left for several days, after being brought home by Tobias Kivell.

'It's Clemency's handwriting. Sit up and read it, Hattie. Please, my dear.'

'No, I don't want to read it.' Hattie was curled up with her hair dragged over the dressing on her gashed cheek. 'You've thanked her on my behalf for her part in my rescue. I know Logan survived although is sadly maimed. I'm not interested in anything else she might have to say.'

'Shall I read it to you? Clemency is your friend. She's probably asking to see you.' Matthew was desperate to get Hattie out of her depression, understandable as it was. She had survived a dreadful ordeal, believing she was going to die in a hideous manner, and the physician he had called in to attend her had confirmed that she would have a permanent noticeable scar on her cheek. To be flawed on the face was one of the worse things possible for a young unattached lady to suffer.

'No! I don't want to see her. I wish I'd never met her. Her father has ruined my life. I don't want to see anyone ever again! Go away, Matthew.' Raising herself awkwardly, her spine and limbs stiff from lack of movement, Hattie tossed a pillow at him. 'Leave me alone. I'm fed up with everyone bothering me. I don't want to hear positive or jolly talk. I don't want promises or to be distracted. My life is as good as over. Go away and let me get used to it.' Shaking throughout the tirade, she gave way to a flood of scalding tears, throwing herself into the remaining pillows and pulling the quilt up over her head.

Matthew saw history repeating itself in his family. He and his siblings had no blood link but he and Jane, and now Hattie, had neither the desire nor the courage to face up to the cruelty of fate. Their parents were mild and vulnerable, and until recent years had done very well in society. They had a good reason to keep themselves safely confined to Poltraze, but they adored company. They were capable of entertaining and, he admitted, feeling ashamed, they could mix socially away from the property if they were escorted and watched over. People would find their mutual devotion and sense of fun delightful. Too much had been denied his family for far too long and he, as the eldest son, was wholly responsible. 'Leave you alone? I will not!'

He strode from the room, where Sandy was patiently waiting. He stroked the dog's broad head. 'Come along, boy,' he said, his teeth gritted with purpose. 'We have work to do.'

He set off to the west wing, ordering that Barker and Mrs Secombe and a bevy of servants be sent after him. He walked abruptly into Jane's room.

'Matthew, how dare you barge your way in here and bring that dog in with you? Get the creature out of here at once before it knocks over some of my precious mementoes of Hugh.' In her black cloth and starched lace, Jane appeared a mere shadow to him in her darkened sitting room.

Her living shadow wrung her hands. 'Really, Mr Matthew, you forget yourself,' whined Adela Miniver.

'Hold your tongue, woman,' Matthew snarled. 'Don't dare to interrupt.'

'What is the meaning of this, Matthew? Have you taken leave of your senses?' Jane was at her most indignant.

'Yes, but it happened some years ago. Today I have re-discovered them and I am thoroughly ashamed of myself. I have allowed you to wallow too long in this pathetic grief and your utter selfishness. Today, you too will live again.'

Barker, Mrs Secombe and four servants came quietly into the room and stood in a humble line. 'You require us, sir?' Mrs Secombe coughed discreetly, eyeing the proceedings warily and with some embarrassment. Her master seemed to be in the throes of some sort of brainstorm. It was all very worrying.

'Indeed I do,' Matthew said with determined emphasis. 'Rip all these black curtains down. Remove every dark and morbid thing from this suite, including the portrait of Captain Hartley. Take it all outside and burn it to ash on a bonfire.' He made a start by yanking off the first curtain and letting in the bright April sun.

Adela Miniver sobbed and held herself in fright as the dutiful, unquestioning Barker, and the startled Mrs Secombe dealt out orders and set to with the task. Jane threw herself at Matthew, clawing him. 'How could you? You've gone mad! I hate you.' Then she fell to her knees and clutched his coat hem. 'No, no, no, Matthew, I beg you, do not touch my dear Hugh's things. I will die without them about me.'

'You shrivelled up and died years ago.' Reaching down, Matthew pulled Jane up and held her at arm's length. He shook her hard. 'Look at me. Your grief has been all for nothing. Hugh Hartley was a scoundrel.'

'What the hell are you doing, Matthew? Stop this!' Kingsley yelled, charging up to him and trying to relieve Jane from his clutches.

'Stand back!' Such was the venom and authority in Matthew's voice that Kingsley obeyed at once. The servants stopped work to listen in respectful silence, every head bowed.

'I'm doing something that you or I should have done long before the tragedy of the fire. I'm telling our sister the truth about her husband, that Hugh Hartley was a womanizer, a hard drinker and a gambler who had run up debts all over London, including many to his brother officers. He deceived you, Jane, and I'm sorry to say he neither loved nor respected you. A handsome philanderer took you in and he was worthless. But you are a very unpleasant woman, Jane; selfish to the core. I, and others too, believe all this grieving is a sham and indeed it's unnatural. You were too spoilt and lazy to devote yourself to anything else.

'You have sorely neglected our wonderful parents and you have shunned dear Hattie, who could have benefited from a kindly older sister's direction. Now Hattie is in despair and she needs long-term devoted, tender care. So, madam, I'll give you ten minutes to come to terms with the revelation about your useless dead husband. Send for a dressmaker and divest yourself of these horrible widow's weeds. And get yourself down to Hattie's room and sit with her, read to her, talk to her. Reassure her that even in the direst of circumstances life is actually worth living, that one only has to seek a new direction, and that you are about to be a living example to her. Tell her that I am to be an example also. This house will no longer be a closed house. I do not own the same amount of property as the Nankervises did, but if Meryen wants a new squire then they shall certainly acquire one.'

Matthew let Jane go and she sank to the floor as her legs gave way completely. Adela rushed to her. Jane put out a hand. 'No, leave me. I . . . just leave me.'

'Bravo, Matthew.' Kingsley gazed down on their deflated sister. 'But I think it will take Jane longer than ten minutes to come to terms with this news, and I'm not sure she'll want to pursue a more selfless way of life. With your permission I'll send Fearne to Hattie. She has wanted to go to her but felt it was not her place, but now . . . ?'

'You and Fearne go to Hattie together. Tell her what has happened. Get her out of that bed and take her outside into this lovely day. Do not listen to her protests. I will not allow another Faraday to shut herself away. Hattie has a scar in a prominent place but between us, somehow, we must make her see that it's not the end of the world for her.'

Thirty-Two

It would be a first for Meryen, a woman having her own business, built from scratch. There were widows who ran their late husbands' shops but that was expected, they had to support themselves. However, they usually had a male relative to oversee the banking side of things. With Verena's approval, Clemency had commissioned premises to be built, next to the newly up and running New Oak, where she would sell musical instruments and offer tuition. A manager would be installed to live in the rooms above the shop and an assistant would be employed so that she could still have plenty of free time, and in recognition of her position in society.

Jowan and Thad were to do the shop fittings. Jowan was a little too interested in the carpentry and cabinet plans, forwarding too many suggestions and seeking endless discussions, preferably alone with her, it seemed. 'Don't lean so close to me,' she had ordered him, a few minutes ago, before leaving the planning office at Chy-Henver, his property, not far past the village.

Jowan had eased back from the desk, where she was sitting, and hit her with a deep smile, while pushing out his chest. 'I was enjoying your perfume, Clemmie.'

So that was his game; he was making advances to her, in a typically direct Kivell manner with very little romance thrown in. He was a fool to think she could be easily impressed. 'Don't be silly.' She had raised her eyes and addressed him as she would an annoying child.

Jowan had met her rebuke with another charming smile, but with some disappointment. He had got the message. Well, he'd better have, she thought. She wasn't in the place where she wanted a man in her life. When she fell in love she wanted it to be sudden, intense and all-consuming, with a man who was her equal, if he existed. She had laughed inwardly at her own musings. No, she definitely wasn't ready yet for love. Her business would be her priority for some time to come.

Clemency rode to the village to go next to the recovering Logan. She would have to pass the graveyard, where her father had been buried in an unannounced ceremony at twilight, to avoid morbid spectators. His name had not been mentioned since then among the Kivells. One day, when she had forgiven him, Clemency would look down on the isolated grave – her father's disgrace did not merit him a headstone – and she would remember the man he had been before he had allowed himself to be taken over by great and foolish ideas.

Matthew had arrived at Wingfield House, with Barker and Sandy with him for guidance, and was now waiting outside. Maudie showed him into the master bedroom.

'It is very good of you to agree to see me, Mr Kivell, in view of your indisposition,' Matthew said. He felt uncomfortable perched near the other man, who was laid up in bed, the left sleeve of his nightshirt almost empty from the loss of his arm, his other arm in a sling. His broken leg was in splints under the bedcovers. Dark circles shadowed his eyes and his features were drawn, but otherwise he seemed calm and content, in a state of mind Matthew had seen before; of one glad to survive an ordeal because he had much to live for. 'I went first to Burnt Oak in the hope of seeing Miss Clemency, and your mother kindly suggested I call here. I was disappointed when the maid informed me that Miss Clemency is presently elsewhere.'

'My sister is due here shortly, Mr Faraday,' Logan said. He had invited Matthew Faraday to join him, curious about the man who would be Meryen's new squire. Faraday's intention was arousing much speculation. He would be tested from all quarters before achieving any such acceptance. However, noting Faraday's sense of presence, despite shutting himself off from all society for so many years, Logan thought he would succeed and quite soon. 'She will be surprised to find you here. Have you come about your sister? How is Miss Hattie? Our shared dreadful experience will be more difficult for her to come to terms with.'

'I'm confident my sister will come through with the family's support. I'm hoping Miss Clemency will be part of that care.

I am also hoping she will not be displeased to see me. You must know of the unfortunate exchange between my brother and yours and your cousin that day. I am eager for there to be no enmity between my family and yours.'

'I once thrived on bad feeling,' Logan said. 'Now I am weary of it. I am alive and will marry the woman I love as soon as I can rise from this bed. I have everything I want. I would do nothing to risk that. I am sure a good relationship between your people and mine could be forged, Mr Faraday.'

'I am gratified to hear that, Mr Kivell. How is Clemency?'

'She is well, but burdened again with that wretched farm. A purchaser reneged on a deal. It was made unlawfully by my father, but Clemency would have preferred it to go ahead. The purchaser didn't relish living in a house that saw such bitterness, apparently.' Logan raised a brow. 'By any chance would you consider buying Trenbarvear? And return it to its original name of Poltraze Farm?'

'I'd be very glad too. I shall pay Clemency a good price.' Matthew was greatly pleased; this would put him in a good light with Clemency. How much longer would she be? He was longing to see her; longing for her to be under Poltraze's roof again, where – ruthlessly if need be – he would ensure he got her all to himself.

If Matthew's sight had been better he would have noticed that Logan was studying him intently. 'I wish to be forthright with you, Mr Faraday. Am I right in thinking you are in love with Clemency?'

'I . . .'

'You should know that my cousin Jowan is also very taken with her, but I'd like to warn you kindly, as I will Jowan, that even allowing for her young age, Clemency is far from ready for a commitment to love and marriage. She will be making her own way in the world for some time to come. Patience may pay off, either for you or for my cousin, or perhaps for neither of you. If you press Clemency you will lose her friendship and respect for good. You will also offend me.'

Matthew sighed but the news was not entirely unexpected. 'This is hard to hear, but I thank you for the advice. I assure you I would never do anything to cause unrest to Clemency.'

'Ah, here she comes now.'

'Logan, I— Matthew!'

Matthew stood up, bowed, and then moved close enough to gain a good view of Clemency. She was as stunning and as gorgeous as ever. 'Forgive me for startling you with my presence, Clemency. It's a pleasure to see you. I have come to extend an invitation to you to dine this evening at Poltraze. Hattie is in very poor spirits and I am hoping your company will cheer her.'

'Of course I will come. I'll do all I can for Hattie. I have been concerned about her. I've learned from Logan what a dreadful ordeal they both suffered.'

'I extend an invitation freely to all your family to come to Poltraze,' Matthew said, to Clemency and Logan.

'I'm sure you'll make many friends now you are venturing out, Matthew,' Clemency said. 'It will be a new era for Meryen. Perhaps in time the Kivells will become close friends with the Faradays.'

'I shall hope for that day to arrive soon,' Matthew said. 'And then I shall write a poem about it. Now I will leave. Mr Kivell surely needs to rest.'

Clemency felt that she would enjoy her future visits to Poltraze now that Matthew seemed to accept that there should be no more than friendship between them. 'I'll take you down, but please stay a while longer, Matthew. I'd like to tell you about my new venture.'